Moon Shadow

Moon Shadow

LUCINDA BETTS

𝒜

APHRODISIA

KENSINGTON PUBLISHING CORP.
http://www.kensingtonbooks.com

For SKK, the Queen of Tough Love, if ever there was one.
For WTT, who casts strong love spells of his own.

1

I needed the perfect man.

So, I prepared to cast the *Rurutu* spell, a spell lost and uncast for millennia. Maybe longer.

With a shrug of my shoulders, my thistle-colored robe fell to my feet, a puddle of silk. My nipples hardened in the room's cool air—and with anticipation. I became increasingly aware of my desire hormones coursing through my system.

The long feathers of my wand vibrated as power gathered and coalesced, and my stomach muscles contracted in the expectation of desire. The intricate hearts carved into the ebony floor began to shimmer with golden light as they channeled the earth's electromagnetic energy.

Now. Now I could begin the perfect spell.

Tracing the ancient *Rurutu* glyph in the air with my wand, the feathers, lavender and orchid, quivered and danced. All was ready. Carefully I stepped into my heart pentagrams, easing the arch of my foot into the proper golden groove. Standing for a moment, I allowed the pulsating energy to reset the rhythm of my heart.

My blood flow slowed, but pulsed with increased force. It inundated my smallest arteries, imbuing them with oxygen and nutritious glycogen. My fingertips, my clitoris, my lips, and the tips of my toes—every small, erogenous part of my being swelled with this thick, slow blood.

My blood carried power.

And the hormones of desire.

Secretions from glands in my cervix moistened and lubricated the walls of my vagina. I was hot. And I was wet.

And I was shocked by the power of this spell.

Under the spell's strength, my tingling feet tracing the heart's lines engraved on the floor, my mind focused on the paper at the center of the hearts. The paper's microfibrils. The shells of long-dead plant cells. These would carry my arcane spell.

Golden sparks falling from my wand made the flames from the beeswax candles flicker. Actively fighting the need to touch myself, to ease the burning desire, I concentrated, hunting specific complementary protein structures within my own chemistry. Deep within the spell casting, my big toe danced over the *Hiva Oa* groove in the small northeastern heart engraved in the floor.

The man I sought had to have particular testosterone distributions. His dopamines and serotonin needed to be just right. Endorphin triggers needed to be easily accessible. His tears and sweat and semen needed to be worth all the effort I'd expend in extracting them.

Deep in this unconventional spell, my toes danced over the heart pentagrams. Power from the etchings pulsed through the balls of my feet, up adrenaline-laden pathways in my calves and legs, through the core of my body and to my brain.

Slick with desire, I knew the time was nearly upon me—the spell's command was not to be ignored, not if I wanted to find the perfect man.

With the right assistant I could cure the anguish suffered by the victims of the most persistent serial rapist in living memory. Perhaps, with the help of the right assistant, we could actually find the rapist and bring him to justice. Bravery would be required, no doubt.

My perfect man also needed some magical abilities. Any little aptitude could flourish in the proper environment. I'd provide that environment.

Since he'd be living with me, it'd be nice if he cooked and cleaned.

In short, I needed a hero, one worthy of the Star Goddess herself.

By necessity, the *Rurutu* spiked my nipples. I couldn't Grab the right hormones unless a cascade of reactions had started. The wetness between my thighs, my pebbled nipples told me the cascade had properly begun.

Now. The time was now.

Carefully, I lay my head back into the vee of the southernmost heart, the *Hiva Ia*. My clitoris throbbed, begging me to hurry. But precision was required. Cautiously, I slid my legs until my labia was positioned exactly in the center of the hearts.

I paused a moment, absorbing the thrumming of the hearts beneath me, then I shifted two degrees west. Now I was perfectly aligned—the electromagnetic energy of my body throbbed in time with that of the earth's field.

Pressing my back against the silky black floor, I gasped at the coolness, a balm to the burning in my core. The spell directed my position—legs spread, my feet flat on the floor, one in the *Hiva Ea* groove and the other in the *Hova Ua*.

I needed the wand, couldn't release it, but my other hand ran the length of my stomach, hard and flat, skimming the curve of my breasts.

Now, bid the spell. *Now.*

I slid my fingers slowly, as slowly as my beating heart. Remembering to breathe, I slid them against the smooth skin that sheltered my clitoris. One finger. Then two.

Lower, the spell bid me. And I obeyed.

I rubbed the slippery nub with featherlight fingertips. Beneath me the throbbing rhythm increased its tempo, telling me to increase the speed of my caress. Back and forth, back and forth my fingers flicked across my clitoris.

Grab, said the spell. And as my heart pentagrams pounded beneath my back and my ass, I Grabbed. Within my personal biochemistry, I sought proteins that would bind perfectly to his.

Stifling a moan—the spell required silence—I pushed my hips hard against the friction of my fingers. I wanted penetration. Real penetration. But that wasn't what I'd get. Not here or now.

Inside, the spell commanded.

With slow deliberation, I slid two fingers into the hot, tight folds of my sex. My thighs quivered, wanting the real thing with a desperate hunger.

Grab, said the spell.

The right hormones were available, and I Grabbed.

But a niggling fear danced in the back of my brain. Were my standards too high? I'd cast this spell three times in the last year with no luck. The resulting fliers each brought back unacceptable prospects, men who'd seemed so promising at the beginning but lacked the proper concentrations of spine or semen or serotonin in the end.

I kept doubt from the spell, though, or I tried to. Worries have a way of backfiring, working themselves into spells and potions with unwanted side effects. Years ago, I'd worked a spell to help an older woman with fertility, doubting the entire time the spell would work. The woman bore triplets.

I didn't want triplets, figurative or otherwise.

Legs spread, my head thrown back, I received inadequate relief. An orgasm, firmly controlled, rippled through me, leaving me panting but not out of breath. The intense burning was gone, but a hunger gnawed my heart.

I'd completed the casting part of the spell.

Careful not to let my feathered wand touch any of my heart's grooves, I stood. I delicately stepped from the *Hiva Ea* and *Hova Ua* grooves, and the power generated by the *Rurutu* spell subsided gently, like waves receding with the tide.

In the thrall of the spell, I'd Grabbed the required proteins from my adrenal gland and my pituitary, from my blood, as hormones were generated and broken down. I'd Grabbed those proteins and put them into my tear ducts. Now, I wiped those protein-laden tears from my eyes with a sterile white handkerchief, and wrung the tears onto my wand.

The tears would go directly onto the paper, onto the flier. Now I could affect the paper, prepare it to travel the city and countryside, riding the breezes, searching and seeking. Serving as my minion.

I wrung the handkerchief onto my feathers, filling the air with an electric sizzle. I held the wand over the paper flier, holding my breath in hope.

Energy sparkled off my wand, dripping golden glitter onto the paper then evaporating as I Pushed the final molecules into position. Satisfied, I lifted myself fully from the spell, brought myself to normal consciousness. The throbbing from the hearts finally quieted and then ceased.

No Wizard had cast the *Rurutu* spell in millennia, but I felt its strength now. Would the Wizard's Guild disapprove of the use of my spell? Had it been retired for a reason, or just lost in time? I didn't know.

My status as a Gold Wizard gave me a lot of freedom, and I doubted any Guild members would complain. I didn't thrive on scorning the opinion of the Guild, but my need for the perfect assistant outweighed any girlish warnings Guild Chair Uriah or his minions might have.

Conventional solutions weren't available to the rape victims who were just recently filling my waiting rooms. To relieve their misery, no spell seemed too arcane, too bizarre to try. Careful not to waste a drop, I wrung the last of my chemical-filled tears onto the advertisement.

I was ready for the final step.

Shrugging into my silky robe, I walked down the narrow stairs to the tiny garden in the back of my brownstone. In the bitter cold air, only the holly and rhododendrons had any color, a withered green. Everything else was brown and gray.

The heat that had permeated my body during the spell still lingered, but the warmth wouldn't last long on this bitter morning. My feet cringed against the icy earth, and I had to force myself to relax them, to flatten them. They couldn't read the electromagnetic field if they were curled defensively against the cold.

Squinting in the late winter sunlight, I climbed to the top of a small hillock covered in hoary, dried grass, just behind my fountain. Glad for the stillness of the air, I again let my robe fall to the grass at my feet. Goosebumps rippled across my skin. Ignoring the scent of my own juices on my hand, I thrust my wand into the sky.

Electrons crackled off my wand into the atmosphere, changing the temperature immediately. A warmth, uncharacteristic of mid-winter, surrounded me. My feet more easily embraced the still-chilled ground.

The temperature change brought a damp wind from the sea, thick with briny salt. At my bidding, the breeze immediately lifted my flier aloft and carried it away.

Now I only had to sit back and wait.

And hope.

2

Huddled against the cold inside my flimsy cardboard box in the alley, I scratched my balls then cupped my hands around them for warmth. Their hairy presence, somehow solid against the night, reminded me that I was a human, a man.

Cold bit through my cloak and trousers, even through the newspaper I'd scavenged from the street. Winter's touch had a way of seeping through the brown cobblestones, through my cardboard and paper, through my once nice clothes, into my bones. The extra newspaper merely slowed the implacable creeping.

With my shoulders huddled against my chin, my knees nearly to my chattering teeth, I wanted to cast a spell to warm my bones. But spells cost energy, and my fat stores were nearly used up. I didn't want to waste muscle—I needed that to survive.

An icy blast of wind attacked my box, ripping through it like it was silk. The night would be hard, and I had just enough fat to get through. I closed my eyes and cast a spell.

With my spell of delusion I found myself back in my wife's

kitchen, a warm fire crackling in the fireplace. "Gage!" she said. "I'm so glad you're home."

"Mmmm," I answered, walking behind her and snugging her tight bum to my groin. I wrapped my arms around her and pulled her tight. "You feel good." I sniffed her hair and said, "And you smell like bread."

She planted a quick kiss on my lips. "That's dinner you smell—pheasant soup with *masawa* tubers."

"And bread?"

"And bread, fresh from the oven with a big thick crust just the way you like it."

Even though I knew I was deluding myself, my stomach started grumbling. My mouth was watering. "And for dessert?" I asked, kissing her longer and slower than she had me.

"Have you been good?" A suggestive smile played on her lips.

"I can show you good." I pulled the kerchief from her shining hair and let it fall over her shoulders. The warm firelight made the strands glow all different shades of gold.

Lyric turned toward me and let the tips of her breasts caress my chest. Tilting her head, she smiled in my eyes and said, "Prove it."

I pulled her with a demanding kiss. I kissed the side of her mouth, then the front, licking her bottom lip and tugging it into my mouth.

Her lips were soft and warm, as welcoming as her kitchen. Her mouth was hot and wet for me. My tongue met hers, tasted her, drank from her. My mouth claimed hers.

She confessed her heavy need to me with a gasp of anticipation.

"Have you missed me?" I asked, the words slurred against her lips.

"When you're gone, Gage, I always miss you."

"Prove it." I threw her words right back at her.

She grabbed my ass and pressed her mound against my thigh, kissing me the whole time. Her kisses demanded something from me, gave no quarter. Her sweetness, her spice, the raw need I tasted amazed me.

Why had I ever stayed away so long?

"Lyric, my love, I can't live without you. Without you I'm nothing. Nothing."

In her arms, It was like yesterday never happened. Time receded into nothingness, right here in Lyric's kitchen.

Lyric swept her arm back across the counter, pushing dishes out of the way. Unashamed, she held her arms out to me, inviting me to join her. I wanted her more than I wanted dinner.

Burying myself in her neck, I kissed that warm spot behind her ear, nipped the curve connecting her neck to her shoulders, stroked her shoulder blade with my fingertips. Sounds of longing escaped her.

Unbuttoning the tiny buttons of her dress, I caressed her soft breast, savoring the feel of it in my hand. Her pink nipple pearled in my mouth under the touch of my tongue, and I palmed the other so it wouldn't get jealous. Her small breasts were perfectly shaped. They melted into my palms.

"These have haunted me," I said to her, teasing the straining tips with my tongue. "Sometimes I'd try to sleep at night, and all I could remember was the taste of your breasts, the way your nipples get hard for me every time I touch them."

"You've haunted me, too, Gage." Lyric stretched to meet my lips, and I shook my head at my luck, to have a woman so faithful and true.

Was ever a man luckier than me to have a beautiful and caring wife waiting for me through the hardships of my quests?

"I've missed your kisses like the desert misses the rain," she said.

I climbed up on the hard countertop with her, my lips not leaving hers. Her tongue danced around mine, and I savored her willingness, her eagerness. She gave a fluttering sound of desire.

My wife moaned for my touch.

"You taste the same," I said, like it'd been years instead of weeks. "You sound the same."

"Do you want to go upstairs?" Her blond hair was tousled around her face, her eyes bright with need.

But I couldn't stand to leave the warmth of her kitchen. "Let's stay here."

I snagged my fingers around her panties and pulled them off. They landed in a puddle on the floor. I closed my eyes and inhaled. She smelled so good, so ready for me. She smelled like she loved me.

I ran my fingertips over her clit and found my nose hadn't tricked me. My wife wanted me. She was hot and ready. I ran my thumb over her clit, felt it throb under me. Pushing her skirt to her waist, I buried my face between her spread thighs, eating her on the counter like she was a banquet.

Lyric tasted salty and tangy, and she went to my head quicker than any wine could have, quicker than any champagne. I laced my tongue across her throbbing nub, sucking her hard. I pushed my tongue inside, lapping her, tickling her clit again.

She thrust her hips toward my face, and my cock throbbed. I loved it when she wanted me. But I knew she was so close to orgasm. I pulled back, wanting to prolong her pleasure.

Her high-set nipples were still pearled in desire. I caught one between my teeth and bit gently. Again she moaned and pushed toward me. I ran my tongue around her nipple and sucked her deep inside me. The scent of her desire filled the room, and she pushed my head down. I knew exactly what she wanted.

I didn't tease. She wanted surcease now. A hard suck on her clit brought her to a clenching climax. I kept my tongue pressed against her until the throbbing subsided, then I sat up to relish the contented beauty of her face. Resting my palm on her flat stomach, I smiled, happy to have done something nice for my wife.

It'd been too long.

"Come here," she said in a dreamy voice. I did. She clasped my erection through my trousers. "You need to take these off."

I did. I stood naked before her, as I did so often.

She grasped me again, slowly rubbing my straining cock, one finger slowly caressing the head, rubbing the moisture seductively over my shaft. I was ready to explode.

The countertop was hard and not quite big enough, but I didn't care. My wife loved me and wanted me. I climbed on.

"Love me, Gage. Hard and fast. Right now."

My cock jerked at her words, wanting her now. I had to come now. With her. I set myself at her entrance and asked, "Are you sure?"

As an answer she pushed her hips to me, thrusting me inside her. One thrust. My breath burst from me in hot gasps. Another thrust. I sunk deep inside her, her wet heat surrounding me. The rhythmic pulsing of my cock matched the pounding of my heart. "Lyric!" I shouted.

With a cry of her own, Lyric's muscles rippled then clamped down, wrapping my cock in her tight warmth. She came with a primal scream: "Gage!"

Her feminine scent mingled with my strong one, and I laid my head against her stomach, careful not to crush her against the hard countertop. I traced her velvet ribs with my fingertips. "You are so beautiful," I said as my finger memorized the groove.

I felt her quiet laughter under my face. "Stop it," she said, but I could tell she was pleased.

And then my stomach gave a wretched gurgle.

"You're hungry!" Lyric said, pushing me up. "Dinner's got to be ready."

I admired her grace as she sat on the counter, buttoning her dress and smoothing the skirt.

"Hand me my panties, please."

I retrieved them from the floor, inhaling their scent as I gave them to her.

"Don't!" she said, but again I heard pleasure in her voice. "Why don't you set the table?"

She lifted the lid on the soup and my stomach grumbled again. It'd been too long since I last ate, and her cooking was delicious. I put plates, bowls, and spoons on the table.

"What would you like to drink, love? I've made some tea."

To drink? I wanted an ale—a Brown Worm. Meeting her eyes across the kitchen, I asked, "How about a beer? Do we have any?"

Sorrow. Consternation. Disappointment. These expressions crossed her face as my spell of delusion exploded into a shower of hard, black boots and wicked cold winds.

Damn reality.

A steel-tipped, patent leather boot just missed my face as my cardboard shelter burst into bits around me. "Look at all these low-life homeless men," I heard the cop mutter to himself, slamming box after box with his heavy boots. Shouts of anger and unhappiness filled the wintry alley.

Then, in keeping with the cruelty of the night, the cop homed in on me. "Get your fucking ass out of here!" He grabbed my shoulders and tossed me into the street. My hands were sticky with come as I pulled them from my trousers. *Lyric!*

As I scrambled to my feet, the cop aimed for my balls, coiling his leg to unleash his worst.

A heartbeat before tasting pain, I Grabbed the man's ankle with my mind and twisted. He fell with a hard thud and an angry cry of pain onto his fat ass, and I spared a moment to gloat. I might only be a Brown, but my magic kicked ass—literally—when I needed it to.

With a roar the cop jumped to his feet and ran toward me, fists bunched.

"Stop, Pike," a woman cop said, making the cop skid to a halt. Her voice was as cold as her eyes. The planes of her cheekbones were interesting, but her lips were toothpick thin. "Bring him here." She sounded like a boss, not an underling. Maybe this woman was a detective then, not a regular cop.

As Pike snatched the scruff of my shirt and frog-marched me toward her, I wondered how the fat-assed cop liked having a woman for a boss.

Not more than I liked getting picked up by cops, I guessed. On the up side, I wouldn't get the shit beat out of me, at least not right away. On the down side, no one in all the Hells wants to be questioned by the cops, particularly when women were getting raped and no one could catch the rapist.

"One of these is the rapist," Pike muttered. "Probably this one. He smells like sex." He shoved me toward the woman, who remained as still as a frozen pond.

So the cops were hungry for roasted scapegoat, but I had no desire to be cooked. I'd have run if I weren't so hungry and tired.

"Bring him to the precinct," the cold woman detective said to Pike.

I'd been sleeping rough for days now, maybe even weeks, not wanting to spend my last talens on a room. I didn't have regular food, and my shelter had been beat to shit by a cop on a mission.

Worse, though, I had no credibility. I could say I was innocent until the Star Goddess walked the earth again, and they'd never believe me. They were going to cook me over the metaphorical roasting pit, marinated in fear.

Faced with Pike and his mistress I could only do one thing. Dropping my shoulders into the picture of humility, I followed the detective past huge harnessed Percherons, black as pitch, into the police cab.

No one said a word the entire ride. Clapping hooves provided the only sound. The detective stared blindly out the window. Pike glared at me, jerking me into an office when we arrived.

Sitting in the stale-smelling office, I wished for any veneer of civility. Couldn't someone offer me a coffee? A cigarette? An ale? Cuffed to a cold hard chair, I wished someone would just treat me politely.

Before I lived on the street, I took these things for granted. But now, how the mighty had fallen. At least this office was warmer than my alley box.

Finally someone remembered I was cuffed to the chair. No-nonsense footsteps approached me from behind. "I'm Detective Habit," the cool woman said in an emotionless voice. "And I have some questions for you."

"I see," I said, wishing I had something intelligent to say. But I had no alibi for anything—I lived on the street.

"Where were you three days ago?" She held a pen to a notebook as she looked right through me.

I couldn't be sure, could I? My life didn't have the usual rhythms of breakfast, lunch, and dinner. Showers in the morning and reading the paper at night were habits I dropped amazingly fast after I left my home. "I don't know exactly," I answered, finally.

Detective Habit looked unsurprised. "Then let's figure it out, shall we? When did you last eat? How did you pay for it?"

I cringed in embarrassment. Was it that obvious I'd been homeless for so long? I'd had a nice job, a wonderful wife, and a great home—not too long ago I'd had those things. "I, uh . . ." I didn't remember. Too much Brown Worm did that to my memories.

"Have you earned any money lately?" Detective Habit prodded. "Panhandling maybe?"

"I don't panhandle."

Habit coolly raised her eyebrows.

"Not unless I'm really hard up."

"How'd you get enough money to eat?"

"Not too long ago a man I knew had a cow having trouble with calving. I helped him."

"With magic." It wasn't a question. She'd seen me Grab her cop.

"Yes," I said. "I'm a Brown."

"You trying to rise in rank?"

"I live on the streets," I said in the same tone one might ask, "Are you stupid?"

"That could mean 'yes' or 'no.' Are you desperate to get off the street? Maybe you've been trying to become a Red?"

"No, I haven't been trying to rise. I've been trying to eat." *Drink. I'd been trying to drink.*

"So you helped the farmer with his cow."

"Yes," I answered.

"And he paid you?"

"Yes, ten talens." I'd saved the cow and the calf, and the cheap bastard paid me nearly nothing. He knew how hard up I was, and he'd taken advantage of it.

And yet I was the one sitting in the police station while he enjoyed his house and his family and his dinner, cow and calf safely stabled in a warm barn, munching hay. I envied the cow.

"So, when was this?" the detective asked through her razor-thin lips.

"I don't know exactly. In the morning, for sure. A few days ago? You might ask him. He'd remember." He wouldn't be pleased to be asked about it, not at all. He should have used a Guild Wizard and paid full price, as he well knew. Serve him right to get a visit from the cops.

"And you still have some of the money?"

"Five talens," I said, patting my pocket, protectively.

"So, not that long ago, then? You helped him maybe two days ago, maybe four?"

"Probably three." I shrugged. I had enough cash left to buy three Brown Worms, and that's all that mattered. In fact, I wished I had the ale right then.

"So, you know another woman was raped three days ago? In Tarawa?"

I'd known it'd come to this. That's all anyone talked about. People acted like the end of the world was approaching. No girls on the street, and no women either. And everyone looked at everyone all suspicious like.

"Were you in Tarawa then?" she asked.

I shrugged again. "Maybe. Probably."

"Did you know her?"

This detective thought she was tricky, but it was impossible to trick an innocent man into a trap like this. "How should I know? You haven't told me her name."

"Melisandra Rockwater."

I thought for a moment. Before I'd lost my life, I'd had a job with clients. I'd known people. I'd known families. But still, my mind came up blank while sifting for this name. "No," I said finally. "I don't know her, or her family either."

"Did you rape her? Or any other woman?"

"No! I'm a drunk, not a criminal."

"They're often the same thing."

"I've never hurt a soul," I said. And then I thought of Lyric. I'd hurt her for sure, but not like that. "I've never forced myself on anyone," I amended.

I don't know what the icy detective thought. I doubted she believed me. Who could blame her? I looked like street scum. After living rough for a month I probably *was* street scum.

"Hmmph," said Detective Habit, which could've meant anything. "Please wait a moment."

Like I had a choice. I watched the detective walk down the

hall, heels clicking on the tile and her brown hair swinging past her shoulders. How had my life come to this?

Detective Habit returned in the company of a familiar face. Recognizing his mossy beard, my fists itched to hit something. Maybe his face. Hard.

"This is Wizard Uriah, Chair of the local Wizard's Guild. Do you mind if he—"

"I know this man," Wizard Uriah said with a hearty clap on my shoulder. "Gage Feldspar! Obadiah's pig!"

"Yes," I said, striving to keep my voice emotionless. "How're you, Wizard?"

"Better than you, apparently. Good thing I'm here to bail you out of trouble, Gage—first the crazed pig, and now this."

I swallowed, biting back a curse. I'd rather chew off my foot than let this man help me again.

"The Chair's been kind enough to help us sort through potential suspects," Habit said. "If you don't object, he'll briefly scan your mind."

"And if I do mind?" Because I did. I didn't want this creep in my brain. He'd saved me once, unasked, at great cost to himself. I never wanted to see him again. I didn't want him crawling through my brain.

"Then you can stay in the cells until tomorrow, when you can try to convince a judge that a mind scan isn't necessary."

For a moment, I was tempted. The night was cold. The cells would be warm. But a night without Brown Worm . . . I needed ale more now than I'd had in weeks—maybe since Obadiah's pig. "He can scan me," I replied finally, looking at the floor.

Uriah held out his hand expectantly, and I laid my palm in his. I'd met half-orcs I'd rather touch.

I'm only a Brown-status Wizard, which is pretty low on the food chain, but with someone like the Guild Chair, who must be a Silver or Gold, conducting a mind scan, I expected to feel something, his smarmy presence oozing through my thoughts.

But I felt nothing.

Guild Chair Uriah must be powerful indeed. Even as I squirmed in my chair, I told myself that his power didn't intimidate me. I lied.

Then he dropped my palm, giving Detective Habit a big, wide smile—yellow teeth above his nearly green beard. "He didn't do it, Detective. You can let him go."

Despite the fact I'd love to punch this man to a bloody pulp, relief flooded through me. The cops wouldn't be roasting me tonight. Thanks to Guild Chair Uriah.

How had I managed to rack up two debts to this oily man?

Pike showed me—ungently—to the door. He opened it for me, with a mocking bow. "Get a job," he said. Then he put his black boot on my ass and pushed me toward the stairs.

I stumbled to my feet, glad I hadn't tumbled down the icy granite. That could've really hurt. Sticking to the un-iced path, I went down the stairs, fighting the biting wind. Then I trudged toward the Slug and Garden, focusing wholly on how good the Brown Worms would taste.

An arctic dust devil swirled across the road and wrapped around my leg. It crawled up to my balls, stealing all heat. It occurred to me in that moment that I had a choice—I had enough talens for a room, if I didn't buy any beer.

My choice was clear.

Brown Worm.

"Leave me alone!" Wind distorted the high-pitched plea, but the words were recognizable. I peered through the darkness, wondering where the shout came from. I didn't want to walk through an ongoing brawl.

"Stop! Go away!"

I guessed the shouts came from the alley. I would have ignored the violent-sounding voices except that I'd heard a decidedly feminine yelp.

The rapist wouldn't be attacking someone this close to the cops, would he?

Maybe I could clear my almost-accused name, at least of this crime.

Maybe I'd get a cash reward—then I could have room *and* a beer.

I might look like street scum to the police, but with my broad shoulders and a determined attitude, I knew I looked dangerous to some of the real scum that seethed on these streets at night.

I straightened my shoulders and strode into the alley like I was the boss. "What're you doing to the lady?" I growled, letting magic make my voice deeper.

But the thugs, both half-orcs, weren't attacking a woman—they were harassing a boy. One of the thugs held the kid by his neck against the red brick wall while the victim kicked valiantly. The other creep looked on and laughed, his pointy teeth glittering in the winter moonlight.

The half-orc pair were preparing to do some serious damage to the kid.

The sensible part of my mind told me to walk away, just walk away. These weren't the rapists, and saving the kid wasn't going to make me a hero with the police. The kid's ratty clothes pegged him as a street rat—he couldn't even give me a cash reward.

But sensibility was never my strong suit.

"Let him go," I rumbled.

"Get out of here," one of them snarled. The closest half-orc towered at least a foot over me. His skin was gray, even for his kind, and his sloping forehead made him look really ugly.

"Yeah," the other half-orc sneered. "Fuck off." He had some sort of tribal tattoo inscribed on the side of his head. In blood red.

I Sensed a big rat lurking in the dark. Good. I could use it. I Sensed another few rats just a little bit farther away. "Leave the kid alone," I said, using a subtle spell to give me the appearance of looking larger than I was.

My legs apart, shoulders back, deep-voiced and thick, I reeked of confidence. Even half-orcs had to think twice before attacking the man they thought they saw before them. Half-orcs aren't known for their intelligence.

I walked in like I belonged there, like the biggest rooster in the barnyard. And I kicked the closest bastard in the knee with all my strength. Hearing the popping, crunching sound, I knew I got him in just the right spot.

He howled in pain, and I snorted, knowing I'd busted the capsule of fluid behind his knee bone. It'd ooze liquid for days. His knee would swell to the size of a goose egg in a matter of hours.

The half-orc prick clutched his knee, still howling, so I slammed the ball of my palm into his nose slits, and he howled louder.

Have fun chasing little kids, buddy.

The other thug abandoned the kid to take a swipe at me with his long ape arms, but just then I convinced the lurking rats that orc eyeballs tasted delicious, like farm-fresh eggs. I could hear the rats laughing as they launched themselves toward the villain's face.

Half a heartbeat later, I heard the rats land with a thud on the half-orc. The creep's fist swung wildly, missing me by an arm's length.

Ha! I punched him solidly in his solar plexus, knocking his lungs straight on, turning them into empty flapping sacks. He doubled over, gasping for air. I jerked my knee up hard then, smashing his nose and his teeth. Sharp pain rushed through my knee to my brain, but blood poured from his nose slits as he collapsed to the ground in a fetal position.

Filled with adrenaline, I strode over and grabbed the kid. Neither creature tried to stop me. It was over and I'd won.

Both half-orcs writhed on the cold cobblestones, gasping for breath.

"The police station's just up the street," I said pointedly to the half-orcs. "I'm going there now to tell them what I've found."

One of them snarled at me, its bloodied yellow teeth glittering in the moon. I wasn't cold anymore.

"Of course," I continued, "you might well be gone by the time they get here."

With that, I left.

Still high on testosterone and adrenaline, I put my hand on the boy's shoulder. He tried to squirm away, but I kept him next to me as we strolled down the street, away from the cops.

Of course I'd been bluffing about that.

When we rounded the corner, I dug three of my five talens out of my trousers. "Here," I said. "Get something to eat. I'd head over to that shelter on Tusrui Street if I were you. There's a real nice lady over there, Mrs. Jericho. She likes kids." Maybe she'd send him to school and find a good home for him, too.

No one should have to live life like this, picking pockets and sleeping rough.

3

My front door rang while I was heating a beaker. *Damn.* I didn't want to spoil the potion.

But maybe the flier had found someone.

Jerking the beaker from the flame, I burned my fingers and swore. I really needed that assistant.

Wiping my hands on the skirt of my fitted kirtle, I flung the door open. "Yes?" But the man waiting for me banished all impatient thoughts from my mind.

"I've come to inquire about the job. Is it filled?" He had the sexiest voice I'd ever heard. The Star Goddess herself would be weak in the knees with his voice.

"I'm Esmenet Sokaris," I said. "What's your name?"

"Fyord Amiln."

Jet-black hair, thick and hanging endearingly in his eyes. A face like a fox, angles and laughter. Eyes the color of turquoise stones and just as bright. They very nearly matched the unusual jerkin he wore. Turquoise leather wasn't something I'd seen before, but if designers saw how this man wore it, blue jerkins would be all over the streets.

"Come in," I said, warmly. "No, the position isn't filled." I said that last word suggestively, letting it roll off my tongue. He had that lean lanky look I've always favored. Like a wolf. Could I drool any more?

"I hadn't realized from the ad," he said, "but you're a Love Wizard, aren't you?" He followed me toward the living room.

Not stupid, then. "What gave it away?" I asked over my shoulder, moving my hips a little more than necessary under the weight of his gaze.

"Too sexy to be anything but," he said, flashing me a grin.

Oh, my flier had finally found the guy I needed, the guy I wanted. I sent a mental kiss of thanks to the Star Goddess.

"Sit here," I said, pointing to a love seat. Retrieving the *Wabizi* hand mirror from the end table, I settled next to him.

If he passed the mirror's test, I'd have the perfect partner. Handing him the mirror, I said, "Look in the depths for a minute while I ask you some questions."

"Okay," he said, obeying.

Over his shoulder I could see the image. The mirror reflected a truth for him nearly immediately. He had strong magic. Promising.

He was touching the face of a woman, both gazes filled with an intense love. She was beautiful. Her chestnut-colored hair was twisted at the top of her head. Wispy tendrils had escaped, and they framed her high-cheekboned face. Her eyes looked kind.

"This is amazing magic," he said. "I've never heard of such a thing." He indicated the gold gilt mirror.

In the depths of the glass, I watched as Fyord presented a box made of rosewood to the beautiful woman. I could see a lip of green velvet lining the hinged edge. With her slender hand to her throat, nervous anticipation crossed her face, as if she knew what lay inside. It both frightened and excited her. Upon opening it, the lady jumped up and threw herself into Fyord's arms.

A shift in the depths. I hoped for someone beside this green-eyed woman, but the hope was in vain.

A fire crackled in a bedroom, sending cozy shadows dancing across huge tapestries. Bathed in the light of flickering flames, the largest tapestry depicted fair maids picking daisies from a huge field of wildflowers while tall hounds stood at their sides.

Lying on a tall four-poster bed made of cherry, the woman wore a filmy gauze of virginal white. More relaxed, Fyord lay naked beside her, holding her hand. She looked ready to bolt.

With a teasing expression he walked his fingers up her side. She swatted him away with a nervous smile. He did it again, getting closer to that ticklish spot beneath her arm. She rolled toward him, thwarting his fingers of their desired goal as she sank into the mattress. Fyord threatened to tickle the other side, and she picked up a pillow and bopped him over his head.

But electricity charged the moment. Her gaze met his, and even at this distance from the mirror I could see the desire in their expressions. Her wedding-night fears had evaporated under the heat of his touch.

Toying with the tie of her gown, he pulled the string and let the cloth float to the floor. The woman made to cover herself, but Fyord didn't let her. Instead, he stood back and admired her.

Fyord crossed the room to stand before her, his cock throbbing. He slowly ran his hand over her stomach, her ivory thigh. She quivered under his touch, but fear wasn't on her face. Anticipation was.

When he placed the lightest of kisses on her breast, I watched her eyes open in surprise and then roll back in pleasure. She relaxed into his arms and—

On the love seat next to me, Fyord placed his hand over the glass protectively. "That's my wedding night," he said, almost with chagrin.

Gently I moved his hand away and reassured him. "I'm sure the scene's shifted."

"What is this magic?" he asked, peering to see what the next image brought.

"It shows me all I need to know to make my decision," I answered, but he was already lost in the mirror-directed reverie.

The same beautiful woman, now thick with child, lay in a bed with a mattress as thin as their wedding night's had been thick. Gone were the tapestries. Cracked plaster decorated these walls. From this bed, a tiny kitchen could be seen. The apartment had an even smaller dining area, with a small desk squirreled away in the corner.

This image must have been from that morning because Fyord was wearing his unusual turquoise jerkin as he told his wife good-bye. She wore a brave smile while her hand rested protectively on her large stomach. The kiss he gave her was long, and with a grin he kissed her belly, too.

The mirror shimmered to a halt, and Fyord made a sound of disappointment. But I'd seen all I needed to see. My decision had been made.

"You love her, don't you?" I asked, knowing the answer before I heard it.

"With all of my heart. Ceara's brother gambled away the family fortune. He forged my name and gambled mine away, too."

"Gambling terrorizes some people," I said. "It's an addiction, like alcoholism."

"Can you treat it?" he asked with a sudden rush of hope.

"No," I said, my mind working the problem as it always did. "Addictions are hard to treat. Wizards can Sense the illness, we can see the disease in the molecular structures of the cells, but we can't change the cellular structures." I looked across the room thinking with frustration of the various addicts

who'd sought my help. It didn't matter what they were addicted to—alcohol, drugs, sex, gambling—I couldn't help them.
"Perhaps someday . . ."

"Well, someday won't help this problem. It's killing us now."

"I can see that."

"Then you can also see I really need a job, a profession. My
parents and I decided a long time ago to ignore my magical aptitude and focus on the family business. I've been trained in
banking and investment, but Ceara's brother . . . after all he did
with my signature, well, I've been blackballed from any of the
money careers."

"I see," I said. But I couldn't give him the job he sought.

"I'm a Tan," he said, his dark hair hanging in his eyes. He
pushed it back with his elegant fingers. "And I work hard. I
know it looks like my life's been charmed, but I always took
my schooling seriously."

I would've loved to hire this guy.

"I can't hire you," I said. The breadth of his shoulders gave
me so many reasons to want to hire him.

Disappointment crossed his face. "But I thought . . ."

"That I liked you?"

"Well, yes."

"I do," I said. "But you've found your heart's mate. If you
take this job with me, the love of your life will be jeopardized.
You don't want to put your relationship with your wife on the
line for this, believe me."

"But she wants me to get this job as badly as I want it. We
have a strong relationship. It can withstand"—Fyord waved his
arms at me—"this."

"Neither of you understand the responsibilities of a Love
Wizard's assistant. You didn't even know I *was* a Love Wizard."

"We didn't know what kind of Wizard you were, but it's

such a respectable line of work we decided that even if you were a Love Wizard I'd take the job."

His earnestness was endearing. So were his piercing blue eyes. If only he weren't so happily married. "Fyord," I said, taking his hand in mine. I worked hard to ignore the chemistry of his cells whispering to mine. "If you were to take this job, you and I would have sex frequently." He looked embarrassed, but I could Sense his interest. I continued, unrelenting. He had to know this. "It's true that many times you'd think—you'd feel like—you were making love to your wife. Those times probably wouldn't hurt your relationship."

"That's what I mean," he said in a voice thick with hope. "Ceara and I are strong together. It wouldn't hurt us."

"But there're other times when you'd have to lead the spell. During those times, you'd know exactly who you were having sex with. Very few human relationships can withstand that, and from what I've seen of you in the mirror, it would kill you and your beloved."

"I'd never hurt my wife," he said, and I wished I'd found him first. Fyord sat silently for a moment, staring at his hands as if they could help him. "I need a job," he said finally.

I stood up and said, "Fyord, I'm a Love Wizard. I fix relationships—not ruin them."

He stood, too, eyes hard with resignation.

"But I can still help a little bit," I said. "I have a friend at the local Guild who might be able to guide you toward a more appropriate apprenticeship."

"That might help," he said. "I'm looking into every possibility."

I scribbled the name and address. "Also," I added a warning, "Ceara is due within the month."

He looked at me and blinked. "No," he said. "She's due in two month's time."

"I saw her only through the mirror, but I Sensed she's due imminently. Love Wizards deliver a lot of babies, and I'll happily deliver your child, free of charge, as one Wizard to another."

After Fyord left, I buried my face in my hands. He'd been so damn perfect. Grabbing the right hormones from his pituitary and his adrenal, pulling proteins from his blood to make love potions would've been so much fun.

Now I needed to make a new flier. I still needed to find my guy.

4

"Let me in!" I bellowed at my own front door. My breath, thick with Brown Worm, condensed into hot clouds in the cold winter air. "By the Hells, Lyric! It's my house, too!" I hammered my fists on the thick oak panels. To no avail.

"Gage," Lyric's voice had a patient edge, and she spoke softly, forcing me to stop pounding so I could hear her. "Please, stop. You're annoying the neighbors."

"Fuck them!" I yelled, mechanically beating the door.

"Gage," she said, so quietly. "I'm sliding some talens under the door. Get a hotel room or get a drink. Just go away. Please."

"Fuck you!" I kicked the door with all my might. *Bang. Bang.* Icicles, crashed from the eaves to the pavement right in front of me. Icy diamonds scattered over my shoes, making me shiver in the cold. "And fuck your talens!" *Bang.*

But when I heard the coins slide under the door, clinking on the weather stripping—weather stripping I'd installed myself— I stopped my attack against the door.

My mouth was watering—I could taste the beer those talens would buy. And I loathed myself.

I considered walking away then, being a bigger man than I was and just walking away. Lyric could retrieve the talens in the morning. Or some other homeless guy could take them, and buy a room for a night. Or a Brown Worm.

I'd find someplace real to live. I'd get a real job. Again. I'd forswear the Brown Worm.

But starlight glittered off the coins, and my hands itched for the pints of Brown Worm. My mind craved the oblivion they promised. One pint and I'd be funny and charming and entertaining. It'd take the edge off. I only needed one pint. Only one.

As I reached to pick up the coins, her voice—as lush as birdcall on a spring morning, but chilling as a winter's night—accosted me. "Don't come back, Gage. We're through. Please, stay away."

I took the talens and ran.

Afraid I'd change my mind, I jogged toward my parents' home. They wouldn't ask questions—not right away. They'd put me up for a night or two. They'd feed me something warm and good for me. I could bathe finally, maybe even get my mother to patch up my shirt.

Cold from the cobblestones chilled my feet as I ran. I didn't have to go to my parents'. I could use the coins for a hotel room, something simple and clean. No one in an inn would ask questions. I could eat and wash my clothes. No pitying looks from my mother or head shakings from my pop. By the Stars, the anonymity of a hotel sounded like just what I needed.

Pausing at the lamp-lit intersection, I panted, deciding on a direction. The closest hotel was . . .

I turned west, heading down the cobblestoned street toward the beckoning glow of the Golden Coach. Candles lit the windows. The night promised warmth and safety—and dignity.

The innkeeper wouldn't know that the talens I gave him were my last. The glittering sign etched with the carriage and horse promised a haven from my problems.

With an eye on the sign, looking neither right nor left, I slowed to a quick walk, my heavy breaths filling the night with puffs of fog. The Slug and Garden lay between my goal and me, and the pub pulled me as strongly as a magnet pulls iron filings. Locking my jaw, I resolutely padded toward the hotel.

As I passed the open pub door, holding my breath, hoping for strength, I envisioned a warm, clean bed. Two steps past the pub, and my feet still headed toward the hotel. Maybe I'd done it. Three steps. I'd done it. I was past the bar. I'd *done* it.

A hot bath, respectful company, would be mine.

A cold breeze skittered down the street, and then the beery smell wafting from the window wrapped itself around me, snaring me. Like a wolf in a trap, I fought it, and like the wolf, I lost.

Just one pint, I told myself.

No one said I was smart.

My regular stool was empty, waiting for my bum to warm it. My drinking buddy, a blue-eyed gnome, waved to me, a happy grin on his face. Clover wore an emerald-green shirt that showed off his thickly muscled arms. They looked like pythons, even when I was sober.

"You think she meant it?" I asked him. Clover's forked beard framed his otherwise naked chin. "When she said to never come back," I clarified, "do you think she meant it?"

"I'd mean it," Clover said.

Slightly high on my third Brown Worm, I elbowed him. "Gnomes are always joking."

"That's true, but being married to you for seven years wouldn't be very funny."

"Was I married to you that long?" But he was right. Lyric had been patient for seven years. Then she'd had enough. Not that I blamed her.

And then, with a dramatic flourish, the pub doors opened in a way that bespoke the entry of someone who thought a lot of himself. I watched heads turn as Guild Chair Uriah entered the pub, his thick, black cloak billowing behind him like bat wings. *Damn.* Couldn't I get away from this man?

Watching Wizard Uriah's grand entry, Clover whispered to me, "We'll get this guy. He's so damn snooty. Just watch."

"Clover," I whispered back. "Just leave him alone." I elbowed him hard in the ribs. "I mean it. I don't want anything to do with him."

But my gnome friend ignored me, getting everyone's attention with a shrill whistle. In the stunned silence, Clover shouted, "I've a taste to tell a tale!"

Everyone loved Clover's tales. "Let's hear Obadiah's Pig!" the bar crowd shouted right back at him, rowdy for a story.

"Ah!" he chirped to them. "An entertaining choice! Especially on this evening."

"Why's that?" someone shouted.

"It's true, it's true—we lack Obadiah. We even lack his pig."

"I've got pork rinds!" some comedian shouted, but Clover ignored him and continued.

"But we have the Wizard who crazed the pig." Clover pointed at me, and the crowd cheered. I gave him a look meant to shut him up, but it was futile. Clover was on a roll.

The little gnome held up his hands, and the barflies quieted. "And we have the Wizard who saved the pig." With a bow rich with flourish, he pointed to Guild Chair Uriah.

"No!" I muttered to Clover, but it was too late.

I shot a look at Uriah. His grin was tight. He was pissed. But he bowed gracefully to the crowd. By the Stars, humiliation followed me everywhere—Uriah's and mine.

Halfway down the bar, with a swish of her golden hair, Sweet Orange held up her lute. She drank here as often as I did. With a strum of her strings, Sweet Orange said, "Clover, tonight I shall accompany you."

"Lucky gnome," I heard someone mutter.

As Wizard Uriah accepted his drink, amber-colored scotch from the barmaid, Clover gave a gleeful cackle next to me. Then he cleared his throat. The gnome sang in a voice as pure as a summer breeze,

> *Sweet Orange the elf, and everybody else*
> *Let me introduce you to Guild Chair Uriah.*

The gnome held up his hand to the crowd and said, "You all sing 'You-rye-ah.'"

"You-rye-ah!"

I wanted to club Clover right there on the spot.

> *Uriah is the Gold who single-handedly saved*
> *The county fair when Obadiah's pig got crazed.*

"Now you sing," said Clover to the crowd.

"You-rye-ah!"

Uriah held up his glass to the crowd, looking very much out of place. Why was a snoot like him drinking in a dive like this? I wasn't nearly drunk enough to find this amusing.

"The prick is following me," I muttered, but nobody listened. I drank the final drops from my stein, wishing I could buy a refill. But I'd drunk my talens away with the last pint.

> *Old Farmer Shade said to Obadiah's wand*
> *The cavage is mine to win at the fair*

Make my pig's nose clean,
Make my pig's nose clear.

Uriah held up his hand. "Please." His voice was cultured, incongruous with his scrappy, mossy beard. "Might we sing a different song?"

Sweet Orange tossed her hair over her shoulder in such a fetching way as she played her lute. "Can't stop now," she insisted with a flirtatious smile. Who could refuse her? Her tresses cascaded like a waterfall.

But I agreed with Uriah. We didn't need to tell this story. Why hadn't I gone to the Golden Coach? Two more steps and I would have been out of the pub's spell.

The job is so simple,
My assistant will do.
Let Gage Feldspar fix your pig for you.

"Ga-age! Ga-age!" The crowd shouted over the playful sounds of Sweet Orange's lute. Only the thick crowd kept me from bolting for the door. That and the fact that the barkeep had just given me a free Brown Worm.

Clover's voice carried easily through the room.

With the wave of his wand
Gage spelled the black hog
Who found a fat truffle under a log.
But he ate that rich mushroom
Which a truffle hog should not do
And then he consumed the fair's rich beefy stew.
The pig ate the biscuits.
He drank golden ale.
He stole ladies' almond cakes
And made them fall pale.

With the last line, Clover put the back of his hand to his forehead and pretended a very ladylike swoon. The crowd ate it up, cheering with laughter.

The weight of Wizard Uriah's gaze felt like an anvil on my chest. Not wanting to look at the laughing faces, I stared at my ale glass. A huge scratch scarred the surface of the pub's counter, and I ran my finger over it.

> Obadiah's pig ate all the fair's food.
> And would have continued to behave oh so rude
> But a savior arrived
> So smart and so brave
> A Gold wand he brandished
> A Gold wand he waved
> But the pig was so fast
> And the pig was so quick
> That each wave of the wand
> Just made the pig shit
> Uriah did chase him
> Over hill, over dale
> But each wave of his wand
> Brought shit from his tail.

"You-rye-ah!" The crowd cheered. "You-rye-ah!"

I couldn't look up, so I pressed my finger into the gouge, hard, wishing I were pressing Clover's eyeballs or his windpipe. Anything to shut him up.

> Each wave of Chair's wand
> Brought shit from pig's tail
> Each wave of Chair's wand
> Brought a squeal and a wail.

Sweet Orange herself was laughing so hard now that tears streamed down her elfin face, but she couldn't wipe them off without interrupting her playing. She played diligently on.

> *Uriah our hero*
> *Stopped the pig in its tracks*
> *But not before he made us all laugh*
> *For when the pig finally ceased*
> *Its mad dash around town*
> *Uriah found pig shit*
> *All over his gown.*

The crowd went wild with the line, so Clover obligingly repeated it.

> *Uriah found pig shit*
> *All over his gown*
> *Now the odor of pig shit*
> *Likes not to leave*
> *It stays and it lingers*
> *It gives no reprieve.*
> *Uriah, he stank all the day, all the night*
> *He stank 'til his beard grew green with the fright!*

What did I need friends for? I couldn't bring myself to look at Uriah. He'd saved me at the fair. He'd saved me at the police station. Expecting him to save me now was too much. He needed to be saved himself.

> *Uriah, he stank all the day, all the night*
> *He stank 'til his beard grew green with the fright.*

Sweet Orange finished the song with a fancy flourish of strings, wiping the tears from her eyes. Clover bowed to the hooting and applauding crowd.

"Zapp! Eeeh! Zappp! Eeeh!" I heard the man sitting next to me tell his friend, mimicking Guild Chair Uriah as he spelled the pig, and the pig dodged out of the way. "It took Uriah himself nearly an hour to undo Gage's spell! Isn't that right, sir?"

Wizard Uriah grunted, but I knew the answer. Guild Chair Uriah had needed two hours to undo it. And the fair committee had to promise free concessions to all the vendors for next year to make up for it. And Obadiah couldn't spell any more mushroom-hunting pigs. I slurped the last drop from my glass.

Obadiah got the shit end of that stick, literally. It wasn't his fault I fucked up the spell. And it wasn't the committee's fault the damn pig ate all the food. And it wasn't Wizard Uriah's fault everyone was laughing at him, imagining him covered in pig shit and laughing at his beard, ugly as it was.

Wizard Uriah held up his glass, bringing silence to the room with his graceful motion. "Gage really has the makings of a remarkable Wizard," he said, the picture of a gracious loser. "My spells actually bounced off the pig's behind. By the time I fixed the error, I was covered in muck and two hours had passed." He smiled, laughing at his own misfortune.

The drunken patrons guffawed, but I saw the tightness behind his eyes, contradicting his bonhomie.

"Pig shit!" Clover shouted and nailed my side with a sharp elbow. To me he muttered, "See? I told you we'd bring his highness down."

"To Obadiah's pig," the half-orc barmaid said, sliding another Brown Worm in front of Clover, Wizard Uriah, and me. "It's on the house."

"Thank you, madam," Uriah said, all elegance and manners.

Slamming back the free ale, a thought occurred to me—maybe I'd get a free Brown Worm each time the bar crowd told the Obadiah's pig story.

The bitter taste of ale rolled down my throat. Maybe I could go to my mother's tonight. If I could just make it to the door . . .

Just then the door opened. A dwarf with fierce-looking skull-shaped beads twined into her beard walked into the bar, accompanied by a cold gust of damp air.

The zephyr surfed a flier right into the room and plastered it to my face. Just like it knew what it was doing.

Since I was halfway plastered myself, I took the cold wet slap as a sign. My brain said to itself, "Self, whatever this sheet says, take it as Word."

Oh Hells, who was I kidding? No Word could save me. I'm just a loser, and there's no way around that. Bosses, even ones as great as Obadiah, get tired of late and hung-over employees. Who could blame them?

So I peeled the supposed life-changing flier off my face. I removed it slowly, not wanting to leave the words stuck on my cheek. The cynical part of my mind expected it to be one of those ubiquitous ads for new fangled tampons or hair-growth spells.

But part of me longed for salvation, and that part knew the flier was a message, a message that could not be ignored. See, for a loser I had this strange ingrained belief that I was meant for bigger things.

The memory of Uriah's overly kind smile flashed through my mind. His tight, nearly angry smile, as the crowd laughed at him. Who was I kidding?

I carefully unfolded the damp, yellowed sheet. The words were surprisingly clear, somehow unsmudged by the rain. The flier read:

Gold Level Wizard looking for magician of beginning level, Gray through Tan, to assist with spells/light housekeeping. Assistant preferably will be interested in pursuing a higher degree. Pay: 48 talens per month, tutoring, room and board. Apply to E. H. Sokaris in person at 73 Bantam Boulevard, Carathay. Serious applicants only.

The job was perfect, upscale address and everything.

Okay, I didn't have much interest in pursuing a higher degree. Too much work. But light housekeeping didn't sound too bad. I could definitely put the "lie" in "light," if you get my meaning. The broom and I weren't exactly friends. And landing this job would save me having to find an apartment. I could catch two fish with one hook.

But mostly I liked this: the Wizard didn't ask for references. For a man who'd been living on the street, for a man who'd been fired from his last ten jobs, this was an important feature.

"Barkeep! Another Brown Worm!" I laughed, and if it sounded a little maniacal, Clover didn't say. I elbowed him and said, "I just got a new job." I waved the flaccid paper at him, all grins.

"That's great, Gage. Maybe you can afford a haircut." Sarcastic bastard. He himself had hair so perfect that it looked like someone had drawn it on his head. "Ah, you're jealous."

Fuck him. I was saved!

"Excuse me, Mr. Feldspar," Guild Chair Uriah said. His nose was twitching. "May I see that, please?"

Reluctantly I handed it to him. I wanted it, but how could I say no?

Wizard Uriah came as close to snatching the flier from me as he could, without actually snatching. He held the yellow paper to his nose, closed his eyes and sniffed. Then his eyes flew wide open, and I was pretty sure I saw shocked anger cross his face. But maybe it was desire.

"May I keep this, please?" the Guild Chair asked, folding the flier up neatly and placing it in his elegant pocket.

"But I—" I started.

"Thank you very much, Mr. Feldspar." Wizard Uriah tipped his hat at me and walked out the door, his black cloak floating behind him.

He left the stink of the ocean in his wake.

5

――――――――――

Hearing the bell ring, I put my textbook down and walked to the door. My latest flier had been out for three days now.

Turning the knob, I would've had more hope, but the last person to stand expectantly on my stoop was a thirteen-year-old boy. That certainly wouldn't do.

But the man waiting for me was no thirteen-year-old.

"Guild Chair Uriah," I said, trying not to stare at his weedy beard. Was it my imagination or was that thing getting greener? "What a pleasant surprise." I stepped back and made room for him. "Please, come in."

"Thank you, Wizard Sokaris. We need to talk." His voice was stern.

Fingers of fear laced my heart. Wizard Uriah was one of only four other Gold Wizards in the land, and, given his political position within the Guild, he was technically my superior, although I was one of the four Golds.

I led him to my sitting room, knowing I should offer tea. But my kitchen was a wreck. One of these days I should clean it and buy at least the basics. I didn't think I even had coffee or anything else suited to polite company.

Sitting opposite of him I asked, "What can I do for you?"

"What is the meaning of this?" he demanded, amber eyes hardened in anger. He flipped one of my fliers onto the cherry-wood table between us. The ad was one imbued with age parameters. No more children at my door, thank you. "It smells like . . . sex! Pure sex! What is this?"

Cold anger flared through my veins. "It's a flier," I said in a chilly voice.

"I see that. But you know the rules."

"I'm breaking no rules." How dare he tell me what spells I could cast?

"Esmenet." Uriah held up a placating hand. "Forgive me. I didn't mean to sound so imperious."

He'd sounded more than imperious, but I let it slide, willing to be gracious—for the moment at least. I nodded for him to continue.

"You're the best Love Wizard we've seen in many generations."

"Thank you," I said, warily.

"I'm not saying that as an accolade. I'm telling you this to remind you how the community relies on you. You've made great breakthroughs in anything to do with endocrinology."

"Thank you," I said again. He was right. Although I was a Love Wizard, I helped with birthing and lactation. I could help many problems based in biochemistry.

"That thyroid elixir you brewed for the Guild last month is still being analyzed. No one's seen anything that effective."

I was appeased. Sort of. "What's this have to do with my flier, Uriah?"

"I'm here to remind you that if you bond with a mate, your

potion-brewing skills will be lost. We—the Guild and the people of this land—will lose our most talented Love Wizard."

Anger raced through my blood via nerve synapses, jolting me from my shoulders to my teeth. Was he telling me my job? Wizard Uriah hadn't brewed a potion in decades.

I cleared my throat, controlling my temper. "The flier doesn't say anything about binding with a mate."

Uriah straightened a crease in his elegant grey trousers. "Of course not. But if you find the man who fits this biochemical profile, I believe you'll have found yourself the perfect mate, at least from a hormonal perspective."

"What're you talking about? If I find this man, I'll be able to brew elixirs that help the victims of these rapes. They'll be able to recover their self esteem and confidence. I've been powerless until now, and this spell gives me hope!"

"This *Rurutu* spell hasn't been used for years, Esmenet, not since the reign of Alfred III, and there's a good reason for that."

I'd found the notes on the glyph scribbled in the margins of one of my old textbooks, but I didn't know any good reason not to use it. The *Rurutu* hurt no one, not the user nor the creator, despite its ancient origins.

"And what's the reason for this moratorium?" I asked.

"If you find the person who compliments all your dopamines, serotonins, vasopressins, and everything else, you'll have found your heart mate."

I straightened in my seat. I wasn't looking for love—I was looking for the man with the perfect biology to help the rape victims. "So you've asserted," I said. "But how do you know that?" I'd never heard of such a contention—and I was a Gold Love Wizard. But still, it might be true.

"As the Guild Chair, I've access to many ancient texts, many of which are unavailable to the public. If you'd like to read them, please stop by my office. You can read them there."

I'd love to read them. Love to. But time wasn't something I had to spare. If I could sift through them in my bedchamber before bed, I might make headway, but there was little chance that traveling halfway across town would be possible, not with my schedule.

"Esmenet, you know I'd never tell you what to do with your love life . . ."

I didn't know any such thing. It seemed like he was doing exactly that.

"But if you stumble across your heart mate with this flier, you'll have to give up your practice."

Helping people was my calling. Brewing potions allowed me to see exactly how molecules within our bodies worked, and how I could manipulate them when things went wrong. I didn't want to find a heart mate, and I didn't want to give up my practice.

Maybe Uriah was right. I didn't want to jeopardize my career. When I cast the ancient *Rurutu*, I thought the Guild might object based on its antiquity. It had never occurred to me that I might use this spell to find my heart mate. I didn't want to take that chance.

"Forgive my quick temper, Uriah. I didn't realize I'd imperil my ability to brew potent elixirs by casting this spell. I don't want to lose that ability any more than the Guild wants me to."

"Then you'll cease?"

"Yes, sir. I'll make no more *Rurutu* fliers."

As I opened the door to let him out, the wind carried a foul scent of rotting fish into my foyer. *Funny,* I thought to myself. *The ocean's several leagues north of here.*

My client doorbell rang, and as I raced to the back entry, I thought about Fyord's wife. Ceara's time wasn't yet, unless the babe decided to come early.

"Hello?" I opened the door. Two teenage girls stood in my garden, maybe seventeen and nineteen years of age. One girl glared at me. The other stared at her shoes. "Would you like to come in?" I asked.

I led them to my office and bade them to sit. "My name's Onyx," the angry girl said before I could speak. "And this is my sister, Ruby. Ruby was raped last night."

Onyx didn't mince words, I noticed. "Where's your mother? Ruby, wouldn't you like her here with you?"

Ruby sniffed, and I saw tears dripping onto her lap. Silently, I handed her a handkerchief from the stack on my desk.

"My mother's been dead for years now," Ruby said. "It's our aunt who takes care of us, and we don't want to tell her about this."

Onyx gave me a hard look, daring me to judge. "Auntie found Ruby kissing her beau not too long ago and convinced herself we're both sluts. She'll think Ruby deserved this," Onyx said. "She'll punish her."

"Our auntie isn't really very nice," said Ruby in a subdued voice.

My Wizard senses told me these girls weren't exaggerating. Their aunt was very strict and not happy in her role as a surrogate mother.

"Would you girls follow me, please?" I led them to a smaller spelling room I kept for clients. "Ruby, please sit in the center, in the middle of all the hearts there. Onyx, you need to stay to the side."

Using my feathered wand to channel the earth's power, I cast my mind over the girl. Strengthened by my heart pentagrams, amid a handful of small injuries, I immediately Sensed a serious complication.

A zygote—Ruby's egg surrounded by thousands of the attacker's sperm—was traveling up her fallopian tube directly toward the uterus.

If I did nothing, the egg and sperm mass would enter the uterus. In three days, the mass would turn into a sphere-shaped ball made up of a handful of cells. Inside that ball would be Ruby's egg. In five or six days the sphere would attach to the internal surface of the uterus, and an embryo would form. In forty weeks, Ruby would have a child.

Right now, though, there was only Ruby's egg, attacked by myriad sperm, swimming up a fallopian tube.

"Ruby, you're not pregnant, but a pregnancy could occur."

"You mean from the rape?" Her face radiated horror.

"If we do nothing, yes. Do you want a child?"

"No! Not now, and especially not his! Whoever he is!"

With a concerned sound, Onyx made to move to her sister's side, but I held up my hand. "Shh," I said. "It's okay, but don't go into the pentagrams."

"Are you going to abort the baby?" asked Onyx.

"There's no baby to abort. There's no new life—only an egg covered by a lot of sperm. Her distinct egg. His distinct sperm. I can convince the sperm to let go."

"Please make them let go," said Ruby. "Make him let go! I feel like I'm being raped all over again."

"Shh, honey," I said. I looped my mind over the embattled egg, and I broke the bond between it and the sperm. "It's over. The egg's free."

"There's no baby?" she asked in a little-girl voice.

"No," I assured her. But there might be worse.

Still connected to Ruby's cells, I did a quick scann for viruses or bacteria. I didn't want this girl getting any horrible sexual disease. But the rapist had left nothing but semen.

Then I Sensed her other injuries. The brute had severely abraded the girl's vaginal opening and walls. He'd scraped her cheek, and the inside of her lips were bruised where he'd clapped his big hand over her face. She'd bit her tongue and bent back several fingernails while trying to fight him off.

I easily healed all of the wounds. Physically, they were all minor in nature.

It was the wounds to her heart I couldn't touch, not without the right assistant.

Pulling myself out of the spell, I looked over at Onyx and said, "You can both follow me back to my office." Ruby carefully stepped out of the pentagram, and I nodded to Onyx. She embraced her sister.

When they sat across from me, I told them both, "I'll do what I can to keep your aunt out of this."

"Thank you," said Onyx. My Wizard senses picked up on how heartfelt her thanks were.

"But we don't want any more girls getting raped," I said. "Especially if we can do anything to stop it."

Ruby shivered. "No other girl should have to go through this."

"Ruby, have you ever heard of a *Wabizi* mirror?"

The girl nodded. So did Onyx.

"If we use one, you'll have to watch the rape all over, but Onyx'll be right next to you, and so will I. I'll watch the whole thing. I'll see everything you know about the rape. Then I'll tell the police. No one else will have to bother you."

Ruby looked paler than she did when she'd arrived, but she nodded. This small slip of a girl had more courage than most men I'd met.

With Ruby ensconced between Onyx and me, I unwrapped the gilt hand mirror and handed it to Ruby. Her magic was strong—a picture appeared right away.

Together the two girls walked on a grassy path at twilight. The sky was nearly black, but not quite at its darkest. I could see their breath in the cold air.

"We were walking home from town," Onyx said. Ruby's undeveloped magical talent was strong enough that the picture in the mirror didn't even waver.

As they rounded a boulder on an otherwise desolate stretch, a man jumped from behind and clubbed Onyx in the head with a big stick. Onyx melted to ground like she had no bones.

Startled, I looked at the girl. "Why didn't you tell me?"

"Ruby here needs help more than I do."

"Let me heal that when we're finished."

In the mirror, the assailant grabbed Ruby's mouth, shoved her to the ground, and raped her from behind. We never saw his face.

Beside me, Ruby was sobbing. I silently took the mirror from her, while Onyx buried her sister's face in her chest.

I could imagine the potion needed to heal the girl. It'd restore her blood chemistry to what it was before the attack. She'd remember the rape, but she'd be distanced from it. Ruby would be free to love and enjoy sex.

As she was now, Ruby would be scarred for life. She'd distrust all men, all dark paths, all nighttimes.

Rage rippled through me at the thought of her loss.

Why had I told Uriah I'd send out no more *Rurutu* fliers? I couldn't remember. There wasn't a good enough reason.

That night, I couldn't sleep. The beginnings of spring were in the air. Yellow crocuses were peaking out from shallow banks of snow on the sidewalk. Purple and white ones were bursting out all over my garden. Spring was sneaking up on winter.

Spring was the time for baby chicks and lambs and bunnies. Spring was the time for babies, and love. And lovemaking.

Maybe that's what was bothering me. It'd been too long since I'd lain with anyone, in a spell or out of it.

My heart mate. That's what Uriah said I'd find with that old spell. In a theoretical sense, I wondered what a heart mate would be like.

When he touched me, would it feel like this? I pressed an icy finger to my nipple and it sprang to a peak, sending ripples of desire through my veins. My nipples engorged so quickly that the silk of my sheets felt like sandpaper against them.

Would his nostrils flare like a stallion scenting a mare when he smelled desire on me? Would his pupils gleam black, making me think of hot, hot mouths and hands?

I was awash in desire. There was a heat low in my belly. I smoothed a hand across myself, across my stomach, tracing the line of my pubic hair.

I couldn't remember the last time I felt this kind of heat without a spell. Was it the rising sap of spring? Or was it the *Rurutu* spell I'd cast?

I pressed a finger hard against myself, slid over the slick wetness. My clitoris was swollen and slippery.

But it wanted a hot, hungry mouth, not my well-trained cold fingers.

I settled back into my bed, preparing to convince this roar of sexual desire to calmly dissipate.

With one hand on my nipple and the other tracing circles around my clitoris, I felt the slow growth of an orgasm. My stomach muscles clenched and I tilted my hips forward. With each stroke I sank my fingers a little deeper inside of me.

Finally, a wave of pleasure swept through me, strong and calm.

It wasn't enough.

I sank two fingers deep inside myself, willing them to give me what I wanted.

Another orgasm washed over me, as solid and dependable as the last.

Would a heart mate be able to rip an orgasm from me? Tear it from me? Would a heart mate leave me gasping for breath, craving more? Pinching a nipple almost painfully, I wanted not a wave of pleasure but a storm. I wanted to crave his ass under my fingernails. I wanted to scream as he buried his cock deep into my heat. I wanted to taste the sweat on his neck as he thrashed beneath me, wracked by an orgasm of his own.

I came again with my own fingers. It was better, but still—it wasn't enough.

As I drifted to sleep I thought back to the components of the *Rurutu* spell. It specified dopamines and vasopressin. It didn't specify penis sizes or tongue temperatures. Uriah was wrong—he had to be.

I sighed, rolling over a final time. I'd told Uriah I wouldn't cast the spell again, and therefore I wouldn't. In the morning I'd go back to my books and see if I could find another way to soothe the minds of Ruby and the women like her.

6

That smarmy Wizard Uriah might have taken the flier from me in the bar, but I wasn't stupid. I'd already memorized the address. No pushy snoot would steal a chance like this from me.

Wishing for better boots, I stepped around an icy-ridged puddle. I was wrong about the upscale address. Carathay might be the place where the snoots lived, but none of them lived on the Bantam Boulevard from the flier. None of them lived on Leghorn Lane, Ancona Avenue, or Cochin Court, either.

The houses on these streets had yellowed patches of grass for lawns, and they were speckled with dog shit. At several addresses, laundry hung flaccidly under the overcast sky. I don't know what genius thought laundry would dry on a cold, gray day like today. Cracked stucco and peeling paint were abundant everywhere.

Carathay's city planners had a twisted sense of humor, making the nonsnoots live on chicken streets. What did they have against poultry?

As I rounded Leghorn Lane, I paused to cast my spell. My

glamour magic is so light most people don't realize it's there. Even a Goldie wouldn't see it unless he were looking for it. I put an elegant spin on this one, too.

E. H. Sokaris would see a man's man, a man of helpful discretion and few complaints, a man who knew just how to handle any situation with subtlety. Yes, Mr. Sokaris would take one look at me and know on the spot that he had to hire me. All other applicants would seem a tired, faded second-best next to me.

Feeling confident, I found 73 Bantam Boulevard, a nice prime number for a ratty brownstone. The gray stairs were worn, the railing rusted. The blue paint on the shutters was peeling. Most impressively, two gargoyles looked down over the door. They were both chickens. I wasn't surprised. One was fierce and laughing. The other looked like it was about to swoop down and stab me with its razored spurs. It was laughing, too.

The cursed things.

My nerves tried to rattle me, but I slapped them back. What did I have to worry about? My clothing might be as tatty as this brownstone in reality, but I looked like a bushel of talens. This spell never failed to impress a man. I swallowed and brought the knocker down firmly on the door.

I swear one of the chickens—the fierce one—cackled. Like it'd just heard a hysterical joke.

Then the door opened.

I nearly lost my breath. Now, I'm not the sort of guy who believes in love at first sight, at least I didn't think I was. But when I saw the chickie who opened the door, I was completely at her mercy. If she'd asked me to lick her boots, I would have. Happily.

She held a feather duster in one hand, and myriad charcoal-colored braids fell over her shoulder. Gold and violet beads decorated the bottoms. Mr. Sokaris must be a man of discriminating tastes to have a maid as fine as this one. She had the longest legs I'd ever seen. I've always been a sucker for long legs, and tiny waists, too. I could have run my tongue around her waist with one lick. I would have paid to try.

"May I help you?" she asked coldly.

Not that I blame her. My glamour spell is aimed at men. It irritates women. Too much machismo or something.

But even now I wasn't worried. The housekeeper wasn't going to hire me. After the Goldie took me on, I'd have plenty of time to make a better impression on this chickie.

Still, I wish I'd have found something better to say than the word that fell out of my mouth. "Chicken?" I asked, like I was a waiter or something.

Her indigo eyes squinted at me, and her full lips pulled into a frown. Gold dust coated both eyelids and lips. Mr. Sokaris liked exotic-looking help, apparently. "Excuse me? What did you say?"

Now that was exactly what I was asking myself. *Chicken?!* "The feather duster," I explained with a lame gesture. "There seems to be a, um, chicken motif in this neighborhood."

Without the spell, she might have laughed at me, if only out of pity for my stupidity, but that's not what happened. No, she looked at me as if I were poultry shit.

I knew the spell made me seem like a condescending, patronizing, manly man, and maybe I should've cut my losses and run. But no, I'd come this far, despite the odds.

I tried to blunder through. "You know, Ancona Avenue? And the, um?" I pointed up to the concrete monsters. "The gargoyles?"

I sounded arrogant, patronizing, even to myself. I didn't mean to, but that's beside the point.

Those luscious lips of hers flattened into an irritated line. "Can I help you?" she repeated again.

There was no escape. Under the weight of my spell, I knew whatever I said would irritate the most gorgeous creature I'd ever met. I took a deep breath and spat it out. "I'm here to interview Mr. E. H. Sokaris for the beginner's wizard position. May I speak to him please?"

Flamed by the spell, I thought my words would bring a frigid wind into the doorway, but her words froze my heart. To its core. "I'm Esmenet Sokaris, and there is no job. I changed my mind."

"But—" I floundered.

"But what?" she demanded.

But I had assumed the wizard was a man. Don't ask me why. I'm a chauvinist, I guess. Who ever heard of a Goldie woman? Not me.

E. H. Sokaris was definitely not a man.

I stood on her doorstep at a loss for words. I considered running away, coward that I am. I considered annihilating the spell on the spot and throwing myself at her mercy. Let her smell my true desperation, see my true colors.

"I—" I said, before my pathetic brain even formulated a game plan.

She held up a hand—the one without the duster—to forestall me. "Please. Don't say another word." Esmenet Sokaris motioned me into her home and said, "The lavatory is to the right. Remove your spell, and then we'll discuss the possibility of your employment, which I must say is exceedingly remote."

With my shoulders slumped, the very picture of humility, I headed where she pointed.

But inside, let me tell you, I was jubilant. Sokaris hadn't thrown me out. I was saved!

"I specialize in love potions," E. H. Sokaris said to me while I sat alone, spell free, on her settee made for two. She sat across from me in a stark black-lacquered chair. Its high back towered above her head, making her look like a queen. Her regal bearing added to that impression.

I thought about a number of smart things to say, smart-assed comments about her and me and love and potions. But for once, I said the smartest of all things: nothing.

"Please," she said, handing me a gilt mirror. "Look into this."

"A *Wabizi* mirror," I said.

"Yes." Did she look surprised that I knew this?

"I've never seen one," I said, taking it. "But I've heard of them." I examined myself. "Is it keyed just to you somehow?"

"Yes," she said. She enunciated perfectly, as if each sound were carefully crafted and controlled. "The particular mirror shows me what I most need to know about the person holding it."

No wonder she didn't ask for references. Like lightning, fear forked through me. I had nothing good at all to show this woman. There was nothing in my life that made me proud.

"Do we have to do this?" I asked.

The Gold Wizard gave me a steady look. She wasn't like Uriah at all. There was nothing oily or smarmy about her. "I need to know the state of your heart."

The state of my heart . . . Empty. Forsaken. Drunk. I had nothing more to lose. Silently I held out my hand for the mirror and looked into its depths.

A different kind of man might've seen lank hair in need of a wash and cut, round dark eyes with even darker circles under them, a wan, sickly pallor seen in street-living drunks.

But I wasn't the man to see myself that way. Instead, I brushed my hair from my eyes and saw finely chiseled cheekbones, twinkling eyes, and a strong chin—in short, a handsome devil that E. H. Sokaris would have a hard time resisting.

"You're missing the point entirely," Sokaris said, with more than a hint of exasperation. "Setting the mirror in your lap may help."

I obediently put the mirror on my thighs and spent some time trying to find my nose hairs appealing. No luck. I was about to give up when something flashed, like a fish deep beneath the surface of a pond.

"Yes," she breathed, her voice huskier now. "You've got it."

A delicate toenail came into focus in the mirror's depths, the palest pink and breathtakingly feminine. Apricot-colored sheets, which may have been satin, provided a fitting backdrop. The nail belonged to a narrow foot with a lovely arch.

The foot couldn't belong to Sokaris. Her skin was the same shade as the midnight sky, so black it approached purple. The foot in the mirror was the shade of barely toasted bread, lighter than honey but just as sweet.

Something about that foot . . .

"Keep looking, please, while you answer my questions."

"Okay," I said. Watching wasn't difficult. The foot was beautiful in its proportions. Delicate and strong at the same time.

But the pink-toenailed foot wasn't alone in those satiny sheets. A thick, manly one had just come into view, too. A few black hairs crinkled along its toes. I blinked. Her foot was easier to look at.

"What's your name, Brown?"

So she could see my level, somehow. "Gage," I answered. "Gage Feldspar." The calf of the mirror girl was coming into focus. The play of muscle beneath her tight skin tantalized me. What a perfectly shaped calf. I wanted to run my hand over it, feel its warm smoothness under my palm.

Mirror Boy apparently had the same thought. His hand traced the length of her leg, obviously enjoying the texture like I would have. The same scant dark hairs that decorated his toes covered his hands. His skin was darker than hers.

For no good reason, I hated him.

"Gage," Sokaris said to me, grabbing only some of my attention.

"Hmm?" I answered. I'd heard of this sort of magic, of course, but never seen it in action. I was Gage Feldspar, proud Brown magician and proud owner of an attractive face and fine physique. I'd never needed a love potion. Ha!

"Gage!"

Until this moment, I'd never appreciated the voyeur's pleasures, never thought that watching a couple enjoying each other's bodies would turn me on. But watching these two people make love . . . I realized I could get to like this. My cock was throbbing, and if Sokaris hadn't been sitting right next to me, I might have grabbed it while I watched.

I shot a look at the Love Wizard. Her erect nipples stuck straight out through her purple kirtle. Maybe there was something more to this interview than I thought. Maybe it included . . . But I couldn't. Lyric was still my wife.

"Watch the mirror, please," Sokaris said with her perfectly formed words.

I swiped my hand across the stubble on my chin as I watched. Mirror Boy worshipped the woman's legs, and her legs were worthy of worship. His palms snaked behind her knees. His lips traveled up her thighs.

Watching his fingertips slide over her skin, I could imagine the silky smoothness of that vulnerable area, so often ignored in lovemaking but worth the effort nonetheless. Mirror Boy took his time, caressing every bit of her long legs.

My cock pulsed watching him savor her. I moved my free hand so that my wrist masked my tented trousers.

Mirror Boy's head was between her thighs now. I watched the woman pull him around, leaving his mouth exquisitely latched to her clit. I could easily imagine his groan of pleasure, muffled to be sure, as she pulled his cock into her mouth.

The sight of the lithe naked woman sucking Mirror Boy's cock while he sucked her clit made me clench my teeth. Despite the beautiful Wizard woman sitting next to me, I pressed my hand against the bulge in my pants.

I suppressed a groan. You had to really like a woman to enjoy this position, and she had to like you, too, since both partners had to give up a little of their own pleasure to give some away. The incessant throb of my cock had long ago become painful.

Mirror Boy was lucky to have this woman, luckier than he deserved . . . but I bet he wasn't properly appreciating the silky spot behind her knees.

"Gage," Sokaris said so softly that I had to strain to hear. The mirror's focus shifted perversely to his hands, which firmly grasped her peach-shaped ass as he suckled like a newborn calf on her clit.

But my mind saw Mirror Boy's cock in her mouth. I knew her lips would be as pink and delicate as her toenail, and pouty to boot. Her eyes would be rolled back in ecstasy as she inhaled his thick cock. I knew she loved to suck and suck hard.

"Gage, I make love potions," Sokaris said.

But I waved her words away with my hand. Watching the pair in the mirror, I felt like a wild animal, trapped. Frustration and tension mounted, and I wanted to be freed. I'd become mad, a little insane.

In the mirror, they'd switched positions. The girl's hand came into view. Long graceful fingers with neatly tapered nails. That pink. Again. Could I really detect boldness and shyness through this magic? She grasped Mirror Boy's hand and tentatively led his fingers to her breast, to her nipples. Did Mirror Boy know what that cost her, that act of courage?

"If you're to be my assistant, do you realize what that entails?" Her voice barely penetrated my concentration. The woman was heartachingly pretty, like someone I'd love to protect and keep safe.

I was aware of myself enough to know I really wanted a Brown Worm. Or three or four. But even if I had them I knew I could get completely shit faced and the heat between my legs wouldn't go away. Neither would the guilt in my heart.

"Do you know what Love Wizards do?" Sokaris asked again.

The mirror shifted its focus now, and I grunted my reply. Young women have such fuckable cunts, and the girl—woman— was no exception. Soft white thighs and the delicious place between them. Mirror Boy's face was buried there. Her cunt was crying for a nice thick cock, and Mirror Boy offered only his tongue. What good is a tongue for a cunt as soft and eager as hers? I felt outrage for the girl.

"I only hire unattached assistants, Gage."

Unattached.

That word brought her to mind—Lyric. My ex. I wanted to kill her. How dare she? "I'm not unattached," my voice choked out.

But I was wrong. My wife had detached me.

Those narrow feet flat on the bed, Lyric thrust up against him, burying his tongue—his ineffectual tongue—deeper into her.

So many fuckable little cunts in the world need to get fucked now and then. So few of them get the fucking they need. My wife. My ex. Lyric wasn't one of the deprived. *The cunt.*

Her cunt wanted a throbbing thick cock, and a fat cock was filling her.

But not by me. I could fuck her senseless. And I wanted to. I wanted to fuck her with my hand around her throat. I wanted to fuck her until she begged me to stop. *The cunt.* How could she?

How could *I?*

Where'd I been when this ill-born relationship was hatching? In the boss's office. Getting reprimanded again. At the Slug and Garden. Drinking my way into nothingness. Sitting halfway across the city in the living room of a breathtakingly beautiful Goldie who wanted my help in making love potions.

Wherever I'd been, I hadn't been attending my own garden, Lyric's garden. And now a snake had moved in.

Not that I blamed him.

I wanted to kill him.

I wanted to be him.

Then the mirror showed his face. Obadiah. My ex-boss.

I could smash his face into the cobblestone street, beat his head against a brick wall. How dare he.

"Are you unattached, Mr. Feldspar?" E. H. Sokaris asked.

I could've answered civilly. I should have. But I didn't.

Instead, I stood and threw the mirror as hard as I could across the room. It shattered into myriad shining pieces as it bounced off the icy blue wall and landed on the marbled floor.

I marched out of that room and out of that house.

I wished I could march out of my life.

I stalked down the cursed chicken streets, blind. Anger and rage burned through my veins. I marched past a pub, Heart and Thigh—no doubt another poultry reference, but I didn't want a beer. I didn't want a job. An image of Sokaris's breathtakingly tiny waist flashed through my mind, but I didn't even want to fuck.

I didn't know what I wanted.

But I did know. I wanted Lyric.

The wintry sky had grown dark while I'd been watching that forsaken mirror, and now nearly frozen rain spat from the clouds, scarce and irregular.

Sokaris. That bitch. Were those images even true?

Sick hope blossomed in my heart. Maybe she was manipulating my emotions for some twisted reason that only a Goldie could understand. I had to know. I spun on my heels and turned back to Bantam Boulevard.

I banged on her door, ignoring the knocker. "Sokaris!" I shouted so loudly even the gargoyles could hear me. Their frozen rictus grins mocked me. "Sokaris!"

When she opened the door this time, I realized that her feather duster was actually a wand.

Fool! Only a complete chauvinist like me could've mistaken this Wizard, who sparked power with every breath, for a parlor maid.

But that was no fucking reason to torture me with pictures—fake pictures—of my wife fucking my ex-boss. They fucked! In her faked mirror. Her cunt in his mouth.

The frigid rain plastered my hair onto my forehead and face, but the raindrops I pushed off my cheeks were curiously hot.

Not rain, then. Tears.

"Why?" I asked her. I'd aimed for an angry tone, a demanding one. But my question came out cracked and filled with sorrow.

In that moment, before Sokaris muttered even a word, I knew the truth. Lyric and Obadiah were truly fucking each other. His cock in her mouth. And I had brought this pain upon myself.

Standing on the doorstep of a Wizard I barely knew, pushing tears and raindrops off my face, still shaking with a hangover from last night's ales, I broke down and wept.

The tears I'd shed should have left me cleansed, released, but I only felt stunned. The trip to the bathhouse up the street—paid for by Sokaris—didn't help either. My knees were weak. So was my stomach.

In a pre-cathartic haze, I followed Sokaris into her spelling room and stepped into the symbols inscribed on the floor. Even in my stupor I knew better than to smudge a line.

She'd hired me. Amazing but true. My official new title was Assistant to Gold Wizard Esmenet Sokaris, and we were to get right to work. Despite my hangover.

The first potion I'd help her brew needed my tears, or the tears of a person in my frame of mind.

I myself use standard star pentagrams on the rare occasions when I brew elixirs, but Sokaris used intricately entwined hearts. The tips of the bottoms faced the cardinal directions, and the tops of smaller hearts softened the edges.

Somehow the hearts matched the space. The room vibrated with the color of lilac, bright but solid. Only candles provided light; the room had no windows. The lines of the hearts shimmered in gold against the ebony floor, like Sokaris's lips and eyelids. And her power resonated throughout the room. The hearts pulsated beneath my feet, and when I reached the center, my cock throbbed in rhythm, despite my misery.

Sokaris followed me to the center. Hers wasn't an air of satisfaction. When I looked in her face, I saw resignation. Maybe empathy.

Probably disgust.

We stood eye to eye, neither taller than the other. She brushed her fingertips over my shoulder and said, "I'm sorry for your pain." Her voice was as silky as the sheets on which Obadiah fucked Lyric.

Or, those on which Lyric fucked Obadiah.

Sokaris hadn't caused my despair exactly, but if she'd kept her mirror to herself, I'd still be trampling through my life, oblivious. Content in my oblivion. I didn't exactly like her in that moment, and I certainly didn't thank her. Instead I looked away, knowing I was acting like a rotten brat.

"Are you ready?" she asked. "You know this won't be pleasant."

"I'm ready," I croaked.

Sokaris traced one of the lines of the east-facing heart with a toe while she traced a dazzling glyph I didn't recognize in the air with her feathered wand.

I stood with my face to the east, the direction of beginnings, and said, "I may need instruction as we . . ." But before I could finish my sentence, the spell had begun acting like morphine on my brain.

I floated back in time. Lyric, on our wedding night. I'd completely forgotten how nice our honeymoon room was. Blue, nearly translucent curtains floating in the spring breeze. Morning sunlight made the pine floors glow. I could even smell the faint scent of cedar that had filled the room.

Hope surged through my blood. I'd found my lost life—the life I'd had before I trashed it as surely and easily as Obadiah's pig trashed the fair.

A smile danced on her lips as Lyric took my hand and dragged me to our nuptial bed. No lines of sorrow marked her face. No disappointment shadowed her eyes. Just clear, pure love as she playfully pushed me onto the bed and straddled me, smothering me with her kisses.

Damn, how had I ever ruined this? What a treasure I'd had. It had slipped through my hands like water.

As a Wizard, I knew the real lips under mine belonged to Sokaris. But, as if I were back in that wedding bed, my lips felt only Lyric's. Lyric's lips—not Sokaris's—began to kindle my fire.

In our wedding bed, I'd captured her velvet mouth in mine and lingered there. Slowly, I'd teased her. I'd danced my tongue to the inside of her top lip and thrilled in her groan of pleasure, the way she'd melted her body into mine. Sunlight shined on her skin and over her hair, and she felt like a dolphin, incredibly smooth and supple.

All that pleasure I relived now, under Sokaris's spell. Under her hands and lips.

Lyric had worn a blue robe that morning. It matched her eyes. Lyric looked like the Star Goddess herself that morning.

Under the spell, I nudged the filmy thing off her shoulders, as I had that morning. Her breasts were perfectly shaped, tiny and high. Her nipples were hard pearls, the palest pink. Like one of those spring flowers she liked to grow in her garden.

I had stifled a groan when I saw them the first time—afraid to overwhelm my virginal bride with the depth of my desire— and I stifled the same groan now.

I don't know what thing in my life made me associate virginal inexperience with a lack of enthusiasm—maybe the same thing that makes me a chauvinist—but I learned my lesson that morning. Lyric wasn't at all frightened by my need for her. She was flattered and charmed. My desire equaled hers, and in her eyes, that meant we were heart mates.

Standing in Sokaris's spelling room, I believed it still—Lyric was my heart's mate.

She had trusted me completely, that morning and for years— until the drink took hold of me, until I started shirking and shrinking.

In bed, on our wedding night, she only shyly asked for what she wanted, requesting more intimate caresses in the subtlest of ways. The smallest shift inched her breasts closer to my hands or my mouth, and when I divined her desire and ran my tongue over a pebbled nipple, Lyric's mewlings, her fingers clutching my back, rewarded my attention to detail.

Lyric's lips hungrily met mine, her face sweetly tipped toward me. I ran my palms down her back, enjoying its silky firmness. She ever so slightly cocked her hip. An invitation. A plea. I accepted and gently palmed her splendid perfection. The small noise that escaped her mouth as she twined her tongue around mine nearly undid me.

A small step back invited my hand to stroke her belly and

lower, and when I explored that wet private spot, Lyric melted into me. I remember feeling like I'd explode.

I also remember feeling I'd lay down my life to keep this precious woman content and safe. That same feeling reverberated through me now.

As in dreams, the mind has a way of radically shifting from one story line to another without missing a beat. Apparently the same was true while working a spell.

Sokaris's spell shifted, and I balked. I caught a whiff of where she was taking me, and I didn't want to go. Not one bit.

But the firm, steady pulse of her magic forced me. Even as I dragged my heels, I marveled at the elegance of her strength. I'd never achieved this finesse, not even with the chickens and pigs with which I'd worked.

Still, I didn't want to go to that dreary room.

On that dreary night.

In the spell's grasp, I walked into the dark kitchen. Lyric sat at the table. I sniffed. No dinner. Then I looked at my wife.

No hope, nor love, nor worry were in her eyes. She shed no tears.

No, on this night, cold hard anger emanated from her. She shook with fury.

Not caring, I let out a big belch, filling the air with the fragrance of half-digested Brown Worm. I sounded just like Obadiah's pig at the fair. The ale didn't smell all that good before it'd spent time in my stomach. Now it stunk.

I stunk.

"What's for dinner, hun?" Inebriation erased any sense I might have had, and I swung in to kiss her cheek.

She moved away and flung a pale green envelope in my face. "This is," she spat. "You can eat this for dinner."

The envelope fluttered to the ground as I sloppily sat in the cheap chair opposite of her. "'Fraid you'll have to read it to me." I scratched my balls.

"You drunken swine," Lyric seethed. Another woman might have ranted, but her fury was much more controlled and focused. "You've gotten us evicted again."

"Brastrards," I slurred, spraying spit everywhere.

"You're the bastard, Gage. You and the forsaken drink."

I let out another burp. "You can say that again."

If I'd thrown myself at her feet, she might have forgiven me, given me another chance to fuck up, which I surely would have done. But I didn't. I didn't throw myself into her arms. Instead, I put my muddy shoes on the table, and said, "You shouldn't wear red, wife. It doesn't flatter you at all. I can see all the veins in your eyes, and they're not pretty. Makes you look old."

I watched something in her harden. Then shatter and break.

"I'm evicting you, Gage. From this marriage."

Blearily, I looked at her. "Whah?"

"It's over. You're a good man, but a lost cause. I can't help you. The Silver couldn't help you. I'm not even sure that *you* can help you."

"Whah?"

"Get out."

"Now?"

"Yes." Before I change my mind. I heard her unspoken words as clearly as if she'd spoken, no magic necessary.

"But, hun—"

"No, Gage, I mean it. I've given you hundreds of opportunities to do the right thing."

"Hundreds? Surely you exagger—"

Angrily she swiped tears from her cheeks. "I've wanted babies for years, but could I lift the spell and let the implantation happen? Not with you coming home drunk every night. 'Look, baby,'" she quipped cruelly, "'Papa's drunk again.'"

I didn't know what to say to this. She'd been thinking of kids? I hadn't thought of them in years.

But Lyric wasn't finished. "And you don't like me in red?"

Outrage. I'd never seen her like this before now. "Well, if you didn't drink away every single spare talen, maybe I could buy something new—just once in a while!"

"Now, you're just being petty, hun." I wanted to reach through the spell and smack the Gage sitting at the table across the head. I should have been racing through the house and throwing out every bottle of ale. I should've been forbidding the old half-orc barkeep at the Slug and Garden to sell me even a drop of Brown Worm.

But I burped again, and reached for her.

"Out!"

Like I was a bad dog.

Maybe I was.

For the first time since Sokaris's spell took hold, I felt vaguely aware of my physical body. Without conscious thought on my part, my toes traced the reverberating lines in the floor, over the top of one small heart and around the base of a large one. I was facing east, the direction of beginnings.

And then her magic had hold again. It had a hard hold.

I shimmered back into our first house, the one Lyric and I had owned, with the help of the moneylenders. Late morning sunlight streamed though the windows and landed on our breakfast table. Green pears in a blue bowl looked like an expensive painting. Lyric and I were sharing a plate of crispy *frawngs*, and my mouth watered.

I didn't recognize the day, and I felt . . . strange. I had more free will now than I'd had in other moments of Sokaris's spell.

Tentatively, I reached my fork toward the *frawng*. I could tell by the way the tines sunk into it that it was done to perfection. I wasn't disappointed when it melted in my mouth. "Mmm," I said. "You were always good at this."

Lyric looked up at me, with an odd look on her face. "Really? I'd no idea."

"Surely I've told you a million times." Hadn't I?

She touched my arm gently and laughed. "No, but I'm glad to know it now."

I looked around, searching for some clue. Where—no, when— was I? The house suggested the beginning of our relationship, but the lines on Lyric's forehead—lines I'd given her—suggested a more recent time.

"Lyric—" I began.

She gave me an expectant look, but I was unsure of myself. "What is it?"

I cleared my throat. "I'm sorry I've hurt you. I mean, I never meant to be such a bad husband."

My wife—my ex-wife—moved her gaze to her plate as she toyed with her food. Her shoulders were so thin and delicate that even now, even after I saw her inhaling Obadiah's cock, I wanted to scoop her into my arms and kiss her.

When she looked up from her plate, I saw resigned sorrow in her eyes. "Our babies would have been beautiful, Gage."

I tried to ignore the verb tense as I said, "And you'd be a great mother."

Happiness lit her expression. "You think so? It seems like such a hard job, and an important one."

I could so easily see a bright-eyed imp clinging to her skirt while she carried a babe in her arms. They'd have her golden hair and solid ways. "The best. You'll be the best mamma."

Lyric grinned, and it clenched my heart. I wanted to be the one to make her dreams come true. They were such good dreams.

And I loved Lyric. I could feel the dopamine oozing from my pores, my tears binding me to this woman in love and affection. That tie, based in and magnified by biology, gave me strength.

I could do it. I could buy back our lovely cottage. I'd become as steady and reliable as she. I'd be a great papa.

I could walk away from the bottle and never look back. I *would* walk away. I would. I would . . .

When I regained my senses, I was sitting in the center of Sokaris's hearts, tears once again streaming down my face. These were thick with hormones, though, and Sokaris caught them gently in a tiny, white silk handkerchief.

The look she gave me while she captured my tears . . . There was something a lot more personal, more intimate even, than the kisses we'd shared deep in the spell. I saw compassion in the set of her lips and eyes. And while I may have touched the Wizard's lips in the spell, Lyric had given me those kisses.

Sokaris wrung the tears into a small vial.

The feeling of fortitude and determination that assaulted me during the spell still rocked me. The feathered wand might have magnified the motivations I felt, but as a Wizard—albeit a pathetic one—I knew enough to know her spell couldn't make me feel anything that wasn't already within me. Magic could magnify emotions and twist them, but wands and elixirs couldn't create nonexistent feelings.

I grabbed that sensation and held on to it, like it was the only ember standing between me and an impossibly cold night. I blew on it, fed it small tinder. And I made myself a solemn vow, a vow I'd never made before today—I would never drink again.

Even as I made that promise, my mouth craved the hops. My throat craved the cool sparkle. More than that, my brain craved the oblivion, the escape from the pressure to live up to everyone's expectations, even mine.

Sitting weak in her circle of hearts, my eyes now dry, I grabbed Sokaris's arm and silently pleaded for help.

Being a Gold, I've no doubt she understood exactly what I wanted, but she didn't offer me a potion like the Silver did. She didn't offer to pray for me like my mother did. She didn't plead with me to find my inner strength like my wife did.

Sokaris took a different strategy. She began to distract me with words.

"Your tears are going into a very particular elixir," she began. "I'm—no, we're—brewing it for a young wife, married only three years. For years before the wedding, she resisted his wooing. See, he was a rogue, devilishly handsome, with sparkling eyes. You know the type."

I grunted at her pointed look. My desire to reform warred with my overwhelming need to find a Brown Worm. I had little energy to reply.

But had she just called me "devilishly handsome"?

Sokaris continued, "But Mathilde, that's her name—" She shot me a doubtful look, and said, "You're officially my assistant now, and any information I give you concerning our clients remains confidential."

I nodded.

"Well, Mathilde wasn't a fool. She didn't want a husband who cheated, and this man had cheating written all over him. He'd slept with any woman who'd have him, and most would."

I grunted again.

"But," she continued, "the rogue wooed Mathilde and begged and wooed some more. He sent her extravagant gifts. He made her parents adore him. In a final heroic effort, he took out his earring, sold his merchant ship, and bought a farm. He settled down."

"Sounds promising," I managed.

"It was," Sokaris said. "His friends found him at the co-op in the evenings, but never in the pubs. His myriad ex-girlfriends gave up hope and married other men. And then, after all this, when the man proposed, the young woman felt inclined to believe him."

"Hope," I croaked. The hero had reformed to live up to the heroine's standards. Her tale gave me hope.

But Sokaris held out her hand, telling me to hold my conclusions. "For the first year of their marriage, Mathilde and her husband were exceedingly happy, both in bed and out. Their farm prospered. A healthy child was born. They bought more land."

I nodded, wondering what the young bride needed Sokaris for.

"But then the husband reverted to his premarital behavior—chasing every petticoat that crossed his path. The husband, when caught, begged forgiveness, told his young wife that he never wanted to hurt her, that he loved her beyond all reason. When he was caught the third time in six months, the wife decided she needed help. The biology of a good man was destroying her happiness—and his, too."

"And can you help him?"

"With your assistance."

The overwhelming need to succeed where I'd failed before coursed through me. I thought of the dopamine spike I'd felt while looking at Lyric at the breakfast table. "The hormones in my tears?"

"Yes. You were craving reformation, and in that moment biological strength was thick in your blood. He and I can use that to reset his biochemistry."

"And that will work?"

"It should." Sokaris nodded. "And if Mathilde's handsome husband ever wrestles again with the need to cheat, a sip of the potion should reset him again."

So, the Goldie would use my desire to overcome my own weaknesses to strengthen the cheating husband. Did that mean I was destined to achieve success? If I failed, would this man fail, too? "But—"

"It's late, Gage, and we're both weary. Let me show you to your room."

I breathed deeply, aware of the fatigue . . . and something more.

For the first time since the Brown Worm latched onto me, I felt I could hold my own against it. Maybe.

A good job, my cottage, Lyric—they could all be mine again. Maybe.

"That's the kitchen," Sokaris said as we passed an open door. In my quick glance I saw a lot of counter space. Dirty dishes, plates of moldy food, randomly placed mugs filled it. Then I caught a rancid whiff. Piles of . . . maybe dishrags cluttered the floor. They looked like they might sprout legs and run away. The table bore candles with mountains of wax piled beneath them and something rotten surrounded by fruit flies.

I could see why Sokaris asked for a housekeeper in her ad. She was a slob.

Mice scurried under our feet as she continued our tour.

"You can have either of these rooms," she said, opening one door and then another. Moths flew out, carried on the odor of wet dog. "And the bathroom's at the end of the hall."

Maybe there'd be worms swimming in the basin.

As I stepped into one bedroom and noted the green mildew oozing up the wallboards, I said, "But the ad said *light* housekeeping."

Sokaris laughed like I'd said something funny and replied, "My room's upstairs, and I like my privacy. Take tomorrow off, and we'll begin work on Dniatday." She swirled up the narrow staircase leaving behind the scent of cinnamon. How did a woman with a kitchen like hers end up smelling like cinnamon?

I flopped on the closest bed, covering my face with the pillow, both of which were bad ideas. Dust roiled out of everything on the bed. My wizard's nose detected dust-mite shit in the mattress, disintegrated duck feathers in the pillow, and bed-bug scales in the blanket. Hacking and coughing I sat up.

This was too much.

Going into the second bedroom, I poked that bed and found the same disgusting components.

I was hungry. I was tired. I was heartsore. And I could not sleep in this. Cooking, which I did terribly, was going to be no fun in the kitchen straight from the Hells.

What was Sokaris thinking? I was to get room and board in exchange for my assistance. I'd given her my assistance, and what did I get in exchange? Room and board? No. I got flea shit.

I marched over to the stairway and banged on its door. "Sokaris!" I shouted, hammering away with my fist. "Sokaris!"

Nothing happened. She didn't answer. I considered jerking the door open and marching up the stairs. But I didn't. The power of her magic scared me. She could squash me like a roach. She could change me into a roach and squash me.

So I pounded a few more times, with less enthusiasm now. I wanted a Brown Worm. If I had a Brown Worm and a broom, I'd clean this mess up. I could walk down to . . . what was the pub? . . . the Heart and Thigh, and get a drink.

I stood, wiping the floor's dust from my ass and knees. I marched to the front door and swung it open. Standing on the granite stoop for a minute, I breathed the cool night air. The air was so clean, I could almost taste stardust.

I could almost taste ale.

With a jaunty little step, I headed down the steps.

"Gage," she said. "Please."

Lyric.

I spun around. Lyric had found me, here at Sokaris's! She loved me still and wanted me back and I'd live up to her expectations this time.

But the doorway was empty.

"Lyric?" I asked quietly. "Lyric!" But I spied only the glittering eye of the gargoyle, the laughing chicken. The other gargoyle—the attacking fowl—looked like it was sleeping.

"Ah, both of you can fuck each other," I said, but my words lacked rancor.

I went back inside and passed out hungry on the bug-shit bed.

7

Wrapping my amethyst robe tightly around my breast, I climbed the tiny stairs to my chambers.

Even Guild Chair Uriah could be wrong, I thought. My *Rurutu* flier had found a man with dopamine and serotonin distributions that perfectly complemented mine, but I don't think anyone could claim this man would be my heart mate. Uriah the fusspot couldn't possibly see Gage Feldspar as a threat to the Guild's supply of love potions, or to my career.

A lesser woman might gloat, but I was too distracted. I didn't usually wish for more power than I had, but I wanted it so badly I could taste it when those rape victims came to me.

And Gage Feldspar made me feel equally inadequate.

With remarkable precision I could Grab four carbon and ten hydrogen atoms from the surrounding air and arrange them in a zigzag chain near the wick of my candle. With a wave of my hand, I could pulse energy through that newly made butane, igniting the taper's wick, filling my room with light. I lit the candles.

But I couldn't cure Gage Feldspar of his alcoholism.

Sensing the mutations in his blood chemistry caused by years of abuse lay well within my grasp. His cell receptors were perfectly molded to accommodate alcohol molecules. If I could hold one of his cells in my hand, I could shape the surface like clay, making it bind to nutrients rather than alcohol. But my mind couldn't Grab cell receptors. The surfaces were too small for any Wizard to manipulate.

When Gage had strutted through my door, pores spewing the aroma of stale beer, I'd nearly slammed that door in his face, Uriah's warning fresh in my ears.

But then . . . But then I wasn't so sure about the guild chair's advice. Gage's chemistry was interesting. Perfect oxytocin, serotonin, vasopressin. Perfect in many ways, but so obviously flawed. No chance of me falling in love with him. Impossible to love a man who loathed himself.

I sat at my oaken desk, a huge thing by any standards but never big enough for all my notes and papers. A new book awaited my attention. *Blood Groups* was its title, simple and basic.

Any breakthrough on this topic was worth a late night, and here's why: opposites attract when it comes to blood groups. Intuitively, someone with B-positive blood will consider any-one but another B-positive person as an interesting bed partner. The more two people differ, the stronger the attraction, the longer the marriage endures. Love Wizards need to know this.

As I skimmed my new book, a thought suddenly occurred to me. I could show Uriah that the *Rurutu* glyph was safe, even for those who were actively avoiding heart mates. All I had to do was show that Gage—with his dopamines and serotonins a perfect complement to mine—overlapped in many or all of my blood groups.

If our blood groups substantially overlapped, we couldn't possibly be heart mates—we'd be relatives!

I leapt out of my chair, excitement rippling through my body. I had to prove Uriah wrong right now.

Snatching a pencil and a notebook I made a list of all the possible antigens: ABO, MNS, Duffy, Kell, Kidd, Lewis, Lutheran, and P. Then I Sensed my own blood, checking off the antigens I had and the ones I lacked.

I needed to sniff Gage to fill in the checklist for him. Hoping he was asleep, I crept downstairs.

His door was closed. *Damn.* And he'd left the key in the keyhole, too. I couldn't stick my nose in it. *Damn it.*

Esmenet, I told myself, *wait until the morning. He'll still be here.*

I quickly squashed that voice of reason. I couldn't wait.

Squatting on the floor, I stuck my nose to the bottom of his door. The crack was just wide enough. I inhaled deeply, searching for his scent. But what I got was a big noseful of dust, and it caused the most unladylike sneeze ever produced by a woman's nose. "Achoo!"

"What the—" I heard him say. At the same time I heard his feet hit the floor. Gage flung open the door and rushed out, but, since I was crouched with my nose to the floor, he tripped over me instead.

We lay in a pile on the floor. And as I opened my mouth to apologize, another sneeze attacked. "Achoo!"

In a voice still thick from sleep, Gage said, "By the sweet Star Goddess herself, it's you." He rubbed his eyes. "The gargoyles. I thought it was those gargoyles."

"I'm so sorry. I can't believe—achoo!" His bleary eyes finally focused on me, my naked legs tangled over his. My purple robe had slid off my shoulders, baring my breast and my stomach to my navel. I quickly closed it.

"Would you like some tea?" he asked, rushing to his feet, embarrassed. He pointed to the kitchen.

"Much more traditional than the hallway as a meeting place," I agreed, rubbing my still-itching nose.

In the dining area, I moved old newspapers off a chair for me and kicked some crap off another chair for him. Gage put water in the kettle with a dubious expression.

"Sorry I woke you," I said.

He was scrubbing out some teacups as he said, "What were you doing? Were you really sniffing under my door, or was I having some weird hallucination?"

"You weren't seeing things," I admitted. Then I told him about the *Rurutu* glyph, the blood groups, and my hypotheses.

"So you can quantify . . . the chemistry of attraction?" he asked skeptically.

I sipped the tea he'd placed before me. "Well, yes. Wizards have been able to do that for a while. The real question is whether the *Rurutu* glyph I used to find you finds potential heart mates. It may find relatives, or it may find someone random."

"I'd have thought any two people were potential heart mates."

"Well, nothing's ever certain. The blood group thing just describes people on average. There're always exceptions: heart mates with identical blood groups, people with no attraction to each other but extremely diverse blood groups. But on average, blood group similarities explain a lot of variation in attraction—more than 90 percent."

"Well, did you figure out how my blood groups compare to yours in the melee?" he asked.

I laughed. "No."

"Well, now's your chance. You don't even have to sniff under my door to do it."

Pulling my robe closed, I squashed my discomfiture. "Give me your hand," I said. "It's a little easier that way."

As his warm palm met mine, a quick jolt of sexual energy zipped through me, surprising me with its strength. I can lecture students about every pathway that sexual energy travels, every nerve it switches, every hormonal change it triggers. As a result, I was rarely surprised by anything sexual in myself.

All the same, my nipples were now hard.

If I were honest with myself, sex with Gage under the veil of the spell had blown me away, like a spring tornado. The unquantifiable way Gage touched me in the spell tore through me, stripped my defenses bare.

Still. The cocky drunk cloaked in the smarmy glamour spell could not be my heart mate.

I pulled my hand away from him, picked up my pencil, and checked down the column. All business. Positive for A antigen in the ABO. Negative in the Kidd. Negative in the Lutheran.

"So what's the verdict?" he asked.

With my heart fiercely pounding in my chest, I passed him the list.

"But we . . ." He looked again, blinking. "Am I reading this right?"

"You are."

Not even one of our antigens overlapped.

8

My day off. I'd go find Lyric and tell her about my job. Maybe Sokaris would pay me, and I could give the talens to Lyric, make my job seem more legit and all that. The day stretched out in front of me, rich with potential. When was the last time I'd felt like this?

Before I got out of bed, I spelled a *Repel* onto the wall's mildew. With great satisfaction, I watched the green patches shrivel and disappear. The yellow patches followed suit. That made me happy. My magic seemed to be stronger and more focused than usual. Perhaps because I hadn't had a drink in almost two days?

Then I made the bedbugs, fleas, roaches, and mice want to leave. I hoped they'd just move upstairs. How could Sokaris offer this room as partial payment for the assistantship?

All the living shitting things had vacated my room, but the mess they'd left was beyond magic, at least beyond my magic.

I groaned. I detested cleaning. Brooms and buckets and scrubbers and soap. Lyric had always been good with them.

I already admitted I was a chauvinist.

I'd vowed to change my ways, though, and I'd scrub this myself, even if it meant putting off my visit to Lyric, even if it meant I had to spend my new income on mops and soap. *Brown Worm.*

But, before I tackled this problem, I needed to eat. *Or drink*, the weak part of my mind whispered. *Brown Worm. Brown Worm.*

Without much hope, I slid on my trousers and headed to the kitchen.

I didn't need much. Some bread and tea. *Brown Worm.* I'd even forgo honey or milk. The kitchen in daylight was worse than it'd seemed last night. I didn't want to touch anything. Too disgusting. Without thinking, I cast another skedaddle spell on the mold. If it oozed to her bedchambers maybe it'd teach her to clean up a little.

With growing irritation I scrubbed at the brown stains in the kettle. I was going to die of starvation before I could make anything to eat or drink in this place.

Then the unmistakable feel of a naked breast sliding across my bare back gave me an instant hard-on. "What the—" I said, half turning.

"Sorry," Sokaris said in a bleary voice. "I just need the—" She pointed to the canister on the shelf above my head. I couldn't help but admire the curve of her breast. Her coffee-colored nipples were rock hard. "Caffeine."

Shocked, I retrieved the jar for her, doing my best not to stare. But she was gorgeous, her spiked nipples, her jet skin. I looked studiously at the ceiling. Gray cobwebs hung from crown molding, which must have been white at some point in the past. I looked at the dirt in the cracks of the floor tiles.

Anywhere but at her luscious body. Those breasts. Her legs.

I could see the minute sleep dropped from her mind, the second she actually woke—to find herself naked, nearly pressed against me. Realization and embarrassment spent microseconds on her face, to be replaced by cool aplomb.

"It seems I'm frequently forgetting my manners around you," she said in an admirably calm voice. "Please excuse me while I get dressed."

I knew I shouldn't, but I couldn't help admiring her perfectly formed ass—two high, tight globes at the base of her tiny waist—as she left the kitchen quickly.

There was no room in my bruised mind for this information.

I took the last of my talens and ran for the market. I'd eat there.

Waiting for Sokaris, I scrubbed the stove until it shone. Everything I did, everywhere I went, Lyric's eyes felt heavy on me. In my mind, she judged everything I did. She'd be pleased with this clean stove. Someday, hopefully soon, she would look at me and smile.

His cock in her mouth, my brain whispered, but I banished the image, now scrubbing the slate countertops hard. When she smiled at me, she would be mine again. Then I'd have re-earned her love.

On Lerodays, Sokaris saw patients, and I worked by her side, learning.

Today was Leroday, and I looked forward to the hard work. But our workday didn't start until three hours after dawn, and that gave me three long hours to fill with something besides drinking.

Last week I'd unburied some ancient cookbooks, dusted them off, and stacked them neatly on the counter. Now I took the oldest out and scanned it for something difficult and time consuming to make for dinner.

Finally, Sokaris stumbled into the kitchen. She woke like a

lizard—very slowly until she warmed up. Strong coffee helped. As she lurched into the nearest chair, I poured a mug for her. She'd learned to put on a robe. Usually.

"Thanks." Sleep made her voice husky. She rubbed her eyes. "How much time do we have?"

"They start banging on your door in about ten minutes," I said, passing her a scone. "And your braids look like striking cobras."

She patted them down, looking at me over her mug. "Who's on our list today?"

"Ceara's on top."

"She's going to pop, but not today," Sokaris said, referring to the impending birth. "Coffee's good." She always said that.

"Thanks. And you've got Old Shade coming with his Parkinson's."

"Another one we can't cure," she muttered.

"You help the symptoms, and he's grateful for it."

"Who else?"

"There's—" A mad banging and shrieking interrupted me.

Together, Sokaris and I flew down the stairs.

We hurried into the back garden where the girl pounded frantically on the door. Ceara and her babe would have to wait. The girl was adorable, and the dog with her was a collie, also adorable. Or it would have been were it not dying in a wheelbarrow.

I did a quick assessment. The collie didn't want to move, suggesting broken ribs. Blood frothed at its lips, suggesting internal damage. Its gums were pale, suggesting shock.

"A cart ran him over, and I think his leg is broken! Please help him," the girl pleaded in a trembling mouselike voice. Nothing like a little pressure.

Sokaris walked over and put her hands on the animal. She'd ask me to take this case—it was an animal, not a person. My heart started pounding.

I couldn't help it. Images of the collie behaving like Obadiah's pig danced through my mind: the dog capering through the market eating all the food he could get his teeth on, bouncing with supernatural power—thanks to me. Sokaris would get covered in shit and become the town laughingstock while getting my bad magic under control.

Better to let the dog die.

But the dog's mistress had huge round eyes, the color of rich earth, and a smattering of freckles across her nose and cheeks. Thick tears ran down her face as she sobbed over her lethargic pet.

I was glad I wasn't in charge.

I glanced over at Sokaris, and I could see she was deep in Sensing. Thank the Star Goddess. But that left me with the sobbing girl.

"There, there, little girl. Don't cry," I said. I sounded like a parody of a veterinarian to my ears, but the child stopped crying.

She turned those huge eyes to me and said, "Can you fix him? Please? He's the best dog in the whole world."

The dog changed from an ebullient pest to a dead pet in my horrified mind. I stood and stared at her for a moment.

"Please?" she asked.

It would take a harder man than me to not rise to this challenge. "Gold Wizard Sokaris is examining him right now, but let's see if we can help, too." I reached to lay my hands on him, but the girl didn't want to let him go. Too many hands lay on the unfortunate creature.

"What's his name, and yours?" I asked.

"Jones and Ada." Her voice was so tiny.

"I need you to be quiet for a minute, Ada. You can pet him, but only on his head and only softly. If you wish him good thoughts with your mind, Jones will hear you. Try not to touch the Wizard's hands. It's distracting and we don't want to get in her way."

"Okay," she said again in that squeaky voice.

And then I violated my own advice, sliding my pinky over Sokaris's, gently melding my mind with hers.

Can we save him? I asked.

Maybe. See what you can do with his bones. I'd start with his legs, if I were you. But his ribs need attention, too.

And you?

Pancreas. Shh. This is hard.

I slid my mind over the bones. An easy break in the foreleg. I Pushed the bones together and knitted them. I knew Sokaris could weld them together as if they'd never been injured, but I was pretty pleased with my efforts. I'd given him the equivalent of about three weeks of healing. He'd be able to walk, a little stiffly, but he'd be sound enough in time. Jones also had two broken ribs, which were just as easily addressed.

Good, the Wizard thought at me. *Now see if you can fix his heart.*

Will do. The pancreas must be a wreck.

I'd never found it easy to send my mind into organs. They slithered away from my Touch. Still, I could explore a little, see what needed repair before I called in the boss.

Jones the dog had a badly bruised heart. Ironically, I'd just been reading about this in the library. I could Sense blood seeping from injured blood vessels to the surface layers of the heart. Jones's heart was bleeding faster than it could push blood out. I needed to either reduce the swelling caused by the extra blood, or I needed to get the extra blood out. Maybe I needed to do both.

Jones's heart may have been bruised, but mine was pounding in near panic. I did not, under any circumstance, want to ruin Sokaris's business like I had Obadiah's. I needed help.

How're you doing on that pancreas? I asked Sokaris in my mind.

Just finishing. Need help?

Yes!

I felt Sokaris Sense the dog's heart. *Do the easiest thing first,* she told me, in full professorial mode.

Get rid of the extra blood, you mean?

Exactly.

It really wasn't difficult. I Pushed fat red and white blood cells into undamaged tissue, into veins and arteries both. I Pushed platelets downstream. Damn the tide. The heart was working easier now. Jones wouldn't have a heart attack in the next few seconds.

Good, she said. *Great. Do you know what an infarct is?*

A definition from Sokaris's library raced through my mind. I said, *Infarct: a portion of dying tissue, caused by obstruction of the blood supply, as by an embolus or thrombus.*

Right. That's the biggest danger right now. We don't want the tissue to swell. What're we going to do?

I slid my mind into the bruised and rapidly swelling tissue, wincing as the tissue pushed me out. I tried again, more slowly. What was the solution to the inflammation? *Cool it? Do we cool it somehow?*

Exactly! Here, I'll help.

Sensing the smallest amount of tissue as I was able, I cooled each handful of cells, literally dropping the temperature. This crude method reduced swelling in handfuls of these cells.

Each time I cooled a handful and moved onto the next, I struggled. Each handful tried to squirm away from me. Sokaris easily cooled much bigger handfuls of cells, and the tissue shrunk back to a nearly normal size.

But by the time I slid back to examine my work, I realized that we'd saved Jones.

We'd saved Jones!

I pulled myself fully out and found Sokaris standing in the doorway. "We saved Jones!" I said, unnecessarily.

The look on her face was, as always, inscrutable. "Unaided

tissue manipulation," she said. She blinked, looking at an area above my head. "You've graduated to Red."

And then she left.

I wanted to celebrate the success we'd had with Ada's dog. But Ada was focused on her pet, and I had to at least appear professional even if I didn't feel it. "Let him ride home in your wheelbarrow, Ada. He needs to rest."

"I'll move him into his bed in front of the stove."

"That sounds perfect," I answered, but I doubt she even heard me.

Can a person think two things at once? I did. In that moment I wished I could celebrate this moment with Lyric—she'd definitely be pleased for me, for us. I also wished I had a Brown Worm. The desire for the beer was so strong I could feel the cool stein in my hand, the weight of the handle.

Success terrified me. People would expect more from me now. *I* might expect more from me. But with an ale in hand I could live up to everyone's hopes.

Today, I thought. Today will be the day I finally visit Lyric, give her the money I've been saving, bask in her pride at my accomplishments and thrill to her touch.

Her mouth, his cock.

But I was afraid. Too afraid. I wanted the Brown Worm so badly that I didn't trust myself. I'd have to walk right past the Slug and Garden, and that seemed to be asking for trouble.

In a dark mood, I went to bed hungry and slept for fourteen hours, right through lunch and right through dinner.

9

Gage Feldspar had passed a test. He hadn't cracked under pressure with the dog, and he'd pushed himself beyond what he believed were his limits. Linked as my mind was to his, I knew he'd been afraid to kill the dog or make it crazy. But that hadn't stopped him.

Gage Feldspar was brave.

Today, though, was a test of a different sort, and it might tax me as well as him. "This is an easy potion, Gage," I said. "The husband's been married to his wife for seven years, wants to keep the flame kindled. He wants both of them to feel like they did when they first met. We'll make them one potion. The husband and wife can share it."

Gage looked at me with that direct gaze of his, and I was increasingly aware of the fact that his pheromones were working on mine. I hoped he couldn't sense my pounding heart. Or Sense it.

Fear laced through my endocrine system, increasing my blood pressure, quickening my heart rate.

I shook my head in disgust with myself. If I stood around

and thought about this, I'd fire him and go hide in my bed-chamber. By the Stars, I needed to get things rolling.

But no, he wanted to discuss it.

"So, you're going to cast me back in time to the first time I made love to my wife?"

I stifled my impatience. I didn't want to talk. I didn't want to look at his chocolate-colored eyes with the gorgeous fan of lines around the side. "No," I said, wishing I didn't sound so curt. "I'm going to take you back to the first time you made love. Ever."

"But I came—"

"I know. You came in a heartbeat. That's fine. All young men do the first time. But the spell will work, trust me. I'll capture the first hormones from the first session, not just the first orgasm."

"Fine," he said, irritated. I was always rubbing him the wrong way. Thank the Goddess.

As he shrugged out of his robe, I looked away. I didn't need to admire his shoulders or his ass, the muscled planes of his stomach.

"Facing east?" he asked, lining his feet up in the appropriate hearts.

"Yes," I croaked. I cleared my throat and said again, "Yes." I had to make this potion—it was my job, my life. So, I must use Gage. There was no help for it. "Ready?" I asked.

"Wait," he commanded. "I need to know—this is going to feel like my very first time making love?"

"Yes," I said, fear making me impatient. "As I explained."

"But that means—" he swallowed and looked chagrined.

"What?"

"But that means I'll be cheating on Lyric."

"Gage," I said. "You know that you and I—" I didn't want to treat him like he was stupid, but I needed to be clear. "I mean, you know that you were actually having sex with me the other day. It should have *felt* like Lyric, but—"

"I know," he growled. "I might be a drunk, but I'm also a Wizard." Gage raked his hand through his hair and said, "But in my mind I was making love with my wife! Now I'm supposed to have sex with Robin? It's cheating on Lyric."

He's worried about this while his wife is rolling in the hay with some other guy? But I kept that thought to myself. He had a point. Weirdly enough.

Gage's dopamine was perfectly placed. My flier had done an amazing job. Although he probably didn't know it, his biology gave him a strong preference toward monogamy and faithfulness. The only creature I'd ever seen with cleaner dopamine distributions were prairie voles, which mated for life without fail.

Just as well he had a biological fixation on his wife. He wouldn't be so quick to notice me, to home in on our chemistry at the cellular level.

"If you want to talk to Lyric before we continue, we can postpone this until after lunch," I said.

He paused for a moment before saying, "No. Let's do it."

So I waved my wand, forming the *Varanasi* glyph.

Finally.

For the briefest moment I wondered if I could cast a spell on myself, shield myself from my own awareness. The apprentice before Gage was pretty unappealing, covered in pimples and tufts of nearly blue hair. He lasted two weeks. If I could make my mind believe I was having sex with him, keeping perspective would be so much easier.

But, no. Someone had to have all of their faculties; they had to Grab each protein and enzyme at exactly the right moment. They had to manipulate the emotions of the donor so that exactly the right hormone appeared.

That someone was I, Esmenet Sokaris, the best damn Love Wizard in the Guild. And I liked sex this way—complete abandonment with a man who thought I was someone else. Using the spell's veil, I was completely in control. And my partners were all thinking of someone else, so there was no possibility of an unwanted emotional tie. I'd given those up to pursue my career. I reaped the benefits of a good sexual release without any of the entanglements.

I could do this.

With a deep breath, I stepped into my spelling hearts, temporarily luxuriating, rejoicing even, in the cleansing feel of my magic thrumming through the balls of my feet.

Then Gage's memories directed the spell. The spell took us to a forest glade.

By the Stars, Gage had certainly lost his virginity in paradise. We lay on the soft sandy shores of a sky-blue lake. White fluffy clouds floated overhead, and the air was filled with the song of meadowlarks and the scent of spring grass. We had a blanket, but I had a hunch we wouldn't stay on it for long.

A moment passed while I oriented myself in his remembered world. Robin was his lover's name.

Fitting name for this spring venue.

Gage sat next to me—next to Robin, rather—and I could feel the warmth of his bare skin against mine. His chin rested on my naked shoulder. The heat of the sun warmed me, but not as much as his touch did. The cells on the side of my neck were overly aware of his breath. Pleasantly aware. My hairs stood up, reaching for him.

I could Sense nervousness in Robin and Gage. Neither had made love before, and the air between them crackled, tight with possibility. I Grabbed Gage's hormones: serotonin, testosterone, vasopressin. Glands and receptors stood at the cusp of switching on. These first secretions provided the foundation of the potion.

"Robin," Gage said, just as he had on that day. His voice was husky, filled with the vibrant energy of a man newly aware of his strength. The power of his voice complemented the might of his thighs and shoulders.

Yum. I could really enjoy this.

"Hmm," I let the spell reply through my lips.

"Your ear."

Robin had giggled at the inane comment, and I did, too. "What about it?"

"I want to bite it."

The spell shrugged my shoulder as if I didn't care, but cells on my neck and ear jumped to attention. Neurons snapped between cells, slamming through a message to my nipples, making me instantly wet. My eyes dilated, and my blood coursed.

Perfect.

Even in the microseconds that Gage's teeth set for my ear, his cells responded to Robin's chemicals. His cock hardened nearly instantly. I Grabbed his hormones again.

Perfect.

He nibbled the back of my ear, and deliciously all the hairs on my neck rippled. Robin leaned back into Gage's chest, and I knew I was in for another great ride.

Gage kissed the side of my neck, slowly. I could tell he savored every moment, but he wanted more. Nerves kept him in check.

Robin rolled her head to the side, inviting more kisses. He might be nervous, but she wasn't going to stop him.

His warm palms caressed my bare shoulders, and as the kisses on my neck started burning lines of pleasure through both of us, his hands traveled lower, to my upper arms. The backs of his fingers brushed the side of my breasts, almost on accident, perhaps asking: Can I touch you here? Robin hadn't squirmed away and I didn't either. That was our answer.

Gage gave a heroic moan of self-restraint.

For deliciously long moments, the pair learned the simple pleasure of his hands on my breasts, of his fingertips on my pearled nipples. Robin arched her back, pressing my tight nipples into his palms.

The sensations of his skin on mine felt so pure and good. The sand felt soft underneath. We had no reason to stop.

"Gage," Robin breathed. "Oh, Gage."

I Sensed the corresponding chemical surge in the man who enjoyed hearing a woman say his name in desire.

Robin shifted around, pressing her naked breasts against Gage's chest. Not satisfied, she sat back and pulled off his thin, sleeveless shirt. "By the Great Star, Gage," she said, tracing a finger over his pecs, over his nipple. "You're gorgeous."

Robin was right. And burying her face in his neck, she inhaled deeply. "And you smell so damn good." She was right about that, too.

I Sensed that Robin considered stopping now, telling Gage she wasn't ready to take this next step. She knew he'd stop if she asked.

Perhaps deducing her thoughts, Gage put his fingers under her chin, meeting her eyes. I felt like I would melt. He didn't say a word, but devotion poured from his gaze. When he captured my lips in his, I knew there wasn't anything I wouldn't do for him.

His tongue danced over mine, over Robin's, and I could appreciate that this wasn't new territory for them, but this kiss held more significance than it had yesterday or the day before.

Today's kisses held a promise of more to come, and that promise would finally be kept.

Heat raced into their kiss, and nervous fear fell to the far background.

Robin ran her hand through his hair, savoring its silky weight, the shape of his skull. Under the barrage of his tongue and lips, I pressed my breasts into his chest, shifting back and forth to maximize the friction. Only fueling my fire, his fingers tweaked her nipples, tearing a gasp from her.

As Robin had, I pulled back for a moment, locking a gaze with him. Then she asked, "Do you think I'm beautiful?"

Gage dipped his head in reply, and flicked a searing tongue over my nipple. He lifted both breasts in his own hands and buried his face there, licking and teasing and biting.

Swamped in the hormones of desire, Robin laid back in the warm sand. "Don't stop," she said to Gage's questioning look. She thrust her breasts toward him, making her desires as clear as could be.

Gage didn't stop.

Robin stretched her hands high above her head, and arched her back as Gage straddled her. He took one breast with his hand and the other with his lips. She rubbed her leg over his thigh, over his cock.

But her words were the thing that undid him.

Robin said, "Honey, that feels so good," in long drawling syllables, as he sucked one nipple hard.

And he came.

With his trousers still on.

I could Sense it, but Robin had had no idea.

The beauty of youth was that I knew it didn't matter. Robin wouldn't find Gage lacking at the appropriate moment, I was certain.

With patience born of temporary satiation, Gage ran his palms over the planes of my stomach. He didn't try to take off my skirt, or try to reach beneath it. He didn't even suggest such a thing.

Instead, the warmth of his hands memorized every detail of my waist and hips, the softness just under my belly button. His fingers tantalized the skin just above my waistband. "Look," his fingers were telling me, as they had told Robin. "Look how nice it would be if I could get in here, just a little bit in here."

And my skin answered with a plea to my brain, "Let him in. Please, let him in."

And the brain can't withstand such a barrage. Robin's didn't. My skirt was shed. I lay in the warm soft sand, naked before him.

I Sensed his pupils dilating, thickening in his blood, the smallest blood vessels opening the tips of his fingers, toes, in his cock. Having a woman spread naked before him, his for the taking, must have been a heady feeling. Through my haze of desire, I Grabbed what I needed.

Reality glimmered around me, not quite tangible. Robin felt—I felt—alive and hungry and weak. "No fair," I said.

"What?" Gage was over me, his voice raspy with lust. "What's not fair?"

"Your trousers. They're still on."

He grinned. Rakish. "Want me to take them off, or do you want to do it?"

Bold enough in her own right, Robin had challenged, "You do it."

He stood, looking self-conscious now. I could think of only one word to describe him: adorable.

But he gamely slid his pants over his hips. I noticed what Robin had missed: his surreptitious swipe at the evidence of his earlier enthusiasm.

Robin held her hand out, and when he took it, she pulled him down. "Come here."

Then Gage was over me, his chest crushing my breasts, his thighs wedging mine apart. Robin had stifled the urge to fight him, and perhaps some part of Gage had sensed that. He pulled back just a bit. Sensitive.

Rolling on his side, he kissed me slowly, gently rolling his lips over mine. With the lightest touch, his tongue teased mine. His fingertips caressed my face, telling me with his every movement that he would not hurt me, that he cherished me.

And I responded. Or Robin had. I thought I might melt into the cushion of magicked sand beneath us.

Gage's thumbs brushed over my nipples, both of them, and it felt so good that I had to urge him on. "Please, don't stop," Robin whispered between kisses, barely loudly enough for him to hear.

"No stopping," he promised as his lips left mine. Then his mouth was there, on my breasts. He teased me, making me want him all the more by kissing everywhere but my nipple. Finally, finally, his mouth, scalding, closed around it, and I arched my back, pleading for more.

Harder. Deeper. My body didn't even know what it was asking for. Robin's didn't, rather.

Gage became languid, and I knew his patience came from his premature release, but Robin didn't. She'd thought him the master of love. She'd thought it proof of his caring.

Even knowing the root of his endurance, I reveled in his touch. With teeth and lips and tongue he lit up every cell in my nipples. Each nerve was firing an erotic message to my fingertips and clit. I Grabbed them. I Grabbed Gage's. Then I rolled over and invited him in.

His fingers were on my bare skin, teasing my abdomen, making my muscles pull tight. Lost in a tangle of pleasure, Robin hadn't even gasped when his fingers looped through her pubic hair. She hadn't even resisted.

I sighed and parted my thighs. I wanted him to touch me. I wanted his magic, his scent surrounding me, the heat of his young muscled body pressing along mine, the gentle, careful way his hands moved over me.

His fingers slid and slipped in places Robin hadn't even imagined, lighting a fire so hot Robin quivered on the edge of an orgasm nearly instantly. Robin hadn't known it was an orgasm. She'd felt like the world opened before her, that if she took the next jump, her entire universe would change.

Gage was over me, his chest crushing me, making me feel safe and protected. He held my gaze and said, "I know I should wait, but I can't."

"No waiting," I'd answered following the spell and opening my legs for him. His hard, swollen cock pressed against my sex, but Robin didn't flinch.

Gage thrust into me, pushing past my spelled hymen in one quick movement.

"Sorry, Robin," he said. I whimpered as Robin had. Stilling himself, he covered my forehead with little kisses. His hand stroked my cheek.

But it didn't hurt as badly as all that, and I melted into him just a tiny bit. The smallest slide against him. The most tentative turn of my hips.

The pleasure of that movement pushed the pain into a memory, and Robin didn't look back. With growing enthusiasm I began to lead the way, sliding his cock right over my clit, plunging him deep inside. Amazingly deep.

He drove into her faster, and harder, but Robin wasn't intimidated. She met him there. And when he shuddered, his whole body stiffening, Robin gave in to her biology, surrendering. Within seconds, I came with him.

This man was a gift from the Star Goddess herself. Even through the intense explosion of pleasure, I Grabbed the right hormones.

With my body still shuddering in orgasmic pleasure, a wintry finger of fear curled around my heart. This man and I were frighteningly good together. Letting go of him, not bonding with him, would be very difficult. Perhaps impossible.

Guild Chair Uriah was right.

I had to fire him.

But as I collapsed into his sweating arms, I had only one thought: this was going to be one kickass potion. The husband and wife would not be able to keep their hands off each other.

Slowly I stood, taking care not to jerk Gage out of the spell prematurely. With my purified handkerchief I wiped his sweat and tears, and my own. The hormones I'd been Grabbing would be concentrated there. Next I dressed. Only then did I wave my feathered wand over Gage.

As I admired the golden glitter falling across his back, I wished I had a stronger totem.

Someday I'd graduate from chickens to something like wolves or badgers. Not that chickens were without merit. They were good mothers and loyal friends. They knew how to tell a loudmouthed brassy rooster from a genuine high-quality one.

But still . . .

The wand had done its job, and Gage stood blinking at me, unabashed in nakedness. He grinned the first uncomplicated smile I'd seen from him since we met, and he said, "Wow, Sokaris, that was great. If you ever want to brew that potion again, let me know."

Ignoring my pounding heart, I tossed him his robe.

I opened my mouth to fire him, to save myself and my career. But he realized then that he was nude. My assistant turned an impressive shade of red and fled.

Gage Feldspar was adorable.

Having Gage in the laboratory with me didn't help at all. Making love with Gage left me giddy—crazy and stupid and I couldn't shut up. I didn't care about Uriah and his dire predictions—Gage and I made powerful potions together.

"Careful," I said to him. "You don't want to spill any."

He walked past me, and the cells within my nose curled lovingly around the scent he left. I wanted to borrow his cloak, just so I could wrap myself in his aroma.

Still, I needed to fire him.

In my laboratory Gage wrung tears from the handkerchief

into an Erlenmeyer flask. Not a drop missed the beaker's lip. I doubted my hands were that steady right now.

"What do we do next?" he asked.

"We use sodium benzoate, we titrate and distill."

"We put things in. We take things out."

"Exactly. And we have to do it now, even though we're tired and hungry." *Deliciously tired, and hungry for more.*

"What happens if we stop for lunch?"

"The hormones evaporate—they're flighty when they aren't in a body." But not as flighty as me. "Would you hand me that bottle over there, the brown one?" I took it from him and read the label to make sure it was the right one. "Great."

"So," he said, glancing across the counter at me. "If we let the hormones evaporate, do we have to cast the spell again?" His grin was wicked. "That doesn't sound too bad."

I ignored the surge of wetness between my thighs and glared at him. My dirty look was a big lie, and I suspected he knew it.

"You need to weigh out an exact amount of this compound," I said shoving the bottle back at him. "The amount's on the notepad over there."

"Okay." As Gage turned to weigh individual grains onto the balance, I tried not to admire his ass. I lost the battle, but at least I didn't caress him. The truth was, I was very happy for Gage's company. I mean—I was happy to have someone to train. In my laboratory.

"Done," he said.

"Good. You can add it to the Erlenmeyer. Put it on the burner until it reaches temperature."

"The temp on the notepad?"

"Yes." We both sat on the stools to wait. I wanted to tell him how good he was in bed, how much fun I'd had. I wanted to fish for compliments from him, hear how he'd enjoyed it.

"You know," I said, flattering him in the only way I felt

comfortable, "I was thinking that the rapist might be collecting stress proteins."

"Yes, but why would they want them?"

"That's exactly what I was wondering, and I have an idea." I could feel my nerves taking over my tongue. Not good, but I was helpless to stop. "See, glucocorticoids help the body adapt to stress, and the most powerful glucocorticoid is cortisol. Someone who's been recently traumatized—like a rape victim—has cortisol thick in her blood." I was on a roll now, in full professorial mode, showing off my brilliance. "The secretion of the cortisol is controlled by adrenocorticotropic hormone," I continued. "That's a mouthful, so the Guild abbreviates it ACTH, which is much easier to say."

Gage nodded in agreement, but I saw a wary look in his eye.

"Regardless," I barreled on, laying my exceptional mind out for him to see, "the pituitary gland makes ACTH and a lot of the other sex and bonding hormones."

"Sokaris, did you have too much coffee this morning?"

"Be quiet and listen! You might learn something. See, sex and stress together might suggest something to do with the pituitary gland."

"Okaaay." Gage was looking at me like I'd lost my mind. "The pituitary."

"But there's another possibility." I got off my stool and started pacing. "See, the adrenal glands make glucocorticoids. More simply, the pituitary gland makes ACTH, which triggers the creation of glucocorticoids in the adrenal gland."

"Where're you going with this?" Gage asked, looking at the thermometer in the Erlenmeyer like it might rescue him.

"Just listen! In looking for a tie between forced sex with virgins and stress, either the pituitary or the adrenal could be implicated. The pituitary is a likely suspect. It makes hormones for growth, lactation, ovulation, implantation, the onset of contractions, and the bonding between mother and child and between lovers."

"Pituitary or adrenal—chicken or beef."

"Stop that! I'm starving."

"Want me to go make some lunch? No coffee for you, I promise."

"Stop and listen." I waved my hand to keep him in his seat. I didn't want him to leave. Ever. "Unlike the pituitary, the adrenal gland doesn't have a whole lot to do with sex. It produces only small amounts of sex hormones, chiefly the male sex hormone—androgen. But adrenal androgens help regulate the development of pubic hair and other early sexual characteristics in both girls and boys during the period just prior to puberty."

"You're hurting my head. And you're probably hurting yours, too."

"But where do these facts leave us?" I demanded.

"They leave me starving for lunch." Gage stood, pointing at the Erlenmeyer. "It's almost ready, and I've something cooking upstairs. I'll be right back."

"Fine," I said, still high on my ideas. But as I eyed the Erlenmeyer's thermometer, I wanted to kick myself in the butt. Didn't I have a spell to seal my mouth shut?

"Okay, Sokaris," Gage said, walking in with a fair-sized platter minutes later. The delicious aroma of some sort of stew wafted through my lab. "I'm going to chalk up that crazy rant of yours to hunger. Let me take over the work here while you eat."

"It smells great. What is it?"

With a smile that met his gorgeous eyes, he walked over to my desk. "Barely bread, which I made myself. I added some of that *Agadez* honey they've been selling in the market these days. New trade routes or something."

"My mouth is watering. Look, I'm almost finished," I answered pointing to the titrator. "Just turn the knob slowly until the liquid below turns the palest blue. Then stop."

Gage laid out a spoon, knife, and napkin before he approached the apparatus. "Okay, boss."

"I can't remember the last time something smelled as good as your stew." Then I thought of the trip to the spelling room and realized I'd lied. Gage smelled this good. I kept my eyes on the bowl.

"Aubergine, tomatoes and *frawng*," he answered, "And herbs from your garden."

"Mmmm," I said in a voice that did no justice to the depth of my gratitude. The stew was absolutely delightful. Delicious. And the bread was heavenly, hot and flakey.

Gage settled next to the titrator with one eye on the beaker. "I've been thinking about your biochemistry lecture," he said.

"What do you think?"

An uncomfortable look crossed his face.

"What is it?" I asked.

"Well, I'm not a Gold or anything," he temporized.

"Spit it out," I said, not helping at all.

"It's just that if I were a bad guy and I were stealing tears of raped virgins, maybe I could use them to make . . ." He looked up at me nervously and cleared his throat.

"What?" I barked again. "Make what?"

"Well, maybe chastity belts or something." He looked a little surer of himself and said, "You know, like a chastity-belt potion." He started speaking faster. "If you took the chemicals from rape victims, especially virgins who've had no other type of sexual experience, and you put those hormones into other women, you could slow down their libido, right? You could make them not want sex."

"And someone would want this potion because . . . ?"

Her mouth, his cock, my mind whispered. "To keep a wife from cheating, Sokaris."

Damn. I knew he was seeing Lyric in the *Wabizi* mirror. Why couldn't I be more sensitive?

And by the Stars, why do I make things harder than they are? All that overblown lecturing about pituitary versus adrenal glands. What had I been thinking?

But then I realized something important.

Gage Feldspar was likely right. If some twisted person fed his wife perfectly prepared hormones from raped virgins, she would be very unlikely to stray from their marital bed. True, the occasional rape victim became more promiscuous, but I wondered if the person behind this hypothetical potion knew that.

I leapt from my seat and kissed him. "Gage," I said, "That's it. That's it! And you're brilliant!"

With that, I fled. Before I could do one more embarrassing thing.

Like fire him.

The woman-child and her mother stood at my door. They couldn't have been wealthy—their wooden clogs and smocks of rough-spun brown cloth spoke of a simple life—but the daughter looked as sweet as they come, despite her red-rimmed eyes and tears.

"Come in," I said, immediately retrieving two handkerchiefs from the stack I kept by the door for this reason. Handing one to each woman, I ushered them to some chairs. "Please, sit. How can I help you?"

A grim expression etched lines on the mother's face. "That horrible brute marauding the streets has violated my Peony, may the Demon of the Hells digest him for eternity." Her bright green eyes dared me to challenge the curse.

Silent tears streamed down the girl's face, but Peony actually looked dewy. Peaches and cream complexion, with summer-sky blue eyes.

"Now she can't stand the sight of any man—not even her father! Not even her betrothed. And the wedding is next month." The mother bristled with fury and frustration.

I thought for a minute looking at the pair. "Mrs . . . ?"

"I'm Dame Gardenese. And I can't pay you full today, but I'll pay over time. I'm good for my word." I had no doubt of that.

"That's fine, Dame Gardenese," I said gently, making a mental note to knock the price down to the bare minimum. "Can I ask when the attack occurred?"

"A fortnight ago," she answered. Well, there would be no semen left, no evidence left with which to pinpoint the rapist.

"And have you told the police, or the night watch?"

"Yes, yes, yes," snorted the Dame. "And we answered all of their questions, but none of that is helping my sweet girl."

"That's true," I said, glancing at Peony. "But it might save another daughter from the same fate."

"I don't want this to happen to anyone else," Peony said, with vehemence. "If there's something else I can do to help, I'll do it. I can't hurt any worse than I do right now."

The rapist had struck for the first time six months ago. Now, I had the ability to do more than heal flesh wounds. With Gage as a partner, I could finally produce the proteins and hormones to ease this girl's mind. I might even be able to help the previous victims.

I took Peony's hand in mine. Her fingers felt exceedingly cold. "I can help you, don't you worry." At a great cost to myself, but I couldn't leave this girl to suffer.

"Thank the Goddess," Peony whimpered. "I was beginning to think I was beyond reprieve."

"Oh no, my dear. I can help you."

"Right now?"

"No," I said. "But tonight. I have to make a special potion, specific to you. But first I need to know more about you, so that I can make the potion just right. And after that, if you feel strong enough, I want to ask you some questions, see if you know anything about this villain that'll help us capture him."

"She's already done all this for the police," Dame Gardenese said. "Do we have to keep torturing her?"

Peony put on a very brave face and wiped her tears. "I can answer your questions."

"Dame, would you please step out for a moment? I'm going to talk only to your daughter."

"I'll stay right here," she said stoutly, taking Peony's hand in her own.

"Dame Gardenese," I began carefully. I didn't want to alienate the woman. "The potion has to be precisely formulated to help your daughter. To make the perfect potion, I must have a very candid conversation, and teenage daughters . . ."

"Don't always tell their mothers everything," finished the mother with resignation. She kindly patted Peony's hand and said, "What the Wizard says may be true, girl, but I'll always love you with all my heart and there's nothing anyone can do to change that. There's nothing *you* can do to change it." With a flounce of her big skirts, the Dame left.

Peony and I stared at each other for a moment, tears now streaming down the girl's face. If her maidenhead had been taken, then she was probably a victim of the serial rapist. But Peony wouldn't be the first maid to dally with her fiancé before the wedding.

"Peony, I have something called a *Wabizi* mirror. It replays the most important highlights of your life, even ones you might not have known about. Do you think you could bear to watch it? It would likely replay your attack, and we might see the attacker."

"I didn't see him," she said, horror written on her face.

"I'll be sitting right next to you, and no one can hurt you here."

"Okay," she said, but she didn't look thrilled about it.

I handed her the mirror, and we waited a long moment. Nothing happened.

"Try crossing your eyes and looking into the depths of the glass," I suggested.

The mirror only reflected her pretty face.

"Keep trying while you tell me about your fiancé. What's his name?"

"Oh, he's such a fair boy. His name is Chase."

The mirror stayed flat.

"When you said 'fair,' did you mean blond?"

Peony smiled the tiniest bit. "No, not blond—dark. He's handsome and kind and gentle and patient." Tears started falling more quickly and she wiped at them with her handkerchief. "I'm so lucky to have such a patient man."

Still the mirror showed nothing.

"Keep looking in the glass, Peony. What does your love look like?" If she thought about him hard enough, it might convince the mirror to bring him into focus. Even the most magically unblessed people have enough latent magic to work the mirror.

"His eyes are the kindest in the kingdom, and brown like the earth, like earth perfect for growing things in. His hair is black as pitch and he has an adorable widow's peak that's just slightly off center. And his hands are powerful strong. You look at them hands and you know Chase can do whatever he wants."

Finally something glimmered in the *Wabizi*, murky and out of focus, but there nonetheless.

The dark-haired boy carried Peony's books back from school while the two walked shoulder to shoulder. They must have been about ten years old.

"Oh, there he is!" said the girl. "Look how little we are!"

The next frame showed them older, perhaps twelve or thirteen. He kissed her chastely on the lips and then ran. I couldn't tell for sure with this murky image, but it looked liked he blushed.

Next the *Wabizi* showed him and her at the same age she looked now, perhaps slightly younger. They kissed passionately alone in a barn. Light from a low, full moon poured into the hayloft. The dark-haired boy pushed her back into the hay, and she succumbed to his lips. I couldn't see their expressions, but I could see arms and hands. His never went near her skirt, near her breast.

"We vowed to wait for our wedding night, and now I wished I'd lain with him in the barn! I saved myself for naught, and now I can't bear the thought of Chase even holding my hand." Peony blew her nose. "I can remember I wanted him, but I can't believe my desire was true!"

"Shh," I said, rubbing her arm. The girl had been a virgin before the rape. She was no doubt a victim of the serial rapist. "Shh."

The *Wabizi* went flat again, and for a moment I thought perhaps it'd drained all of the magic possible from this girl. Then the quality of the darkness changed. The mirror still showed a dark background, but now it had some depth.

Next to me, Peony started shaking. The mirror showed her walking through town at night.

"I should've waited for my brother, but I didn't want to rush him, and no one has ever gotten hurt in our village!"

"Shh, Peony. This isn't your fault. This villain's been raping women all over the countryside. If he didn't take you here, he'd have found another way at you."

The girl shook some more. Her lack of magic made the mirror so murky, but a shadow grew thicker behind a fat adobe wall. When Peony walked passed it, the shadow jumped out, kicked her feet from under her, and took her from behind. His hand was over her mouth, and even through the foggy picture I could see that he outweighed her substantially.

"See," I said. "There was nothing you could do. You kicked

and fought, but you couldn't dent a man that size. You couldn't scream."

The attacker's hand left her mouth. *Did I see a flash of white? A handkerchief in his hand?* Then he melted away into the shadows from whence he came.

"Peony, did he wipe your eyes? Did he wipe your tears away?"

The girl shook her head. "I really don't remember. Maybe?"

The *Wabizi* flickered again, and this time showed a kitchen, warm and cozy with a bright orange fire in the hearth. Peony sat at the table, knitting something long and green. Her beloved entered, and she dropped her needles. Through the fog I saw her pale and start to shake.

Next to me, she had much the same reaction. "How can I marry him?" she pleaded. "I can't even sit next to him now." The girl let angry tears run unchecked down her cheeks. "I need help!" The last came out as a wail.

I couldn't fire Gage.

I'd pulled that *Rurutu* glyph out of retirement for only one reason: to help heal the young women who'd been raped. Over the last few months I'd had to send the other victims to the Guild to help their mental pain, and the Guild was days away. Time and travel added to their suffering.

Peony needed help *now.*

Helping those victims was the only reason I'd stood up to Guild Chair Uriah. It was the only reason I'd hired Gage even after I'd been warned to the dangers.

After watching him graduate to from Brown to Red, after seeing his strength within the *Varanasi* spell, after he came up with the chastity-belt idea, I knew. Gage Feldspar was strong enough to help me. His perfect vasopressin molecules would finally be useful. Gage could work the spell and Grab the healing proteins from me.

And I should've been jerking him right now into my spelling room. But there was one problem.

I was afraid. Terrified.

If having sex catalyzed the process of falling in love, then I might be putting myself in danger. That danger would be heightened for this potion because Gage's perception of our lovemaking couldn't be hidden behind the veil of the spell. The oxytocin bond within him that tied him to the memory of his wife would begin to unravel.

As Guild Chair Uriah said, I could lose all my ability to brew a potion. I could lose my practice.

I weighed my fear against Peony's tears, and there was no choice.

I wiped my sweaty palms on my skirt.

Damn.

10

Sokaris approached me with a command. "You have to lead this spell. So, link your mind with mine, and I'll show you exactly what to Grab. Don't try anything fancy."

Her precise, repetitive instructions made it clear: she was nervous. She didn't trust me.

"Just do what I tell you, nothing more, nothing less," she said.

I hadn't had a drink in a long time, but I wasn't surprised that she didn't have confidence in me. I wasn't surprised—but I wasn't happy, either.

Since taking this job with Sokaris, I'd spent a lot of time and effort making myself a better person. I worked hard. I didn't complain. I spent all my free time actually learning things, growing things, brewing things. I'd hoped my efforts would be obvious to her.

But they weren't. She didn't trust me.

Lyric would appreciate my efforts. *She certainly appreciated Obadiah's,* the evil part of my mind whispered.

Cramming the urge to yell to the back of my mind, I put a

pleasant smile on my face and listened as Sokaris, who had no faith in me, led me to her spelling hearts.

"Step into the *Hiva Oa* groove," she said, stepping into the opposite groves on the northern heart. "South's the direction for learning." Sokaris held out her hand to me, inviting me to link with her mind. I did.

We whooshed right to the pituitary.

It's amazing your purple walls and black floor can't be seen through this spell, I said.

You can cast translucent spells, she said. *But when you need to learn something very specific—like which proteins to Grab—being aware of your location isn't usually helpful.*

We raced past veins and arteries and other organs I didn't quite recognize at this speed. I had the feeling she was traveling faster than she needed. She probably didn't want to distract me.

Here, I heard her say in my mind. *This is where the ACTH'll come from.* A small indentation on the pituitary gland lit up.

Are we looking at your gland? I asked.

Yes.

So when do I take the hormone?

You want to Grab the ACTH before it binds or triggers any-thing. Grab it, and put it in the tear duct. But then let it go, be-cause you're going to want to let it trigger the creation of glucocorticoids. Here, let me show you where to find these and what they look like.

Here's one, I said.

Yes. Great. You've got it. Can you find an ACTH?

This is one, isn't it? These hormones weren't as difficult to manipulate as tissue, although some of them differed from each other only subtly.

Yes. Good, she said. *We're finished. I'm going to lift the spell.*

She finished and the purple walls of her spelling room once again surrounded us. "I have a question," I said.

She gave me that look, but I forged ahead. "It's not that I mind doing this but—"

"Spit it out," she said, always the paragon of patience.

"Well, if you Grabbed your own hormones for that seven-year-itch potion—"

She looked at me blankly and I said, "You know, the lakeshore with Robin?"

The expression on her face could have frozen a summer shower. By the Stars, what had I done to piss her off?

"You want to know why I can't Grab my own hormones for this concoction?" she asked.

"Yes."

"This potion has to be very powerful to overcome the effect of the rape. What started off as physical assault has culminated in emotional turmoil, which changed Peony's chemistry."

"So you can't make a strong potion by Grabbing your own chemistry?"

"That's right. You need to run this spell to elicit the right emotions from me. I'm not strong enough to elicit the emotions and Grab the results simultaneously. No Wizard is."

"And you can't Grab the chemistry from me because I'm male."

"Exactly."

I couldn't read the strange look that crossed her face. An arched eyebrow, an almost-smile on her lips. Sokaris wasn't angry anymore. "You're male."

And then the laughter was gone. She was all business. "Here's the spell to use," Sokaris said, priming her wand with an intricate wave. "It'll cast right if you just complete the *Koror* glyph."

She handed her feathered wand to me. Sweat from her palms clung to it. Then she shrugged out of her robe and placed her feet in the lines of the hearts on the floor.

I stood there a moment appreciating the view. It's a good

thing she detested me; it's a good thing I had Lyric; otherwise I could get a serious crush on her.

Her skin shone like a brown horse under the summer's sun, rich and deep and mouthwatering. Her eyes were the color of those purple flowers that came up before all the others in springtime—muscari, I think. Her eyelids and lips were the same gold color that dripped in sparkles from her wand. Her lips looked like some exotic fruit—

"Are you going to continue staring at me, or can we get to work now?" Her toe tapped impatiently on the heart's line.

I cleared my throat, and said, "Yes, of course," as I waved her wand.

With that, we began the magic dance.

I thought at first I'd used the wand incorrectly, that I'd bungled this job like I had so many others. I saw immediately that she'd been transported nowhere in her past, nowhere in her future. The purple walls were solid around us.

She was right in front of me, herself. Naked and waiting.

By the Stars.

But I saw in her eyes that the glyph I'd waved, the glyph she'd directed me to wave, was the right one. We had to have sex without a spell's veil. The glyph prodded my feet into action. My toes danced across the golden lines of her hearts.

Why had she done this?

I gently touched her face; my heart still pounded with fear. Fear that I had done something wrong. Fear that I would yet screw up. But under my fingertips, her skin felt warm and yielding.

The room faded away, and I found us in a bed of stars.

When her gaze locked on mine, my heart nearly stopped. What I saw there looked like adoration, even love.

Well, no one said I was smart.

I realized then that the spell *was* responsible. Sokaris's patient, Peony, needed to rediscover the touch of her true love.

Sokaris had simply summoned up an experience to cure her client.

I froze. Could I play her true love? Lyric was my heart mate. I'd be betraying her by making love to my boss. I couldn't do it. I couldn't cheat on Lyric.

But no. I wasn't fucking Sokaris for my own amusement. I wasn't even doing it for revenge after Lyric's betrayal. Peony's well-being depended on my ability to pull specific hormones from Sokaris while Sokaris experienced a seduction by her true love.

I wouldn't turn this into something it wasn't. I, Gage Feldspar, would not be making love to Esmenet Sokaris. I was only Grabbing the appropriate hormones. And if I ended up liking my job, that was fine.

I could make love to this beautiful woman, and I could do it well.

11

Deceiving Gage was beneath me, and I wished I hadn't done it. Or, to tell the truth, I wished I hadn't had to do it. He hadn't learned many glyphs, luckily, because the *Koror* glyph was mostly a sham. It didn't do anything but make the naive spell-caster think he'd cast a spell.

To save Peony, I needed the proteins from a woman who was seduced very much against her will. No, that's not accurate. I needed the hormones from a woman who had to erase a lot of emotional turmoil in order to enjoy unadulterated sex. Love. Whatever.

I didn't need a spell to produce these hormones. I needed a lover to pull them from me.

But I hoped he had the patience I thought he did. As strongly as my body yearned for his, my mind longed to be free of these chains. I wished he would just go away as much as I wished he'd take me in his arms and carry me to my room.

I'd tossed an unreal location into the *Koror* glyph. To both Gage and me, when the spell took hold, it appeared that we floated in a blanket of golden stars, free of gravity.

I'd also made the music of my cells audible, and a steady thrumming filled the air. The last trick I'd woven into the spell was clothing. Gage and I both wore long robes. I was tempted to make them amber, but I tend to overuse gold and purple. So I cast them midnight blue, nearly the same hue as the sky behind the stars.

"My love," Gage said, stepping toward me. And despite the fact that I knew—hoped—he was only playing his role, my heart skipped a beat.

I had only a moment to hope he was Grabbing the hormones and their precursors before he touched me. At that point, most rational thought fled my mind.

12

Sokaris's spell was amazing, like we were in heaven. And she was so delectable that I wanted to dive in and devour her. But I knew the game, and it had to be played slowly.

For Peony's sake. For her sake alone.

Curbing my passion, I collected Sokaris in my arms, gently. Under this spell, I could barely recognize the haughty, proud woman who'd come to play such a strong role in my wrecked life. This Sokaris seemed like a scared animal, one liable to bolt. I held her tightly for a long moment, resting my cheek against hers, enjoying the pleasure of her skin against mine.

The eerie music told me when I'd made progress. The first time I touched her, the haunting humming had taken on a nervous edge. But now it was more steady, even if it held an anticipatory note.

But only as I felt her heart harken to mine, when her breaths calmed to match mine, did I remember to start Grabbing. And Grab I did. I found my way easily to the correct indentation in her pituitary, and I Grabbed the hormone triggers. Putting them in the tear ducts for storage was remarkably easy.

My cock was throbbing.

"I've waited so long to hold you like this," I said, stroking the warm area between her shoulder blades. The silky robe only heightened my awareness of her hot skin beneath. I savored each vertebra beneath my thumb. I caressed each, letting the frightened creature in my arms get used to my touch.

From her tutorial, I knew the moment the ACTH started a cascade effect in her endocrine system.

And from my experience with Robin and with Lyric, I knew I'd been rewarded by my slow approach. I didn't recognize most of the chemicals zipping past, but I Grabbed the ones I'd been instructed to capture. Not too difficult.

My lips just touched her ear. I didn't kiss her but lingered long enough to make her wonder if I would. "So luscious." My voice was thick as my caress shifted to her lower back. Even though my teeth longed to nibble her ear and my hands longed to grab her perfect ass, my passion stayed under wraps.

The music, which was somehow linked to her, lost its flavor of fear and began to sound more longing.

My hands moved up to her shoulders. She needed it. Her spelled self was taut with nerves. I massaged those tight muscles with my thumbs and whispered, "I'll never hurt you. I'll stop when you want me to, at your word."

The music lost its anxious flavor, and Sokaris gave a small purr of pleasure. She tilted her head, letting me massage the sides of her neck. She was so incredibly soft, so tender. My cock throbbed.

She relaxed, so my lips grazed her earlobe at the most tender spot. Mistake. A typically cocky mistake.

A jarring note rose through the air, and she stiffened beneath my hands. I stopped immediately. By the Stars, this spelled woman was nervous.

My tone would have soothed a wild animal. "It's okay. "We won't do anything you don't want to do."

"I'm sorry—"

"Shhh. Don't apologize." Pulling her tightly against me again, her heart pounded against my chest. "Shh."

We'd been floating in a standing position, but now I cajoled her around until she drifted onto her stomach. I wished for her robe to disappear, for warm oil in my palms. And the robe vanished while the oil appeared. The strength of her magic. Astounding.

The musical humming was muted to near silence as my hands oiled her back and shoulders. But as I caressed deeper into her rigid muscles, she groaned in pleasure. The humming grew bolder.

"So, what's got you so upset?" I asked. "If you tell me, maybe we can talk it through." Playing my role, I used the same words that had worked with Robin, just before she moved across the country with her family.

Sokaris's shoulders shimmered in the starlight as she shrugged her reply. "Nothing."

The lie hung in the air between us. "There's no problem that can't be helped with someone to listen."

Her beads clacked as she shook her head.

"Is it me?" I could feel her ropey muscles under her velvet skin.

"Maybe." Her voice harmonized perfectly with the humming.

I didn't massage her ass, although at that moment I would have paid to. Instead, my hands luxuriated over her thighs and calves. The plump muscles of her delectable legs loosened under my attention.

The music sang counterpoint to her voice. "A Love Wizard can't fall in love. It messes up her chemistry."

Well. This seemed outside of the script. I probably didn't understand the rules correctly. I massaged high on her thighs, just beneath her gorgeous ass. More to buy time than anything else, my knuckles grazed her ass. Not insisting, just teasing. Just testing. Then I said, "But Love Wizards have to adjust for their chemistry all the time. Don't you need to hold different hormones in check when you're ovulating? Don't the phases of the moon do things to your blood?"

"Yes . . ."

I ran my hand boldly over her hips, her waist. Perhaps distracted, she didn't balk. "If you fall in love, why can't you do to your hormones what you do when you ovulate?"

"The chemistry is much more unpredictable. It's a lot trickier."

"But you're the highest ranked Wizard there is," I said, wondering if I had wandered too far off the script. "I can't believe you'd ever have a hard time controlling your own love hormones, even as you were moving someone else's." With those last words, I ran my palms boldly over her ass. Literally, she made my mouth water.

The melody grew eerie, taking on unusual but not unpleasant notes. She didn't answer either the spoken words or the ones shouted by my hands. She said nothing, and she didn't move.

So I didn't stop. Her heart-shaped ass tempted me, but I danced on the edge. I wanted in. I wanted to delve and explore and slide and glide. I wanted the music to scream to a thundering bass.

But the spelled woman lying before me didn't want to grow attached. Or, that's what she thought—in this moment. So I held back, waiting for her to decide.

"The Guild prohibits it." Sokaris's voice was almost a whisper. "They expressly prohibit long-term love matches. I'd only be able to teach. I'd have to give up my practice. I've worked my whole life to have a practice like this."

"I never found following rules to be all that rewarding."

"But the rules . . ."

"Are merely rules."

Though the spelled Sokaris said nothing, the melodic strains grew with a subdued hope. Then her ass arched up, inviting me.

My hammering heart took that as an answer, and my fingertips cheered to slide along her delicious wetness. Once. Twice.

"It's so good," she breathed, and I could only agree. With my fingers and my heart.

Then her robe reappeared, and she stood before me.

"Slower," I said, refusing to be shocked by the power of her magic.

The desire of her flesh asserted itself again, and she gazed into my eyes for an instant. Hers brimmed with moisture, and the gold flecks within them pulsed in rhythm with our blanket of stars.

I held my hands out to her, willing her to come to me. When she grasped them, every cell in my being rejoiced.

With her first step toward me, her midnight robe melted away, leaving behind a chemisette made of gauze. The shift fell halfway to her knees. That was all that covered her trembling beauty.

With her second step, she was in my arms.

I could have wished her chemisette away. Or she could have. But delight could be found in a more traditional disrobing.

My hands were shaking with excitement as I undid the fastening, and the garment fell open at the neck. Only the peaks of her nipples and two tiny straps held it on her.

With the slightest movement I slid a strap down her shoulder. I pushed down the other strap. With the whisper of silk against silk, it melted away into the stars.

My entire body quivered as my eyes drank her. Her hands and feet were tiny. Her arms and legs were exquisitely formed, and she radiated strength. Then she pulled me toward her and hung her arms around my neck. Her gaze, locked on mine, burned with intensity.

However hot I was, my control was nearly complete. I Grabbed from her. Running my fingers down her elegant throat, I traced a line between her breasts, over her navel, stopping just above her silky nest. Her head was thrown back, and she trembled beneath my eager caress.

Finally I kissed her, joining my burning lips to hers. She tasted like honey, and as my tongue found hers, a wave of dizziness washed over me—dizzy like the first buzz from three or four pints. Better. Delicious dizzy. Addictive dizzy.

I kissed her long then, and deep, and she kissed me in return. She pressed against me, finally. And as my cock pulsed against her, another wave of dizziness washed over me.

What an amazing spell. I didn't want it to end. After the tortured beginning, I knew the sweet delight that yet awaited. And she knew, too.

We fell back on our bed of stars, our lips seeking each other's. Languor gave way to ardor. When I took her nipple in my mouth, she pressed to me, and I nearly came. Knowing a woman wants me has always been my biggest turn-on, and I could tell that under this spell, Sokaris wanted me with her every fiber.

Rolling beside her, one arm snaked beneath her shoulders and neck; the other snaked around her body and pulled her full length against me. As she twined her arms around my neck, her breasts came to my face, and I licked and sucked until she writhed in delight.

She rolled beneath me. Her clitoris, swollen and hot, throbbed with mad anticipation. I slid my fingers over her, and she pressed against me. Sokaris could not remain quiet then. She moaned and gasped with every stroke of my fingers.

I wanted, needed, to claim her, to bind and brand her. She met my mouth with a strength equal to mine, and it shook me to my core.

Her lips were soft and welcoming. They were sweeter than

Agadez honey. Within the confines of the spell, her mouth was soft and hot and wet for me. For me. My tongue met hers. I ran the tip of it along her bottom teeth, tasting her. Claiming her as mine.

My cock would wait no longer. I gathered her close, feeling her nipples graze my chest. With her breasts in my hands, I slid my cock inside her warmth, and stayed there a heartbeat.

Being enveloped in her heat felt right. She felt right. In that quiet moment I felt almost like she could be savored without the thrusting of the impending lovemaking.

But staying there became impossible. The smallest tilt of her hips left me breathless, and my cock wanted to have every inch of it caressed by her heat. The tip of my cock wanted her pressure; the base wanted it, too.

With a wild cry echoed by the magical music, our very hearts rushed into mutual ecstasy. An amazing crescendo washed over us, bathing us in the sound of fulfillment.

The way we melted together was madness, something I'd never experienced, not even with Lyric, the love of my life.

When I'd first joined Sokaris in the magic space, I'd thought that the music came from her, maybe from her cells. But now I heard a distinct syncopation—the music's accent had been shifted to the weak beat. And in tandem, I also heard a distinct counterpoint, beautifully highlighting the existing melody.

Even as it faded, I clung to the spell, wanting it to be real.

13

I absorbed my hormone-laden tears with the silk handkerchief. He'd done a fantastic job, collected exactly what we needed.

Gage fumbled through the fog of the spell. When his eyes finally focused, I handed him his robe, my heart pounding with trepidation. What would he think of me? My insubstantial spell couldn't deceive him for long. If he had any instincts at all, he must know about our chemistry.

My knees were too weak to flee.

But Gage looked at me and grinned. My heart froze, expecting . . . I don't know what. He just said, "By the Stars, Sokaris. I never knew spells to have such power. Remind me not to tangle with you."

But there'd been no spell, not in the way he was expecting. And I could never tell him.

I didn't know whether to laugh in relief at the success of my ruse or cry in frustration.

14

Sokaris's cinnamon scent clung to me like perfume. I wanted to soak in the bath, wash the scent of lovemaking—and that's what it had felt like—off my skin. Not that Sokaris didn't smell good; she did. But even as that sound of our hearts haunted my head, I hated myself.

I'd never cheated on Lyric. Not in the seven years we were married, or the two years we knew each other before that. True, I flirted outrageously, particularly with barmaids, even the half-orc ugly who manned the Slug and Garden. I also ogled shamelessly and made a lot of lewd suggestions, none of which were meant. But I never so much as touched the breast or lips of another woman, not in lust or love.

Not until today.

I'd helped Sokaris make her earlier potions—it's true. But my mind and heart were reliving my love with Lyric. I was remembering my youth with Robin.

But somehow that last spell with Sokaris felt like treason to my marriage—more treasonous than even the drinking.

By the Stars, I wanted a drink. I wanted to go home.

I needed Lyric's cleansing presence.

I'd saved up quite a pile of talens. She'd be so happy to have some money, and I bet she felt worried sick about me. I'd sent a brief note home weeks ago, maybe months, saying that everything was fine and I'd be contacting her shortly. Maybe now was the right time.

The biggest impediment to my visit was the Brown Worm. (*His cock, her mouth,* my brain whispered.) But I finally believed I was strong enough to walk past the pubs, even the Slug and Garden.

I decided to try.

When I stepped onto the brownstone's porch into the balmy spring air, I looked up at the gray stone gargoyles and asked, "Well, birdbrains, what do you think? Can I do it?"

They didn't answer. I don't know why I was surprised at the silence. I shrugged and walked down the stairs.

But just before I stepped onto the walk, I swear I heard them say, "Good luck."

I was glad somebody was rooting for me. I whistled a happy little tune as I turned toward home. Crocus buds were beginning to unfurl—pinks, purples, and whites. I couldn't wait to see Lyric.

My carefree mood lasted about halfway there, and then I couldn't help it: pictures of Obadiah's cock in Lyric's pretty cherry mouth tormented my mind. I vacillated between hating her, hating him, and hating myself.

I should have turned around then. I knew it. My mind kept seeing Lyric's nails digging into that bastard's back. Why couldn't it have been my back? Was I such a bad—

My dark thoughts were interrupted as I turned the corner and came face to face with the Slug and Garden. The wooden sign swung in the slight breeze. The familiar snail oozing up the rake, gold painted against blue, made my heart pound.

I should've run, run as fast as I could.

But I didn't. I never did, did I? The open door was a siren's call.

The beery waft enveloped me like my mother's arms. I was home.

"Long time, no see, Gage," said Clover with a grin. Sweet Orange flashed me a smile and tossed her hair over her ass. As I walked past her, she wiggled her butt invitingly. The barkeep nodded toward me, his teeth as snaggled as ever, and he turned to get me a Brown Worm. I didn't even have to ask.

My mind did the same calculation it always did when I approached my favorite barstool: how many Worms could I buy with the talens in my pocket? Today's answer: a lot.

"Buy a round for the house," I croaked at the barkeep, like I always did when I was flush. And I was certainly flush, thanks to Sokaris.

My favorite barstool loomed ahead of me. Three steps and I'd be there. I lacked the strength to leave. I lacked the strength to order water. I didn't want the Worm—I really didn't. But my cell receptors did. And I was helpless in their grasp.

So I did the only thing I could do to fight it: instead of sitting on the barstool I'd come to think of as mine, I eschewed my longtime friends and sat in one of the booths.

Alone.

In the back.

In the dark.

Elves I didn't know threw darts with amazing accuracy, and each time they let one fly, the wall behind me *thumped*. Each thud made me jump.

I lurked in shame, waiting with a watering mouth for the barkeep to find me. When he did, I'd send the drink back. Or I'd pay and leave without taking a sip. Or maybe I'd take just one sip. What could one sip do?

Sweet oblivion beckoned.

While I waited, fingers drumming nervously on the sticky

table, my mind sought distraction. Sweet Orange's bare midriff would have distracted most people, but I was forever bound to Lyric. I thrust the image of Obadiah's cock away. His black crinkled hairs.

People—humans—sat in the booth neighboring mine, and their hushed voices caught my attention. If they'd been shouting, my brain would have tuned them out.

Breaking all polite conventions, I Sensed their conversation. Most Wizard's wouldn't have spied; it was too rude. But this Wizard was in no mood for social niceties. I wanted a Brown Worm, consequences be damned.

"... don't drink it then," whispered one of them. That was a sentiment with which I could agree. (*Drink it, drink it,* my cells urged me.)

The barkeep pulled the tap for my ale, the Brown Worm logo shining brightly across the barroom. My mouth watered. My brain craved.

"Gives courage, though, don't it. You *should* down it. I'll drink yours, you don't want it." This was the whispered voice of the second man. I couldn't see either of them.

Across the room I watched golden ale fill the glass. Next to me I heard, "He needs three more virgins—I need courage."

"Three more! Pwa, I hate this!"

"Shh!"

"Don't be silly. No one can hear us, no one in here anyway." Little did they know.

My distracted brain realized they were using a silence spell, and even as a Brown I wouldn't have been able to hear them. But I was a Red now, a Red craving a drink.

Across the room, the glass was now half filled with my nectar. Stars, was this the slowest tap in here? "Barkeep!" I bellowed. "Hurry it up!" I didn't want to think. I didn't want to listen. I wanted a drink.

"But I *do* hate it," the second man continued. "I don't like to hurt them pretty girls." His voice was deeper than the other man's.

This conversation was getting difficult to ignore.

"Well, at least we're not killing them."

"Still. My sister's the right age. She's a virgin. Glad she lives in Kankinada."

"Like your sister's a virgin."

At this point, the barkeep put the Worm on a tray, and the ugly half-orc barmaid scanned the room for me. But even as I flagged her, my brain chewed on the conversation going on next to me.

"He says 'do it,' we do it. Ain't no two ways about that."

"I don't got to like it any, though. Give me my drink back."

Were these men responsible for the rapes? And was it part of a plan, not just some rapacious idiot?

No matter how my neurons flipped around what I'd heard, I could draw no other conclusion.

The huge barmaid, a bronze shield covering each breast, started to slide the drink in front of me. I shooed her away. "Bring me a—a lemonade instead. No, apple cider. Bring me cider, please."

She arched a ragged eyebrow at me, shrugged, and walked away.

"Gage!" shouted Clover. "Come sit with us."

"Come sit *on* us," Sweet Orange said. "It's been too long, sweet boy, and you look refreshing."

"What am I?" Clover demanded. "Old and stale?"

I waved my hand impatiently at them. Didn't they have jobs or something?

I waited for more conversation from the men at the other table, but none came. I Sensed only silence. The two were gone. I slammed some talens on the table, enough for the round I'd bought the house, and ran after the two men.

"Stay," invited Clover. "I'll buy the next round."

I shoved the door open.

"Goddess tits," I heard Sweet Orange mutter. "Ever since the Guild snoot started coming here, Gage's too good for us."

Scanning the street from the pub's doorway, I wondered what the Hells she was talking about. Guild snoot? Did she mean Guild Chair Uriah? Strange that he would make the Slug and Garden his new hangout. The clientele alone scares off most snoots.

But then I saw the two men scurry across the street and slink down an alley. Why had I never learned invisibility, or even silence?

No time like the present, I told myself striding purposefully toward the alley. Invisibility was nothing more than bending light. I bent it, racing down the street to the alley.

Once in, I stopped. It was a dead end. The foul stench of their armpits and beer breath lingered. And the smell of someone else, probably the last bum who'd slept here. But the men from the Slug and Garden weren't here.

At least, I couldn't see them.

With that thought, I sought bent light, but either I wasn't good enough to detect it, or they were truly gone. I spent another moment looking for hidden doors, only to be stymied again.

Damn.

With my hands in my pockets I looked at the sky. If I were a better Wizard, these pubic hairs wouldn't be running free, hurting young women.

I palmed the soft leather purse I'd put together for Lyric. She was just around the corner. Giving it to her would take just a minute. (*His cock, her mouth, her sweet mouth.*)

But, no. Lyric could wait. Sokaris needed to know about these men now.

* * *

"By the Great Star, Gage," Sokaris said when I walked in. "Why're you invisible?" Standing in the doorway to her parlor, she held a thick package wrapped in grocer's paper.

"Am I? I wasn't sure the spell worked, but I needed—"

"Darn. I'm going to have to return this now." Sokaris threw the package unerringly at me.

"If I'm invisible, how did you do that?"

She rolled her eyes at me, not deigning to answer. Her expression said it all: I'm a Gold, you fool. She walked into the room, and I followed.

"What is it?" I asked, holding up the package.

"Open it," she said, sitting in her lacquered chair.

Inside was a fantastic red cloak. The weight was perfect—400-thread, maybe 450. "Wow," I said, shrugging it on. "This is probably the nicest cloak I've ever had." I'd have killed for a cloak like this when I lived on the streets.

And it showed off my new Red status, which Sokaris knew, obviously. I'd been vain long enough to know the cloak also showed off my shoulders and chest. It was slightly fitted at the waist, and it snugged against my thighs.

Grinning, I finally looked at her and said, "Why do you have to return it?"

For the third time in as many minutes, I got that look. I caught the "you fool" part, but I didn't understand the cause. "What?" I demanded.

"Reverse your invisibility. You're a Blue now. At this rate, I should just skip yellow and get you a green robe."

"You mean—" but I shut up. I didn't need that look again. "Wow," I said. I'm sure my vocabulary impressed the Hells out of her.

Sokaris stood and took the cloak off my back. I tried to ignore the heat of her fingers on my pecs. Maybe her fingertips lingered longer than strictly necessary, but my vanity can be loose with the facts. Likely, she touched me only as long as strictly needed.

Sokaris folded the cloak neatly. Why she couldn't do that with the dish towels in the kitchen, I had no idea. "I'll get you a blue one," she said. "Congratulations." She turned on those perfect legs and headed out the door.

A strange part of my heart was going out the door with her, and the loneliness that remained reminded me of ale. Which reminded me of my news. "Wait!" I said.

"What?"

Then I told her what I'd heard in the pub—reluctant rapists, three more virgins needed, men disappearing into an alley, their breath still detectable.

"And you've been sitting here trying on clothes! Why didn't you tell me when you came in?"

"I tried—" The woman would try the patience of—

"Do their voices," she commanded. "Let me hear their voices."

"What are you talking about? How do I—"

"You're a Blue."

This woman.

But I saw her point. Grabbing my vocal cords, I shifted them a little and said, "Is this what they—" No. That wasn't deep enough. "How about this?" No. Still not right. I Grabbed the cords a little farther back and up. "Maybe this is— Yes! The most reluctant guy sounded like this! And he said, 'Three more! Pwa, I hate this!' Who says, 'Pwa?' I ask you." And then, back in my own voice, I said, "That's a strange interjection."

"And the other? What did the other man sound like?"

I thought for a minute, listening to him in my mind's ear. Then I Grabbed my vocal cords again and tried, "What about this. No, wait." I grabbed more centrally. "This. He sounded like this, and he said, 'Well, at least we're not killing them.'"

"Very nice," Sokaris said. Great praise from her.

"The one with the deeper voice has a sister in Kankinada."

"That might be interesting." She thought for a minute and asked, "You didn't see their faces. Is that right? Not even a glimpse."

"Not their faces," I agreed. "But I saw them walking down the street, almost running. I saw their backs."

"That might help," Sokaris said. "Now that you're a Blue, you might be able to recognize them even from that brief glimpse. The set of a shoulder, the hip-to-waist ratio, anything might trigger recognition."

"Okay," I answered. "And something else—they were good enough to disappear in the alley. Maybe they're Wizards?"

This time she sighed, sitting back down in her regal chair. "If someone is brewing potions to impede the sexuality of women from the tears of rape victims, a Wizard has to be involved. They may have been Wizards themselves, or a Wizard may have lent them a wand loaded with an invisibility spell."

"Not Guild Wizards," I said, almost a question.

Sokaris shrugged her shoulders, making her beads clack. "A Guild Wizard or a rogue. There's no way to tell. Not yet." Lines of worry settled on her brow. "Whoever it is has a high rank, at least a Silver."

Did she suspect one of her friends? A colleague? I didn't want to ask.

"I have to tell the officials what you heard," Sokaris said. "It's too late tonight, but tomorrow will do."

"Who are the officials?" Stars, the last time I spoke with an "official," I was being questioned for the rapes myself.

"The guild chair—the local chair, not the national one. And the mayor. It's her city. She needs to know what she's up against." She leaned back and thought. "And obviously, the police chief."

"Guild Chair Uriah? The police?"

"You know Wizard Uriah?"

And Detective Habit. And Police Officer Pike. "Guild Chair—" I thought of the barroom crowd laughing at the image of him getting bested by a pig and ran my fingers through my hair.

"Yes?" she asked, expectantly.

"Wizard Uriah helped me with a spell that went awry." And he exonerated me when I'd been picked up as a rape suspect, but I didn't see any need to tell Sokaris that.

"Wizard Uriah's a Gold." Did a look of discomfort cross her face? "I'm sure he was very . . . helpful." Yes, Sokaris looked peeved.

"Helpful," I agreed. "Yes, he was that." Having Uriah save me from not one, but two fiascos hadn't made me like him. At all. Perhaps he had the same affect on Sokaris.

And that made me like her. I liked her a lot.

"Will you invite them over tomorrow evening?" she asked. "If you have time, could you organize hors d'oeuvres and something to drink? No wine or beer."

After Sokaris left, I walked up the stairs to the kitchen and put on some tea. As I poured myself a cup, I saw that my hand was shaking.

Only then did I realize how close I'd come to having an alcoholic relapse.

By the Star Goddess and all her children, I was going to be a slave to the Brown Worm for the rest of my life. If the rapists hadn't been there, I'd probably be drunk, pounding on Lyric's door, closing her out of my life forever.

I should change my name to Lou—then I could really put the "lou" in loser.

But as I drifted off to sleep in my clean and comfortable bed, I remembered that Sokaris had never asked me if I'd had a drink in the pub.

Maybe I was stronger than I thought. And maybe she knew it.

15

"You must be Mister Feldspar," the mayor said, grasping my hand firmly.

The mayor and her husband arrived at exactly the appointed hour.

"Yes, I am," I said, opening the door for them, inviting them in with a gesture. "Pleased to meet you."

Mayor Astra was surprisingly tall with gaunt cheeks and intelligent eyes. "This is my husband, Fan." Her husband looked too dandy for my taste—powdered face and red lips. Was he wearing lipstick? But then I'm not married to him. What do I know? I shook his hand.

"And I brought the chief of police, too, Chief Axiom," she explained.

With dread, I shook his hand, too, as he came in. He had a strong, thick jaw and sad eyes, like he'd seen every terrible thing and expected to see more. "Hello, Feldspar. I brought my top detective. That acceptable?" The chief stood nearly as tall as the mayor.

"Of course," I said to him. Could the ex-hobo actually say "no"? His top detective was Detective Habit, the same woman who'd brought me in for questioning all those months ago. She stepped through the door.

"Come in, Detective. How've you been?" As if this were a social call.

"Mister Feldspar," she said, her thin lips unsmiling. "I see you've risen in rank, despite our previous conversation."

Guilt raced through me. All those months ago, she'd asked me if I were trying to rise in rank, and I'd said no. What a memory. Everyone's eyes were on me, waiting for my reply, but I could think of nothing.

"You know each other then?" asked Axiom into the awkward silence.

I looked at Habit, wondering how she'd answer. Would she say: Yes, I questioned him as a rape suspect.

"We met briefly," she replied to her superior.

Stepping onto the porch, I breathed in deeply, letting some of the cool night air fill my lungs. The gargoyles caught my eye. I swear the fierce-looking one winked at me.

If these people knew I'd lived out of trash bins, they'd never respect me. "Wizard Sokaris is waiting for us in the sitting room," I said. "I'll lead the way."

"Is Guild Chair Uriah here yet?" asked the mayor.

"No, but I expect him shortly." He couldn't be worse than Habit; at least he didn't suspect me of mauling these women. "May I take your cloaks?"

"I brought some growlers," Fan the Dandy Man said, holding up double pints of Badgers Best Bitter.

Even as the blood drained from my face, my mouth watered. If I drank some of those, I could give a shit what these snoots thought.

Detective Habit watched my reaction.

By the Stars, the night was going to be difficult. Wordlessly, I walked to the sitting room with the group traipsing behind me.

When Sokaris saw my face, she knew. She knew, and she didn't think less of me.

Instead, her eyes scanned the entering crowd and stopped at the growlers. "Fan!" she said, "How nice of you to join us." She kissed him on his cheek, and some low-down part of me wanted to punch his rouged face. "But I'm sorry, I've got a tricky potion brewing right now, and I can't have any ale in the house. No alcohol. Please, could you put it in the garden? Right now?"

May her Star shine brightly. I could fall at her feet.

"You Wizards," the dandy said. "Never any fun." And then Fan started to hand the growlers to me, saying, "Surely you know the way better than I."

Just as I reached for them, someone knocked on the door. Guild Chair Uriah.

"Gage," Sokaris intercepted. "Please get the door. I'll take these out."

"Sure," I muttered. As I bolted, I caught Detective Habit's glance again. She was definitely watching me. Those cold eyes missed nothing.

I tried to calm myself on the way to the door. It's not as though I'd lived a life of crime. But who'd believe the word of a bum? And so much of tonight's information relied on my word.

The oblivion promised by the growlers in the garden seemed a hell of a lot easier than the night that stretched ahead of me.

The brass knob slid in my moist palm. Not attractive. With a deep breath, I opened the door. "Chair Uriah," I said to the man. "How nice to see you again." He must have sensed the blatant lie. His beard, fringy and green, clashed with his electric-blue robe.

"Yes, Mister Feldspar," he said in a rich voice. "I'd heard you'd come up in the world. Your friends at the Slug and Garden seem to think you've been avoiding them. And Oh! I see you've progressed to Blue. Congratulations!"

"Thank you." I'd have to ask Sokaris how he knew what level I was. And I guessed I'd heard Sweet Orange right—Uriah had been hanging at my old pub.

"How is it that I so often see you in the center of one disaster or another?"

"I don't know, sir. The group's this way." I didn't like the way this guy smelled.

Fan's voice floated down the hallway as we approached the parlor. ". . . his wand went 'Zapp!' and the pig went 'Eeeh!' and his wand went 'Zappp!' 'Eeeh!' went the pig!"

By the Goddess herself, not the Obadiah's pig story again, not with Uriah walking right behind me. If I were him, I'd want to kill me.

Fan again. "And by the time he'd fixed the spell, our illustrious guild chair himself was covered in pig shit!"

No one laughed at the punch line, and when Uriah and I appeared in the doorway the silence became even more profound.

Sokaris stood. "Wizard Uriah," she said. "Welcome to my home."

"Thank you," he replied. "I was here not too long ago, if you recall." He shot a displeased look in my direction that I didn't comprehend.

"Ah, yes," Sokaris answered, understanding where I hadn't—and still didn't. "Perhaps we can discuss that later?"

"As you wish, Wizard Sokaris."

"Mister Feldspar," Chief Axiom said, rubbing his jaw. "Perhaps you can tell us exactly what you heard and saw yesterday." Detective Habit took out a notebook and pencil.

"At the Slug and Garden," added Uriah. Guilt surged through my veins.

Everyone stared as I stuttered through my story.

"So, Mister Feldspar," the mayor asked when I finished. "How long have you been working with Wizard Sokaris?"

Her question could be polite small talk, or the mayor could be interrogating me, politely, subtly.

How little she knew. Eager women are my vice. Wet, happy, languorous women turn me on. Grown-up women get me hard. Scared almost-girls? Never.

Detective Habit got in my face. "Tell me again what the men looked like," she demanded.

I needed a drink.

"Where did you work before this, Mister Feldspar?" asked Chief Axiom.

Alcoholism can cause lesions, and I wondered if I'd damaged my brain: either I was mad, or this group thought I'd raped those girls. This wasn't the meeting I'd imagined when I'd made the vinegared artichoke hearts. I thought we'd civilly exchange information and then make a plan to catch the villains.

Seeking a friendly face, I locked eyes with Sokaris. Her expression counseled patience. Did she sense the bloodlust, too?

And there were growlers in the garden.

When Sokaris touched my elbow, I jumped, my wracked nerves hypersensitive. Detective Habit saw.

"Gage," Sokaris said. "Could you please see how our potion's coming along in the laboratory?"

I could've kissed her.

I went, wanting to strangle someone, anyone.

Fan was lurking in the hallway. "You want to go out back?" He winked an eyelid, painted an iridescent blue.

I shoved him against the wall.

"Hey!" he shouted. "You're such an asshole."

Fan was probably right, but he was lucky I left him his ultra-white teeth. I stalked past him.

But as I opened the door to the lab, I hoped I wasn't running out on Sokaris. Maybe she needed my help. A hero might try to figure out what in all the Hells the rabid guests were thinking—he wouldn't run away. He certainly wouldn't have nearly beaten the shit out of the mayor's husband.

But no one would call me a hero.

Lucky for my brain, which craved the distraction of something hard to do, the love potion was ready for the next step.

I turned the knob on the titrator, dropping a miniscule bit of calcium benzoate into the tear-filled beaker below. The clear drop hit the translucent, waterlike fluid below, making a glistening blue pond just below the surface. Perhaps Peony's eyes were just this color.

As I counted to ten, I watched the blue spot grow and deepen. Each new color was more amazing than the one before. Blue green, pale purple, light green. Small traces of chemical vapor rose from the surface, adding to the surreal quality of the substance in my beaker.

The chemical fog thickened, coalesced, and by the time I finished counting, a viscous pomegranate-colored liquid pulsated in my beaker.

Peony's salvation.

I hoped it worked. I didn't want to Grab those hormones again.

Making love with Sokaris might be my undoing.

I held the beaker to the light, studying its color and texture, and a thought filled my mind. One single, protein-filled tear could facilitate an amazing change in a girl's life.

The laboratory door opened slowly, and quiet footsteps followed.

"It looks perfect, Gage, exactly right."

"Thanks. Are they gone?"

"Yes." Her purple and gold beads clicked as she approached me. "I brought this pomegranate down so you could see exactly when to stop." Sokaris held the sliced fruit next to my beaker. "But you've already done it perfectly. They're exactly the same."

After fucking up with Obadiah's pig so badly, I was glad to have some successes under my belt. Of course, I'd been drunk when I'd spelled Obadiah's pig.

"You've got great instincts," she said to me.

I looked at her. She had no idea.

It was almost like she could sense my thoughts. "Look, Gage, I know you're frustrated with your . . . addiction."

I kept my silent gaze on her.

"Has anyone ever showed you how to Sense your own cell receptors?"

Was such a thing possible? "No."

"Give me your mind." She took my hands in hers, which were warm and dry. My cock couldn't help itself: it instantly hardened as I remembered the feel of her hands sliding over my shaft.

But I easily linked with her. Her strength amazed me yet again. Linking with people had always been difficult for me, but with her, it was like jumping into a warm lake.

Sokaris wasted no time. She showed me cell after cell, each having normal external receptors. "Dozens of glycoproteins can hook up perfectly with these, telling the cells it's time to make a protein, divide, or release some energy."

"I understand," I said.

"But look at these." She showed me dozens more cells. Glyco-proteins couldn't fit. Only alcohol could.

She gently gave my mind back to me. By the Stars, what had I done to myself? "By the Goddess, I've fucked myself up good."

"I think you misunderstand." Her voice was as soft as whis-pery nightjar calls on a summer night.

"What do you mean?"

"When I first met you, finding normal, healthy cells within

you was much more difficult. Almost all your cell receptors were twisted. What you've done's remarkable. So many are healed."

Anger poured through me. I didn't feel better. Those snoots upstairs had looked at me like I was half a man. "But then why am I always craving it?" I slammed my fists on the bench, and Sokaris deftly caught the precious beaker.

The air turned frigid. "Look, I'm just giving you a tool so you can measure your own progress. I don't have a cure for addiction or for self pity."

She was right, damn her. I thought she'd just leave, but she surprised me. "What'd you think about the meeting?"

I almost said, "I don't think I'm any judge of that," but the small rational part of my brain asserted itself. "Strangely tense," I said.

"Yes," she said.

"They think I'm the rapist, don't they?"

She paused before she answered, perhaps weighing her answer in her mind. "Yes."

So it wasn't just paranoia. "Sokaris, I have to tell you something."

Her gaze locked on mine. Maybe she thought I was going to confess to slaughtering infants in their beds. "What?"

"Before I came here—" I had to tell her, but, by the Stars, what would she think when she knew she'd been having sex with a bum?

"Yes?" That curt tone never made it easy for me.

"It's just that I used to live on the streets before I came to you."

Sokaris blinked.

"I mean, I begged talens for ale. I ate out of the trash. The whole thing." The whole thing. No bathing. No self-respect. No ties to anything.

"Oh."

Now, she'd walk out and leave me to my life.

But she said, "I'm sorry, Gage. I see this is important to you, but I don't get the relevance."

"That's why the cops suspect me! They arrested me for loitering more than once. Detective Habit even questioned me about the rapes. Guild Chair Uriah scanned my mind before they let me go. Those people are never going to believe a word I say, and this whole story hinges on my word." My fists nearly pummeled the bench again.

"Detectives don't arrest the homeless, Gage. Police do."

She'd never struck me as thick before tonight. I slammed my hands in exasperation.

"Honestly, they didn't mention homelessness," she said.

"What did they mention?"

"The detective interviewed a victim who described her assailant perfectly."

My heart froze.

"With a *Wabizi* mirror, a Guild Wizard saw what she saw: her assailant."

"Let me guess," I said caustically, as if sarcasm could make this all go away. "It's me."

Sokaris paused, then said, "Yes, the rapist looked just like you."

I stalked off to the garden. Six growlers wouldn't begin to put a dent in my fury.

16

Gage wouldn't find the ale in the garden. Fan, always cheap, had taken the growlers with him.

My assistant needed a friend, now more than ever, and I needed to rise above myself—lock my forsaken hormones under wraps—and be that person for him. He'd be hating himself for stupid reasons, and someone needed to tell him how stupid.

With images of blood groups in mind, I trudged to my tiny garden.

He sat on the wooden bench next to the fountain. The trickling water sparkled deep blue and silver under the light of the nearly full moon, but the clematis-covered trellis cast a lacy shadow over his face.

"I looked all over for it," he said, holding up his nicked and bloody hands for me to see. "The growlers obviously aren't under the roses."

"Fan took them."

"Cheap prick."

I laughed. "He always is."

"Still, I looked for them, would have drunk them if I'd found them." The shadows hid his face from me.

"When they weren't here, did you run to the pub?"

"No."

"Well."

Water trickled in the fountain, filling the silence that followed.

"So they think I did it," he finally said, not a question.

"None of the victims ever 'saw' her assailant. Some sort of spell blurred his face—or their faces." I thought back to my questioning with Peony. Did she truly lack magic, or had someone somehow blurred my *Wabizi*? Frightening implications.

"Then how—"

"Except the last girl, the one after Peony. She saw you."

"But I've never even met her—"

"I know! Listen. She's the only girl attacked after you saw the men in the Slug and Garden, after you followed them."

"Why does this matter?" he demanded, nearly shouting.

"Shh. We'll get to the bottom of this. I'm on your side."

"Then tell me," he said in a calmer voice, "why this matters."

"The rapist or rapists changed their behavior—from showing no face, to showing your face—only after you followed them."

"And that suggests someone's framing me."

"Exactly. And that sort of mischief's hard to come by."

"What do you mean?" Gage asked.

"Listen, can you change your face?"

"I've never tried. I like the one I've got."

"Stars," I complained. But still, it was nice to hear him cocky again.

"There's one problem with your idea," he said.

"What's that?"

"I was invisible when I chased them."

"Not in the bar, though, right? And you changed on the street, didn't you?"

He paused, thinking. "Yes. You're right, I guess."

"It's difficult to change your face. You can make your nose longer or shorter, but to make yourself closely resemble someone else takes strong magic."

"A Wizard then. One of the metallics."

"Yes," I agreed. "Bronze, Silver, or Gold. A strong Wizard is framing you."

"Oh."

The musical notes of a nightjar song tripped down the scale, filling the night air.

"A metallic Wizard," he said finally. "That's not good. So why do they think I'm behind it?"

"Chief Axiom thinks you might've made up the part about hearing those men in the pub so you don't have to hide your face anymore when you attack the girls."

Gage clenched his fist, frustration etched in his every movement. "But can't someone link with me to see what I saw?"

"That was suggested." By me, but he didn't need to know that. "But Guild Chair Uriah pointed out that you can lie that way, if you have any talent at all."

"Did anyone offer a motivation?"

"A motivation for rape is rarely necessary."

After another long moment of silence, he said, "I'm going to bed."

He stood, sliding out of the moon's shadow. I could see despair imprinted on his face, and I wanted to kiss those lines away. We could crush the ferns under our backs, forget the world's troubles, at least for a night.

Ignoring my desire, I let the sounds wash over me. Nightjars. Falling water. The moon had risen higher, and the garden was nearly as bright as daytime.

The garden door clicked shut as he entered the house.

Guild Chair Uriah had taken every opportunity tonight to suggest Gage was guilty. Habit watched closely, and I took her silence as agreement. Did that mean that Uriah actually thought Gage was guilty, or had another Wizard suggested the idea to the chair? The only certainty was this: the Guild was involved, somehow.

Not for a minute did I think Gage guilty of this. When I'd sent out that flier to find a hero, I never thought the Guild would try to make him into a scapegoat. But that was exactly what was happening.

"Sokaris!" His voice carried from his room upstairs to my spot by the fountain. Panic laced his call. "Sokaris!"

I ran, clutching my long robe so I didn't stumble as I pounded up the stairs.

"What?" I asked, throwing his door open.

Wordlessly, he pointed to a growler of Badger's Best Bitter. It was sitting on his nightstand, looking as lethal as a Lezmiri asp.

"Where did it come from?" I asked. Stupidly.

"You didn't put it here?"

"Of course not! Why would I do a thing like that?" I reached for the huge bottle. "Here, let me—"

"I can—" he said, reaching for it himself.

But there was no way I could let him touch it. I grabbed his wrist. "No."

He shook, vibrating with horror.

"Sokaris—" he said, but he didn't finish.

My arms wrapped behind his neck, twining like ivy over a country manor, and I pulled him tightly to me. I shouldn't have.

But I did.

And I kissed him. My lips slid over his, velvet against velvet. His tongue slipped just inside, teasing the inside of my top lip. His kiss tasted like something from the Stars—sweet and strong.

He pulled back and looked at me. The same look of horror he gave to the bottle of beer, Gage now gave to me. My heart stopped.

"Get out," he said, his voice as raspy as a file over a horse hoof.

"But—"

"Leave." He must've known how that sounded because his voice softened. "Please."

I turned and fled, but not before grabbing the bottle.

17

Sunlight streamed into my window in the morning, annoyingly optimistic in the face of the facts. The meeting had been tense, and somebody—Fan? Uriah? Habit?—had put a beer in his bedroom. We were both stressed, so the kiss could be ignored. Should be ignored. I stepped out of bed and dressed, as was my new routine, and went to the kitchen for something hot. To drink.

I'd spent the night oscillating between rage at whoever planted the ale, burning curiosity of that villain's identity, and shameful desire. And even as I went downstairs these thoughts haunted me.

If nothing else, last night's meeting proved I was becoming a powerful member of the community. After all, I had Police Chief Axiom, Mayor Astra, and Guild Chair Uriah in my sitting room. I couldn't toss away that power for biologically perfect lust.

I couldn't.

Before I could get to the kitchen, the patients' doorbell rang. I shrugged, knowing that coffee was likely off the morning's menu.

The woman who waited for me was tall and gorgeous, or she

would've been if her eyes hadn't been rimmed in red and her skin wasn't blotchy from tears. "Come in," I said, handing her a handkerchief.

I showed her to my office and bade her sit, which she did, but only for a moment. Then she started her mad pacing, reminding me of a wild horse newly penned. "Please," I said. "Tell me your name."

"Ibex. I'm Ibex. My mother wanted to come with me but I wouldn't let her. She's outside."

Surprised, I looked at Ibex again. Her height and strength deceived me—she was only about sixteen. Then I recognized her. "I know you," I said. "You're the farrier's assistant."

Ibex stopped her pacing and really looked at me, as if I'd already exhibited great magical works. But the truth was I'd seen this woman-child assisting my farrier, handling hot tongs, burning iron and massive beasts like other women handled cut flowers. "Yes." She ran her hand through her thick red hair and said, "I am. You have that nice Lezmiri mare. She's got great lines."

"Thanks. She's a lovely horse. But if you don't mind me saying, you look . . . greatly distraught."

She slammed her huge beautiful fists on my table and shouted, "I am!" Then her voice dropped to nearly a whisper. "I've been violated."

By the Stars. Another victim.

"Oh, I'm so sorry." I tried to pat her hand, but she jerked it away from me.

"Don't feel sorry for me! I care nothing"—she spat the word—"for my virginity! Society may value it, but I don't, and I won't wed any man who cares about it."

Well. She was strong, talented, and beautiful. She'd need a strong man, whether or not she'd been attacked. But why was she here?

"Can I ask," I said carefully, "why your mother sent you to me?"

"I don't know." Again, that anger. "I'm here because she bade me. She wouldn't allow me to continue my blacksmithing apprenticeship if I didn't seek your counsel."

Ah, so the mother knew something.

"Ibex?"

"What?" Exasperation.

"Are you angry with the men you work with? Are you angry at the horses you shoe?"

"Why would I be?" she snarled.

"Do you snap at them?"

"What do you think?"

"I think you probably do. Let me tell you what else I think, and you can tell me if I'm wrong."

She looked at me suspiciously but nodded tightly anyway.

"I think you're surprised that a man bested you physically." I'd seen this woman wrestle an unruly two-year-old colt to the ground to trim its feet.

"That bastard jumped off the wall and landed on my back. He knocked my head with a rock. By the time I came to, he had tied my hands and feet up, and was doing his nasty, nasty thing." Tears rolled down her face, and she pushed them off defiantly, daring me to comment.

"And it makes you scared it'll happen again, that you'll be helpless again."

She nodded mutely, but I could see her anger had receded, leaving mostly sorrow and humiliation.

I could see Ibex needed something very particular. For her, her pride in her physical capabilities had taken a blow, amplifying the torment of her violation. I bet she doubted her own strength, which would be incapacitating when dealing with masses of molten iron and huge, reluctant horses.

"I think I can help you, but I need to talk to your mother first."

Ibex was too weary to object. "I'll send her in." She left.

Alone in the room, I rubbed my forehead. The potion that would help Ibex would come from an encounter where he roughed her up and nearly won, but she capitulated and liked it.

I suspected that Gage didn't particularly like rough sex under any conditions, and given what Guild Chair Uriah was accusing him of, he'd be supremely unhappy about this.

Before her mother came in, Ibex stuck her head through the door and said, "I saw the bastard, by the way."

"You did?" I said in a weak voice.

"I did. Dark hair worn in a fancy club. Brown wide eyes. Smarmy."

"Oh," I said, thinking of Gage—or rather, Gage when he'd first appeared on my doorstep. The smarmy look had melted away under the heat of humility.

"And if I see him again, I'm going to kill him. I'll rip him apart."

"I'm going home, Sokaris," Gage said as I walked into the kitchen. "I need to see my wife."

His wife— But she— My thoughts tumbled. But then I remembered his oxytocin distributions and concentrations. When this man bonded, he bonded for the long ride, faithless wife or otherwise. But still, I must have looked stunned, because he fell over himself in a rush of words.

"I'm leaving first thing this morning, and I—"

"Ibex." I threw out the word like it could save me.

"What?"

"Another victim showed up today, needing help—needing *our* help."

Blood drained from his face, and he said in a thick voice, "I can't, Sokaris. Not another spell like that." He raked his hand through his hair. "At least not until I talk to Lyric. I need to talk to her."

And then I understood. Gage was torn in two directions, just like I was. Fear zipped through me. I didn't want to become attached to this guy. And I didn't want to lose him.

I let a chill settle over me as I said, "This spell calls for rough sex if that helps. It might leave you feeling dirty, but it won't break your heart. Go home to Lyric right after that. Please."

I turned on my heels and headed to the spelling room, before he could read anything on my face.

Before he could say no.

18

"Are you tired? Can you do this?" Sokaris asked, so solicitous now that she knew I'd stay.

I sighed, trying to rein in my irritation. "Yes, I'm tired, but Ibex can't wait, can she. Let's get to work." Let her think it was just work for me. I hoped the barb stung just a little.

She shrugged out of her robe, all business. But her ebony nipples were already erect, and I knew she was wet. My newly honed Wizard senses could smell her excitement. As she headed for the pentagram hearts my cock started throbbing. She made it hard to hate my job.

"Okay," Sokaris said. "I've loaded the wand already. You need to use the *Palikir* glyph. Do you know it?"

"You better show it to me."

"This spell is going to take us to a little rougher environment," she said, showing me the spell.

I suspected understatement but replied, "Yes, and I'm to Grab all the same proteins I did for Peony, with the addition of androgen."

"That's right, for female aggression. And go heavy on it, especially in the beginning. You know what androgen molecules look like?"

"Yes, I've got it," I said, stepping into the hearts.

I might've known what molecules to Grab, but I wasn't at all prepared for where the spell took me. After a heartbeat of dizzying disorientation, I found myself in a room, shimmering walls alternating between plum and gold. A seductive scent hung in the air, patchouli maybe. Perhaps a touch of almond.

A table stood to my left, big enough to fuck on and covered in a black velvet cloth. I ran my hand over it, appreciating the crushed softness. I could imagine Lyric's ass pressed against the velvet, soft against soft. Her white skin would be a stark contrast to the black.

Then my mind painted a different picture, a black ass writhing on the table. Wanting. Inviting.

But I was only the apprentice. Lyric was my wife.

I blinked, and the table changed. Now it bore an assortment of things I'd never dreamed of using on a woman: blindfolds, masks, a paddle, whips, ties.

Each implement was a thing of beauty. The blindfolds were made of crimson chenille, and the ties were gold cord that slid through my fingers like silk. Intricately arranged feathers of magenta, royal blue, gold, and black formed one of the masks. Black and gold feathers lent the second mask a leopard look. The whip was made of the softest calf leather, and the paddle, so cold in my hand, was made of silver. A thrill of delight ran through me, despite myself.

At the end of the table I spied bottles and jars. Opening one, the scent of vanilla wafted around me. I scanned the labels. Jasmine. Honey Buttermilk. Pomegranate mint. Cocoa. In real life, cinnamon would be the obvious choice for Sokaris, but in this unreal world anything might be possible.

Maybe not buttermilk. Sokaris wasn't a pancake.

Where was she? An amethyst door with a golden handle stood to my right. With my cock standing at attention, I opened it and found the Love Wizard. She stood in the corner wearing an inscrutable expression. She might attack me with malice, or she might attack me with lust. Either option looked likely from her face.

I stepped warily into the room, as I might were she a tiger.

Her clothing—or lack of it—took my breath away. A chain of small gold links circled her tiny waist. The thinnest black strings served as panties, and these had large gold rings at each hipbone. More black string ran from the rings to another, nestled between her breasts. A brassiere pushed her full breasts together and up, but no cloth covered her soot-black nipples. Her perfect calves were encased in heliotrope-colored boots with spiked heels the length of my hand.

By the Stars, never had I wanted to lose myself in every crevasse of a woman as I did right now. Her nipples, thrust toward me as they were, begged to be sucked and nipped. Like my cock, they were rock hard. I knew the string running between her thighs would be soaking wet.

"Sokaris," I said, holding my hand out to her. "Come here."

"No fucking way. Get away from me."

A woman tells me to leave, I leave. I began to turn, but the spell kicked in a little pressure. I had a part to play.

I stepped toward her, and she lunged away. "Fuck off, I said."

"Don't talk to me that way," I said feinting to the right. She bolted right past me, giving me the best view of the string running over her ass. I wanted to run the length of it with my tongue.

"You did that on purpose, didn't you? You love to show off that ass."

"What makes you think that?" she asked, turning slowly so I had another great view. The height of her heels pushed her breasts out and her ass up. My mouth watered, and she knew it. Sokaris ran her fingers lingeringly over the back of her thigh, and then she pulled the string away from her clit, tracing its path with a fingertip.

"Come here. I'm too hard to chase you," I said to her.

"That's your problem." Her lidded eyes were heated. "You want me, you have to catch me."

I made another halfhearted lunge in her direction, which she easily sidestepped, even in those amazing boots.

"You don't want me that badly, do you?" she asked. "You're really not trying very hard."

Desire made me clumsy. My mouth wanted to suck her. My fingers wanted to caress her, explore her. My cock wanted inside of her.

But I could only stare.

She was worth staring at as she ran her index finger over the string covering her swollen sex, up her ebony cheek.

Sokaris faced me and pretended to sulk. "You keep admiring my ass so much, my tits are going to feel left out." She put a finger into her luscious mouth and sucked. I groaned. Then she traced an areola with that glistening finger, pebbling that nipple.

I had to have her.

I made a heroic dive at her as she turned to leap away. My fingertips caught the gold chain around her waist. I yanked it toward me and tossed her onto the ground. Starting at one hipbone I licked just under that belt, across her quivering stomach and across the next hipbone. Then, not too gently, I flipped her over and traced that tiny path across her lower back.

"I've been wanting to do that since I first saw you in the doorway with that feather duster." My fist was holding the small of her back to the floor, and my knees separated her thighs.

I saw then what should've been immediately obvious. Sokaris's string-clad ass was in my face. Mouthwatering. My tongue found another path it wanted to taste. I buried my face, savoring her salty tang. Under my tongue her clit felt like liquid silk. She was swollen and wet—I know she loved it.

But she twisted out from under me. Despite her absurdly high heels, she leapt from my grasp.

"You're going to be sorry you did that," I growled. And then I stalked her, like a cat stalks a mouse. She was mine. I lashed out and caught her. She might've resisted but instead she molded herself against me, rubbing her tits against my bare chest like she'd never been trying to get away. I grabbed the hair on the back of her head, not painfully, but so she couldn't escape again.

I brought her mouth to mine, but I didn't kiss her—I devoured her. Sucking each of her full lips into my mouth, I ran my tongue over hers. She met my every move. Sokaris set me on fire.

I couldn't help it: My hand loosened its grasp on her hair. Her fingers danced seductively, hungrily over my ribs, down my stomach. Then my balls were in her palm, and she squeezed. Not enough to cause damage, but she certainly had my attention. I let go of her braids and held my empty hands up for her to see.

She smiled wickedly, laughter in her eyes as she winked and sprinted away.

But she wasn't fast enough this time. I grabbed that chain around her waist and led my captive to the bed, which had magically appeared, a hedonistic concoction of silk spreads and satin sheets in a deep garnet. The intricate mahogany headboard and footboard had many newels from which to tie my willing captive.

I should've tied her right away, knowing her dirty tricks and her desire to run. But I couldn't resist using some of the toys on the table, which had appeared next to the bed.

The magical appearance of the table and bed gave this spell a flavor of unreality, a dreamlike quality, but the woman in front of me was as real as the Lezmiri desert. I tossed her over my lap, displaying her gorgeous ass for my pleasure. She glistened with desire. She wasn't fooling anyone; her escapes were a complete charade. I ran my fingers over that inviting trail, throbbing myself as she wiggled against me.

"You've been naughty," I said, taking the silver paddle in my hand. And then I spanked her. Hard. Well, not that hard, but hard enough.

She yelped, and I immediately felt chagrined. What was I doing? This was no way to treat—

And then she bit my calf—hard—and simultaneously thrust her ass up invitingly. The vixen liked it! I spanked her again. And then again.

"Are you sorry?" I asked.

"No," she said, her voice husky. For good measure, she wiggled in my lap, not appearing sorry at all.

"Then it's time for harsher measures," I said. I put the paddle down and spanked her with my open palm.

"Are you sorry yet?"

She bit my knee.

Standing, I flipped her over and scooped her into my arms. It must have been the magic. I knew she was nearly the same height as I am, but she seemed like a pixie in my arms. I'd dated one in high school.

"I'm sorry! I'm sorry!" she cried. She kicked her legs fetchingly, the long spikes on her heels making her legs seem longer and leaner. The pixie version of Sokaris tossed back her head and used her hands to push her breasts closer together and in my face. A gold ring had appeared through one nipple, and I groaned in appreciation. This woman was a marvel.

Well, I had to accept her apology, didn't I? How else would a gentleman behave? I grabbed the nipple ring between my teeth and pulled, gently, yes, but insistently. She arched her back in my arms and moaned, kneading the breasts offered to me.

And then she kneed me in the ear. Hard.

"That's it," I said, dumping her onto her feet. I grabbed that nipple ring in my fingers and marched her to the bed. She sank into its pillowy folds, and I pushed her back, using the chenille cords to tie a hand to each bedpost above her head. I tied her booted ankles to the opposite post.

And then I took a moment to savor the view.

Can words do justice to the shape of her breasts, pushed and bared? Her clit was swollen, almost pink against her black thighs, and throbbing behind the thin black string of her outfit.

And her eyes laughed at the power she had over me, desire clear in her expression.

Then I remembered the blindfold. And the whip.

While she watched, tied to the bed, I picked the whip off the table. I ran it threatening up her thigh, stopping at the fleshiest part. The vixen winked a lidded eye at me and strained the ties to open her legs wider.

I blindfolded her, the bold creature.

Did she feel vulnerable, tied helpless before me? Did she feel scared? If I took off the blindfold, would she still have that air of superiority, or would she be cowed?

No, her expression would be flushed with unadulterated desire.

I couldn't bring myself to whip her. Instead, I knelt above her, straddling her luscious body. I teased her nipples with the textured end of the crop, alternating the rough woven leather of its handle with my tongue until I could sense that she wanted fulfillment more than she'd ever wanted it in her life.

I ran the crop handle down her waist, tickled her navel with it. Turning, I slid the rough part over her clit, and when she groaned and pushed against me, I nearly exploded.

Enough of the toys. The crop rolled onto the floor.

I ran my hands over her silky thighs, caressing that extra-soft place behind her knees. That caress, though, reminded me of Lyric—of Lyric and Obadiah. I couldn't go down on Sokaris. She lay open before me, nearly begging me for fulfillment, but all I could do was look on helplessly.

I wished I could just run away.

The spell didn't have complete control of me, since I was the one Grabbing. But it could strongly suggest a particular direction, and that's what it did now. It shifted my attention.

Leaving Sokaris deliciously blindfolded, I caressed her face with my palm. I caressed her waist, her stomach, her breasts.

Normal desire filled me. I didn't think it would affect the hormones we were hoping to Grab. The fact that the spell let me continue in a more traditional manner reassured me.

I buried my cock in the warmth of her. Like the last time, she felt so good, so right.

I imagined the ties away, I imagined her string suit gone. They evaporated. I made love to her, and she made love to me.

She smelled so good, so right.

Sokaris came almost immediately, and her orgasm prompted mine.

Her tears would be the perfect antidote to Ibex's issues, although Ibex would definitely need her mother's wisdom when she took the cure.

For a change I came out of the spell before Sokaris did. After grabbing my robe and quickly bathing, I headed out the front door before she sought me. I imagined Sokaris riding the delicious post-orgasm waves into a soothing nap. Could a wish turn that into reality?

The gargoyles said not a word to me as I walked down the steps.

I needed to find my wife.

Hiking from Carathay to my old neighborhood, I walked past handfuls of pubs unscathed. None called to me; surprising, given how badly I'd wanted a drink the night before. The Ox and Plough, no problem. The Horse and Jockey, ditto. I steeled myself as I walked past the Slug and Garden, but again, it was easy.

And then I turned onto Pinked Street, onto our street. Who would have guessed that one little road could mean so much to me? When I heard the word "Pinked" I thought of my wife's warm kitchen, made cozy by her efforts rather than by the cheap architecture. I thought of rumpled sheets smelling of love. I thought of the shape of her lips, fantastically swollen, first thing in the morning.

Walking down Pinked Street, I thought of nights spent pounding on the front door, of keys that no longer worked. Of talens shoved under the door to get my drunken self out of her face.

Three blocks from my house, I didn't know what I was going to say to my wife. I didn't know what I wanted from her. For months, I'd been striving to win her back, unbeknownst to her. I'd striven to improve myself, to cage my inner demons, to become someone of which she could feel proud.

But instead I'd become something worse than I'd been before: I'd become an adulterer.

In my heart—and with my body when I couldn't help it—I lusted for Sokaris. With her clacking braids and long black limbs, she was everything Lyric wasn't. Where Lyric was patient, Sokaris was haughty and cold. She had more magic in her little finger than Lyric could even imagine. Where Lyric embodied love, Sokaris and lust went hand in hand. And I couldn't get enough of her.

But even comparing these two amazing women meant I was insulting my wife. And probably Sokaris, too.

I stood on the corner, looking past the flower sellers to my house, one block up the street. Dragging my heels, I decided to get bluebells for Lyric. The color would match her eyes, and she always liked flowers with musical names.

I bought the flowers and, in a moment stood stupidly holding them, staring at our front door. The afternoon sun made them gleam. My hand had forgotten how to knock, how to knock on my own front door.

But I didn't have to.

Lyric walked toward our house, wrapped in a cloak against the cold. Her cloak was the same color as the flowers in my hand, and I took that as a sign that our meeting was fated.

I stepped toward her, her name on my lips. "Lyric."

She turned at the sound of her name, and when she recognized me, she smiled. The curve of her lips melted my heart. She was so classically beautiful, as beautiful as the girl next door.

The antithesis to Sokaris's exotic splendor.

"Lyric," I said, thrusting the bluebells at her like a lifeline.

"Gage!" Her joy lightened my heart. "Gage," she said again. "We've been so worried about you."

I hated that "we've," but she was opening our front door, welcoming me. I followed her to the kitchen, the same kitchen I'd seen in that spell with Sokaris. My heart quivered.

"Sit," she said. "I'll make some tea."

While she tinkered with the water and stove, I sat, looking around. The room was unchanged. She'd somehow thwarted our eviction.

No thanks to me.

Finally, she sat across from me and looked me over carefully. "You look good . . . somehow healthier."

"You do, too." And it was true. She actually glowed with beauty. "Your eyes are shining." Without me, she looked great.

Lyric dropped her lashes, not wanting me to see her pleasure in my compliment. That familiar expression did something to my guts: I hadn't seen it in so long, but I'd seen it throughout my entire adult life.

"So," she said, sipping her tea. "What've you been doing? Where do you live?"

"I'm assistant to a Goldie in Carathay. I live in one of her spare rooms."

"Her?"

I laughed, remembering how I'd so colossally bungled that myself. "Yes, she's definitely a she. Wizard Esmenet Sokaris."

"Wow, Gage, that's great. And has she, you know . . . helped you with your problem?"

I raked my hair with my fingers. "No, not exactly. She tells me it isn't really possible for a Wizard to cure me."

"Oh," she said, and maybe she sounded a little forlorn, which I found encouraging. If she still cared about me, there was hope for us. "But you look so good," Lyric continued, "like you did when we first met. Your eyes look . . . I don't know . . . clear?"

"Well, I haven't been drinking. Not since I started working with her." I'd waited months to say these words to her, years probably. I waited for pride to surge through my veins but the pink of her nails reminded me of Obadiah's back.

"Amazing!" She said it like the Star Goddess herself had just appeared.

It was, and I'd done it for her. I looked at her supposedly happy expression and saw worry.

"What do you do? What's your job?" she asked, pushing a plate of perfectly sliced *wataws* in my direction. Their tangy aroma made my mouth water.

"I help extract hormones and proteins for potions," I said,

bragging a little. This was the sort of stuff I'd only imagined doing when I was married to her. "You know, I Sense molecules and I Grab them. I've learned a handful of new glyphs. Not that I have my own wand yet or anything."

I'd expected Lyric to be a little impressed, but her eyes had glazed over. I could tell I'd lost her. "Sokaris's a Love Wizard," I clarified, trying to get her attention. "And you'll never believe this: I've become a Blue."

"Wow, Gage! You've gone up—what is it?—one whole level?"

"No," I said, "I've gone up two." I ate a *wataw*, savoring the salty vinegar of it.

"That's amazing. Obadiah will be so impressed." Him again. I'd put in all this effort to impress my wife and all she could talk about was Obadiah.

She must have realized how that sounded, referring to that man, because she quickly added, "He always knew you had it in you, though. So did I."

His hands on her bare thigh. His cock between her pretty pink lips. The *wataw* turned to mud in my mouth. I wanted to kill him.

"It's funny." Lyric rushed in to fill the awkward silence. "We were just talking about finding a Love Wizard."

Funny, indeed. Obadiah and Lyric didn't look like they needed any love potion from what I saw in my mirror.

She laughed nervously at my expression and said, "No, nothing like that. It's just that— Do you remember my cousin Cantabile?"

"The little girl?"

"Well, not exactly little anymore. She turned eighteen last summer and married Doctor Sforzando."

"That old guy? He must be seventy." I barely choked out these civilized words.

"Yes, and he could drown the world in all his talens."

"The family must've been happy. Can't the old guy get it up for the girl? Girl hate the sight of him?"

The rage behind my words made Lyric pause. She'd lived with me long enough to read my moods.

"No, no. Nothing like that," Lyric said, ignoring my anger. "At least not that I know of."

"Then why do you need a Love Wizard?"

"It's just that Cantabile's changed so."

"Changed?" I asked. I could tell her about change.

"Well, you remember how she used to be so outgoing and happy?"

"Yes," I said. Despite my seething resentment, an image of the girl filled my mind. Shining auburn hair and bright eyes to match. Always wanting to play. "I remember."

"She's just lost all that sparkle, become so downhearted. Almost blue."

"Is the old guy cruel?"

"She says not. She claims he's as nice as could be."

"It's probably the marriage," I said curtly.

"She doesn't know," Lyric continued, like we were girl-friends having lunch. Not like she was my wife. "She says it's a strange feeling, like something she had once is gone forever."

"She's pregnant."

"She's not pregnant, but it does sound hormonal, doesn't it? That's why we thought a good Love Wizard could help. What about your Sokaris? Is she good?"

All these fucking "we's." "Sokaris's good." With patients. In bed. I had a lot of nerve to get pissed at Lyric. If my wife took me back, we could call it even.

"Well then," Lyric said firmly. "I'll send her your way. In Carathay you said?"

"Yes. Bantam Boulevard."

We sat there awkwardly for a moment, my mind racing with questions that I didn't want answered. I glanced quickly up at my wife, taking in her absurdly shiny hair. It reflected light from the window and bounced back honey and almond with slivers of chestnut.

I clasped my china teacup to keep my fingers from thumping the table. When I noticed the tea sloshing from my cup onto the saucer, I set down the cup and shoved my hands into my pockets. There, I found my sack of talens for her, a small fortune by our previous standards.

"Here," I said, almost slamming the leather bag onto the table. "These are for you. You can pay off our debt. If you can wait just a little longer, I can save enough to get our cottage back."

Her sad look took my words away, and we sat there a moment, staring at the bag like it might bite us.

"Gage," she said hesitantly into the quiet.

I looked at her questioningly as she pulled her cloak tighter around her chest, burying her nose in the trim. Protectively. She needed fortification against me, I guess.

She put her palm over the back of my hand and said, "I'm so glad you've found a good space."

"I am, too," I said, even though I could smell the sharpened blade she held above my head.

"No, I mean it. Is Sokaris a friend? Someone you can count on when you're in trouble?"

I tried to think about how Esmenet had taken the ale from my room, not the kiss she'd scalded me with moments before. "Yes, she's a friend."

"And she's home now?"

"Damn the Stars, Lyric!" I slammed my fist on the table and the teacups skittered toward me. "Just spit out whatever you have to say!"

Lyric carefully pulled the teacups away from the table's edge. "Obadiah and I want to marry, Gage."

Her words punched me right in the solar plexus. They left me gasping for air, like a fish netted into a boat, flopping and gaping. Breathing hurt.

"Drink some tea," she said, but the pity I saw in her eyes made me want to choke.

"I saw you fucking him, sucking his . . ." But I couldn't talk to her that way. I'd given her that line of worry on her forehead. It wasn't there before we married, and now it was a deep furrow.

"Our marriage is over, Gage. And it's been over for a long time." For the first time since I'd arrived at her home, she looked angry. "And I don't like you peering through the window!"

"No, it wasn't like that!" But it was, in a way. "Lyric—" I raked my hand through my hair. "I'm sorry. I'm sorry for all the horrible things I've done to you."

Lyric pulled her cloak more tightly around her.

"Do you love him?" I asked.

"Gage." Admonishment. "I don't want to have this conversation, not with you."

"But do you?" I needed to know. I didn't know if knowing would make it easier or harder, but I needed to know.

"He bought this house for me, Gage. Since we've been together, not a single bill collector has knocked on my door. He comes home every night, just when he says he will. And when he can't, he sends a message."

"Do you—"

"Shut up. He adores me. I have to be careful not to admire anything while we're shopping because he buys it for me. The community respects him, and the mayor sometimes has dinner with us. The DA brings his flute and plays while Obadiah plays the piano and I sing. And I never have to apologize for him, because he never embarrasses me."

Her beautiful blue eyes hardened as she continued.

"He never comes home drunk. Never. So, let me ask you this . . ."

I looked at her while she paused. She'd never looked so lovely: flushed cheeks, a high shine in her hair, her eyes sparkling.

"What?" I said, breathless from a sense of loss.

"How could I do anything but love him?"

19

I walked blindly down the street wishing I were someone else. Like if I were Obadiah I'd be making love to my wife tonight. Happy, worthwhile people filled this world. They'd be laughing and talking and enjoying each other. They'd be raising children and making plans.

What would it take to be someone else? A different look? Obadiah wasn't better looking than I. He had permanent bags under his eyes, thinning hair, and his nose was too long. His chin was underslung, too, like a turtle's.

But he was sleeping with my wife. My beautiful, beautiful wife.

I concentrated on my nose. Could I make it longer? Could I put bags under my eyes? I stumbled down the sidewalk, oblivious to those in my way.

The stale scent of beer wafted out the door as I walked past a building. Could I make my hairline appear receding? Make my Adam's apple look protruding?

I looked up. I was in the *Rohas* district, where every imaginable vice could be satisfied. How'd I gotten here? I stood right in front of an open door.

A pub, seedier than the Slug and Garden, welcomed me. The rich smell of hops called me in.

I could go in and get a—

But I wouldn't give in. I turned tightly on my heels. Not now. Not even for this. I turned toward home. My clean kitchen.

Sokaris.

At least Lyric would have a real man now, not some lowlife who perpetually put the slug in the Slug and Garden. If I loved her, that should bring me some happiness.

But I didn't feel happy; I wanted to cry. Lyric was my heart mate.

Was I man enough to let her go?

Suddenly the hair on the back of my neck stood on end. There was something creepy about the man loitering on the corner ahead, something creepy and familiar. The light shining around him, or the set of his shoulders, or maybe his scent floating vaguely toward me in the air. I knew him.

He was one of the men from the alley, the one who'd been talking about not wanting to rape more girls.

That man looked my way, scanning the sidewalk for someone.

Me?

But his gaze slid over me. Not me. I breathed a sigh of relief.

Then I caught my reflection in an oversized picture window. The face looking back at me wasn't mine. It wasn't Obadiah's either, but it was close.

I'd proclaimed to Sokaris that this skill—taking on someone else's appearance—lay beyond my ability. Apparently, it wasn't. By the Stars, this was cool!

The bitter part of my brain noted the irony: the first face I took was the face of my wife's lover. Maybe if I made love to

Lyric looking like this, happiness would be mine. I could knock on her door and—

But not even I could sink that low.

Movement on the glass's reflection caught my eye—the loitering man lit a cigarette. Curiosity made me forget about my face. Who was the rapist-for-hire looking for?

Lying in neat rows on the other side of the glass were an assortment of dildos carved from polished hematite. Thick ones and thin ones, long and short. A woman also sat on the other side of the glass. She was perched on a barstool, naked, knees primly together. Her blond hair fell neatly to her shoulders, and she'd painted her lips a schoolgirl pink.

Mistaking my fascination with the window's reflective properties for a fascination with her, the woman winked at me, cat-like. Her long black lashes fluttered against her pale cheeks.

I couldn't turn away; I could observe the loitering man from here without his knowledge.

And should he happen to see me watching the naked comely woman? So what. Obadiah deserved a little shit in his life. I hoped a dozen of his closest friends saw him ogling the nubile woman. Wife-stealing bastard.

With her eyes locked on my face, the woman slid her knees in my direction, keeping them together. Seductively, she tilted her head to one side. Then she ran her hands up her sides, held her breasts as if in offering.

My eyes danced between the seductive woman and Loitering Man. I wanted to turn away, but I couldn't, not until the man made a move. With long, elegant fingers, the woman in the window pinched her nipples, turning them into hot pink spikes.

Loitering Man looked south expectantly, but he didn't move. He wasn't watching the woman any more than I was.

In the window, the woman flipped her fine yellow hair over her shoulder and slowly sucked on her index finger. She used her slippery finger to make her nipples harder, shinier. I could tell she was confident in her beauty. She had every right to be.

A young guy, tough looking, entered the woman's shop. His muscled biceps were tattooed with a pattern of overlapping animal eyes, cat eyes peering from a forest glade. But Loitering Man didn't budge, and the woman didn't stop her show for me.

She spread her legs the tiniest bit. I tried to watch Loitering Man, but her wet sex was hard to ignore. Despite myself, I found myself peering toward that dark tunnel. The woman in the window smiled a catlike smile and curled an index finger at me, inviting me into her shop.

I could almost hear her purr as I stood mesmerized by her fingers and her eyes and her sex.

Then a giant thumped past my window, obscuring the reflection of everything else behind me with his massive form. He wore ill-fitting clothes, not surprising, given his size. His casual look was so careful he screamed for attention.

When he passed, Loitering Man was gone.

I whirled around. Where was he?

Then I spied him, walking right toward me. No, not to me—to the door. Loitering Man followed the giant into the woman's shop. They must be working together.

The woman, seeing me move toward the door, picked a huge hematite shaft from the table. Candlelight made its silvery hue glow in her hand. With a quiet movement, she licked the fat head, sliding her tongue seductively along the edge. Then she slid it into her mouth, her lidded eyes locked on mine. When it seemed the dildo must be halfway down her throat, she winked at me again. Her message was clear, but I needed to keep my eye on Loitering Man.

As I followed the giant and Loitering Man into her shop, the woman gave me her feline smile and closed her shade. Her self satisfaction gave me pause, but what could I do?

I blinked in the smoky dark air. The place smelled like cheap whiskey and sex, and the smoke burned my eyes. I followed the narrow hallway, paying a talen to a bouncer, who then let me enter the main room.

A number of men were gathered around a sunken pit: the man with the animal-eyes tattoo, the giant, Loitering Man, and a handful of others.

Wearing Obadiah's face, I walked over to the pit. My disguise filled me with pleasure and guilt. More pleasure than guilt, though. I wished Lyric's flute-playing DA would show up. Obadiah would have fun explaining that.

The woman from the window sauntered to the bed, looked up at her audience, and spun a little flirty twirl. Her hair sparkled in the candlelight, and the pirouette showed off her perfect legs.

"Begin the show!" someone shouted.

"Move it, Hot Ass!"

"Mreow, Pussy Cat!"

The men hooted their approval. Loitering Man and the giant stood next to each other, but they appeared not to know each other. Both whistled to the girl. Feeling like a fraud, I hooted too. I wondered how many people in this room knew Obadiah. A lot, I hoped.

In the center of the pit stood a round bed covered in red velvet, and with her audience hyped up, the woman climbed in on all fours. She stood on her knees a moment, running her hands over her small breasts. When her nipples were pearled, she crouched to her hands and knees, arching her back delicately to give her audience the perfect view of her shining sex.

The show was good, I had to admit, especially when she threw that feral grin over her shoulder.

"Show us the good stuff!" someone called, and she obliged.

She arched her back even farther and caressed the tips of her breasts with the shining dildo. Her nipples grew harder and pinker and the audience hooted some more.

Then gently, she ran the hematite over her flat stomach, teased us as she trailed it toward her sex. When she slid it over her clit, all eyes were on the woman.

Taking a chance, I used the moment to cast my Wizard senses across the pit toward Loitering Man.

I could smell him. He'd had eggs with tomato sauce and mango juice for breakfast, and he exuded a nervous sweat. The nervousness was interesting, suggesting this meeting wasn't his desire. Did he worry something might go wrong?

I kept my eyes on the woman. Everyone in the shop watched her, and she wasn't teasing us anymore. She wasn't teasing herself either. She slid the thick hematite dildo completely inside, then she began thrusting it. Each thrust grew more insistent. She wasn't faking it. From my vantage, I could see her swollen clit; I could see her throb and gleam.

With a little more difficulty my Wizard senses could hear the villain. His breath was tight. His body was prepared to bolt. Was it the excitement of watching the show? Or was he nervous?

The woman switched positions with a catlike grace. Now she lay on her back, guiding the hematite in and out. It glistened with her excitement in the lamplight. With her free hand, she stroked her clit, stroked its sides and its tip.

I'd love to be that hematite shaft, but I wanted to hear what Loitering Man was saying. I wasn't expecting to hear the villain speak, not really. When I glanced up, his lips weren't moving, and this wasn't the place for words, anyway.

But still I heard his voice, and those hairs on the back of my neck prickled again. The man was definitely the same guy as the one in the Slug and Garden, the one who said he hated hurting the girls.

The bastard was in the wrong line of business then.

What he said chilled me further. "That sounds dangerous, sir," I heard. "Are you certain, sir?"

"You dare question me?" The words didn't come from the giant; they came from the man on the opposite side of Loitering Man.

By the Stars, the giant was just a distraction! He had nothing to do with this.

The woman began to make small mewling sounds as she thrust her hips toward the ceiling, toward relief. I could smell male arousal all around me.

I stepped a little to the left to get a better view of Loitering Man and the man giving him orders. The boss was average height and very well dressed. The cloth of his coat was at least 400-thread count, and the coat fell to his calves in luxurious folds. His boots were beautiful, supple leather and had well-formed heels. Talens.

In the pit below, a second woman crept onto the bed with amazing stealth. Where the blonde was gracile and feline, the brunette joining her had huge breasts and muscular arms. Her long hair fell to her plump ass.

Like the blonde, she was naked. The blonde, fingers sliding around her clit, appeared not to notice the newcomer. Maybe she just didn't care. As she thrust the hematite deep inside, she added her fingers, burying them inside, too. Now only her thumb slipped over her throbbing clit. She was close to orgasm, and I Sensed it was real.

I quietly looped my senses over the villain's boss, suspecting he had strong magic. Sensing him, I noted that he'd not had breakfast. His breath smelled hungry. Had he been in a hurry? I tried to Sense his words, and at first I had no luck. What I heard was distorted and twisted. Was that some sort of spell?

Without any warning, the stocky brunette captured the blonde's nipple in her mouth. The blonde girl cried in pleasure. With her peasant's hand, the brunette grabbed the lithe blonde's free breast and massaged it, almost roughly. Panting, the blonde grasped the bigger woman's hand and slid it between her thighs.

I couldn't make any sense of the spell-twisted words being muttered on the other side of the pit. I might've given up at this point, bringing the information I had to Sokaris who'd put it to the best use. But I was feeling surly, punchy.

I glanced down at the pair below me as the brunette's hand slid the hematite between the blonde's thighs, and I realized I was incredibly turned on. Against my will. My cock as hard as it'd ever been.

The brunette flipped her long hair so that it didn't obscure our view, then she tossed the hematite to the floor. In a lightning quick move, she grabbed the blonde's hands and held her immobile. She nodded toward someone I couldn't see, and a muscular man entered the room. He wore a wolf mask, complete with a feral grin and wicked teeth. His huge erection throbbed.

The man next to me began to moan. He quietly put his hand in his trousers.

I focused on those twisted words, willing them to unravel.

And they did.

By the Stars, if I'd know how rewarding it was to be a higher-ranking Wizard, I might have pushed beyond Brown years ago.

Unraveled from their spell, I heard his words. "I don't need to justify myself to a two-bit thug like you. You'll follow my orders or the police with get an anonymous tip telling them where to find you."

"Yes, sir." Loitering Man sighed, and then he tried again. I can say this; he didn't lack courage. "But three more girls, sir? Even you might get caught with that many more."

But the crowd started hooting then, and the words were lost.

Below me the brunette stood behind the blond woman, presenting her to the man. The blonde didn't seem to mind having her arms twisted behind her. Appearing to relish it, she writhed, and as the wolf man walked toward her she thrust her breasts up and spread her legs. I could smell her desire; I could see it.

The audience watched transfixed. Would the wolf devour this feline girl? Each man in the audience held his breath, waiting to see the story unfurl.

The man in the mask didn't dive in for the obvious kill. Instead, he pinched the wide brown nipple of the brunette. He lifted a heavy breast and ran a thumb gently over her hardening nipple. She didn't object, but she didn't relinquish her hold on the blonde either. The man in the wolf mask strode behind her, and still she didn't move, holding her writhing captive.

The man ran a hand down the brunette's back, almost lovingly, and I wondered if he was going to spank her. Instead, he snaked a muscular arm around her waist and wrapped his fingers between her thighs. I saw one of his huge fingers on either side of her swollen clit. The scent of her desire began to mingle with that of the blonde's. Both women were now wet and willing.

I could hear the villain and his boss again.

"Are you threatening me, little rat?" the boss asked.

"No! Of course not. I would never—" The alarm was genuine.

"Good, because if you were, I'd have to—"

Below me, the man ordered the women to bed with one authoritarian gesture. The brunette shoved the willing blonde into the bed. With her feline grace, the blonde eagerly wrapped her legs around the man's hips, and he thrust into her while the brunette stood and watched. He plunged deeper than even the hematite had gone.

While impaling the blonde, the wolf man wrapped his hand around the length of the brunette's hair so that he controlled her head. Her hard nipples and the scent of her desire told me how she employed her role. He pushed her toward the small breasts of the blonde, and the brunette eagerly licked and sucked. Clearly lost in pleasure, the blonde's eyes were rolled back in ecstasy.

"Violet!" someone shouted into the pit. It was the man with the animal eyes tattooed on his biceps. "I'm going to kill you, you cheating whore!" With that, he pulled out a small tube and blew into it hard. A dart flew from the tube into the ass of the man below.

The muscular man grabbed for the dart, but almost immediately his body started convulsing. He died right away as whatever poison was in the dart filled his blood.

Violet, the blonde below, screamed frantically. The tattooed man—elven, I saw now—jumped the railing and landed in the pit below where he grabbed the woman's neck and began to throttle her.

The floor shook behind me as the giant left. The audience poured out of the shop, not wanting to meet the cops who would surely arrive, but I jumped into the pit. I couldn't let the blonde—Violet—come to a bad end.

I grabbed the tattooed man by the scruff of his neck and shook him. "What do you think you're doing?" I demanded, but it was rhetorical and he knew it. The elf held up his spidery hands in surrender. I twisted the nerve at the base of his neck until he passed out, then I quickly tied him up, using the implements from Violet's side table. The cops could take care of him.

A quick glance above told me nearly everyone was gone. The thick brunette who'd been part of the show was gone, too.

I tried to help Violet shrug into some clothing, but her grip was stronger than I expected, as if she was trying to hold on to the man in the wolf mask's life.

"He's dead, isn't he?" she asked, trying to yank the mask off his face.

"Yes," I answered. "But I don't think the guy with the tattoos is. Keep your eye on him." I worked the wolf mask off the muscular guy. He must have been only eighteen or so. What a waste.

"You okay?" I asked Violet, looking around for the bouncer.

"Obadiah," she said. "Thank you so much for helping me. I can't believe you finally came to watch my show. I'm just sorry that it had to end like this . . ."

I floundered for a response. Obadiah just saved a whore he'd paid to watch. I'd been hoping for something like this, but now I just felt . . . dirty.

Then Loitering Man and his boss looked down at us from the pit's lip.

The boss looked at me, making my blood run cold. My disguise didn't fool him for a heartbeat. He could see right through me. I Sensed it.

And then another realization struck me. I could see he wore a disguise. This man wasn't who he appeared to be.

I Sensed he was a Wizard.

"Are you harmed, sir?" he asked in a cold voice I knew not to be his own. "One can get injured when involving oneself in another's fight."

I straightened my cloak, dusting off my shoulder to buy a second. "One cannot simply ignore injustice," I replied.

"Well said, Obadiah," said Violet. She sniffed at the disguised man and said, "No gentleman lets a lady come to harm."

He just nodded sardonically and tipped his hat. He strode off with Loitering Man, his minion, in tow.

I could do nothing now but go home.

"Can I help you?" Sokaris said coolly as I walked in the door. By the Stars, was I getting fired?

"What do you mean?" I asked.

"Gage?" Recognition. "What've you done to your face?"

Obadiah again. I couldn't get away from him. "It's a long story," I said. "Longer even than this nose." I concentrated for a heartbeat, then two, before I felt my features melt back into place.

"Was that someone in particular or a random face?" she asked.

"That was the face of my wife's lover. No," I corrected myself. "That was the face of my ex-wife's soon-to-be-husband."

The Love Wizard nodded, understanding. She didn't ignore my pain, but she didn't dwell on it, either. This woman was a dream. "Not to change the subject," she said, "but do you know what you've done?"

My mind raced over the afternoon: Lyric, Loitering Man, Violet and her lover, the man with animal-eyes tattoos, the rich man in the impenetrable disguise. Probably a Wizard. "You can't even imagine what I've done."

"I think we might be even," Sokaris said.

"Why? What'd you do?"

She laughed and shook her head. "No. I meant I don't think you can imagine what you've done. Hold up your hand a minute. In front of your face."

I did, looking at her like she was absurd.

"Now kind of blur your vision while looking at the edge of your fingers."

"Okaaay."

"You should see a shimmering light. Do you?"

"Yes," I said. "It's yellow."

"When you left here this morning, it was blue. When I first met you, it was brown."

"I'm a Yellow." Awe.

"Yes, you are. Can I take you out to dinner to celebrate?"

I didn't answer, looking for the gold that must shimmer around her. Then I saw it, glittering around her shoulders, her head—like the Star Goddess herself. It cascaded down her back, like a cloak of light, filled with tiny starbursts and amber explosions. I said, "It's absolutely beautiful. You glow!"

Sokaris smiled. "Congratulations. Most Wizards can't see the auras until they're at least a Bronze. When you get a little more practice, you'll be able to see everyone's, whether you're looking or not."

I suddenly saw the inevitability of Lyric's defection to Obadiah. I saw it as clearly as the glimmering yellow around my hand. And it didn't hurt so much. I'd lost her months ago, maybe years, but I'd been unable to face the failure and sorrow head on. Today, the hurt was scabbed over.

"Let's go to dinner. I'm starving."

20

As I glossed my lips with a shimmering purple color, I told myself I wasn't taking extra care dressing for this dinner. I patted my braids into shape, selecting two with orchid-colored beads and draping them over my shoulder. I repeated the phrase to myself: I was not preening for him.

It was a lie.

A lack of self knowledge was never one of my shortcomings, and one particular fact kept jumping out at me: I was a hair's breadth away from falling madly in love with this guy. As a Love Wizard, I knew chemistry played a huge role—our complementary blood groups lit up the opiate receptors in my brain. And his, too.

But it was more than that.

Reconciling the strong man who chewed through Wizard levels like chocolate cake with the hungover fool who'd stood on my doorstep not so many months ago wasn't easy.

Gage Feldspar wasn't the same guy. Any man who could overcome mutated cell receptors with discipline and focus won my admiration.

And the chemistry. When he was near, even the hairs on my arms reached for him. I could smell him—his masculine scent—and he never failed to catch my attention. Even at the molecular level, my body sought to bind with his. My heart was a lost cause.

I selected a simple gown of deep amethyst trimmed in indigo. Its long sleeves and full-length skirt implied a modesty belied by its tight fit. I loved the way it flared when I walked. And we'd be walking to the restaurant.

Slipping into my low-heeled boots and my cape, violet lined with black satin, I knew I looked fabulous. I ignored the voice inside my head warning me about playing with fire. Even knowing that the Guild would revoke my license if I bonded with this man didn't give me pause.

"Are you ready?" I asked him with false cheerfulness. I wasn't happy; I was besotted.

"I am," he answered. "You know where we're going?"

"Mm-hmm," I hummed. "There's a place a few blocks from here. Looks like a wreck from the outside, but the foods unbelievable." I didn't add that they used the dimmest candlelight and that a handsome elf played a lute in the shadowy darkness.

What was I doing? I had to stop. As we walked in silence down the oil-lamp-lit street, I cast a subtle spell, a mild force field only strong enough to repel his hormones. I hoped it'd be enough to save me from myself.

The waitress seated us outside, at a table near a moonlit pond. Someone had used a clever spell to keep the gnats and mosquitoes away, and someone else had lit dozens of little candles and set them afloat on the water. Thick trees filtered light from the moon, casting lacy shadows on the water. The pond looked like a fairyland.

"So you busted through the cryptic speech spell," I said, referring to his afternoon adventures.

"I did," Gage said. "But I don't know that I'd recognize

him. His voice wasn't his own. I could see he wore a disguise, but I couldn't see what he really looked like."

This was interesting. "What made you think he was disguised?"

"You don't believe me?"

Still so prickly. Then I saw the waitress walk by, a tray with two pints of beer balanced gracefully on her upturned palm. Of course he was prickly.

"I believe you," I assured him. Which was true—I did. "But figuring out what kind of disguise he wore might help us figure out who he is."

As graceful as the moonflowers climbing up the side of the red-bricked restaurant, the waitress floated over and slid glasses of water to us. She handed us menus and said, "I'll be back."

When she left, Gage said, "His smell didn't match his face. That's what made me think he wasn't him."

Even more interesting. When Gage came home looking like Obadiah, his smell didn't clash with his face. But if he'd been trying to look like Lyric or a child . . .

"I've got a bad feeling about this," Gage said.

"I think that's normal given these vicious and unrelenting attacks."

"No, it's more than that. It's like . . ." The song of pond frogs filled the air while he searched for the right words. "It's like everything's about to come to a head. I've just got this feeling things are about to explode." He laughed and said, "That sounds stupid."

It didn't sound stupid to me at all. I said, "A girl had a feeling that a particular boy liked her, even though he'd given no outward sign. Independently I learned that their blood groups complemented each other."

"What're you talking about?" Gage asked.

"What feels like 'intuition' is often based on biological fact."

"Oh."

Seeing he wasn't following yet, I clarified. "There might be a reason behind your feeling, is what I mean."

His eyes were directed at the menu, but they weren't reading. Then he looked up and snapped his fingers. "The supposed rich guy was essentially bullying the minion—and not just to attack more girls. There was a sense of urgency in the way he spoke. The rich guy hadn't even had time to eat breakfast."

"So something's pushing him? Them?"

"Maybe . . ." he mused. "Like maybe the plans had changed, and he felt out of control."

He might've added something more, but the waitress approached, pad in hand. Her chestnut hair hung in thick ringlets down her back. "You ready to order?" she asked. "Just so you know, the quail's especially good tonight. Roasted with mango sauce, butter, and almonds. It melts in your mouth."

"Sounds perfect," I said. I hadn't even looked at the menu.

"Make it two," Gage said, and the waitress left.

Make it two, indeed, I thought to myself, and I didn't mean quails. Moonlight filtered through a vine-covered trellis casting shadows over his face, highlighting the planes of his face. I wanted to lose myself in the depths of his nearly black irises. I wanted to run my finger over the light fan of lines that radiated from his eyes.

What I really wanted was to make love to him without any spells.

"Gage—" I said.

"Excuse me?" the waitress interrupted.

"What is it?" If she asked me if I preferred vinaigrette to Roquefort I was going to scream.

"I'm sorry to interrupt," she said, "but there's a woman outside looking for Love Wizard Sokaris. You're the only one here who fits her description." Her pretty eyebrows arched upward, and I nodded for her to continue. "She asked me to give you this note."

I opened it and read:

My daughter was just attacked. We need your help.
Please.

I couldn't read the scrawled signature.

"Thank you. I'll be right out," I said, dismissing her.

"What is it?" Gage asked.

"Another rape." I showed him the note. "I've got to go."

"Of course," he said, standing. "I should go with you."

"Not if the attacker looked like you again," I reminded him. "Eat your dinner and meet me at home. We might have to create a potion for her right away."

Gage sat back down. Hurrying out the door, I realized—thankfully—that adrenaline had wiped away all traces of lust.

Love.

Whatever it was.

21

After Esmenet left, I sat feeling very alone. Tiny fish jumped in the pond, sending moonlight-garlanded ripples across the surface. Metaphoric fish jumped in my guts. Something wasn't right.

I strode out to the street and sent a messenger to tell the cops there'd been another attack, that Sokaris was talking to the girl right now at our house—no, at Sokaris's house.

The victim, her parents, or Sokaris herself had probably done this already, but I couldn't think of what else to do.

And an overwhelming feeling that something needed to be done haunted me.

The waitress brought the quail immediately after I sat back down, and I found she was right. It was very good. But growing unease stole my appetite.

Ignoring the strong, sweet scent of moonflower, I fingered the note Sokaris had left. There was nothing sinister about it, but something about it raised my hackles.

The handwriting was unfamiliar, as it should be. The ink was the same blueblack used by everyone. The paper was the hand-made stuff available in all the markets.

But still . . . I loathed the thing. It screamed danger.

Because it caused your precious Wizard to leave, the cynical part of my mind taunted.

I waved that thought away. Esmenet had said that intuition shouldn't be so quickly dismissed, that a biological basis formed gut feelings.

Using my newly developed power, I Sensed the note. I sent my mind to the note's surface.

Cellulose fibers, thick as trees from this perspective, sur-rounded me. The microfibrils of the cell walls were laid out in parallel lines, about half running horizontally and the other half running vertically from this vantage point. But I didn't see any-thing fishy.

I Sensed the ink. Soot from burned petroleum formed the colorant. Nothing untoward. Resin. Water. Again, nothing sus-picious.

Perhaps my unease was entirely of my own making, stress making me edgy.

I zoomed back for one last quick glance at the note, scan-ning for anything not paper or ink. Just before giving up I found something—an irregularity—on the northeast corner. What was it?

Zooming in, as close as I did when I Grabbed proteins for the love potions, I found a human cell, smaller in size than the plant cell walls of the paper.

Fine, I thought. A person held this note, and a cell from her finger stuck to the paper. Not much help.

But still, maybe it was the source of my unease.

I Sensed the cell's surface, looking at the receptors for the neurotransmitters, growth-promoting substances, and hor-mones unique to the person who had left it.

And finally, I struck gold. The membrane proteins looked familiar. Or it looked like it should smell familiar.

Whose was it? Not mine, certainly. Not Sokaris's. I knew those well. But if it were Lyric's or Obadiah's I wouldn't know it necessarily. I wasn't used to identifying people from their membrane proteins.

Using skills I hadn't imagined before this moment, in my mind I multiplied this cell with its unplaceable membrane proteins until it formed an entire organism, a person. My heart raced as I realized that it worked. An image danced through my brain, an image of a woman.

Though I created only her silhouette from the cell, I could see that she was of middling height with full breasts. But I didn't recognize her, not the slope of her shoulders or the curve of her chin. How could I recognize her proteins, but not her silhouette?

Frustrated, I sniffed her in my mind. Strangely familiar. Encouraged, I sniffed again.

Images began to dance through my mind, and I panicked, overwhelmed by a feeling of incompetence. It was going too fast! I forced patience upon myself as snippets raced past, trusting an answer would surface if I let my brain filter the information.

Things slowed. First I saw Chair Uriah, leader of the local Wizard's Guild, as he chased Obadiah's pig across the fairground. He leaned over me at the police station, saying something kind. Then I saw the alley where I'd followed the men from the Slug and Garden and they'd disappeared. Paper sacks, balled and discarded, blew across the chipped cobbles, but a scent still hung in the air pungent and fishy. Lastly I saw the rich guy, disguised, obliquely threatening me as I helped the blonde in the pit.

How were these things tied together?

I dropped the note and let the world come into its traditional focus.

Could they be the same people? Could Uriah be the big-bosomed lady reconstructed from the cell—and the rich guy bullying the reluctant minion into more rapes? Could his scent be the one lingering in the alley?

It couldn't be true. Uriah wasn't a woman. He wasn't a villain! Sure, he was nasty, but that was *my* problem. No man likes being saved again and again by the same guy. It's humiliating.

I cast my memory back to try to remember what Uriah had smelled like. Incongruous, I now realized. He didn't smell right, but I'd been too nervous to notice at the time. Did he smell like the rich guy I'd seen disguised on the street? I went back and sniffed in my memory.

Yes!

By the Star Goddess! Uriah was not Uriah—he was a she and he was the villain! I had to tell Sokaris right now.

And then the cold fingers of dread trailed over my spine. Adrenaline spurted through my system to promote flight.

Uriah had sent the note that had lured Sokaris away.

22

I raced home, hoping I was wrong, hoping Sokaris was caring for another victim.

But as I sprinted up the stairs, my heart froze. The chicken gargoyles were unrecognizable, melted like clay under a hot summer sun. No mocking cackle greeted me.

I'd guessed these were somehow linked to Sokaris's magic and now I knew it. Their absence screeched volumes.

Esmenet was in trouble.

I leapt up the stairs, adrenaline coursing from my adrenal glands through my veins, catalyzing the conversion of glycogen into glucose. What had they done to her?

Burning up glucose with my rage and fear, I attacked the front door with ferocious power. Under the force of my open palms, her maple doors slammed open and the doorknobs cracked against the interior walls. Plaster dust flew through the air.

"Esmenet!" I shouted into the cold, dark foyer. "Esmenet!"

"She's not down here," a man said from the shadows, his voice familiar.

I blinked and saw Obadiah. *Obadiah*?

"You bastard!" I said. "I'm going to kill you." I jumped toward him, ready to throttle him blue with my bare hands. "Where's Sokaris?"

But just as I touched his ugly, wattled throat, my outstretched hand bounced off him. Like he was ice or granite, Obadiah stood frozen, unmoving.

"You're not going to kill him yet," the voice said. "He's in stasis."

I peered into the darkness, searching for the speaker. Lurking in the shadow cast by the heavy door I found him. Or her. Now that I knew to look, her underlying scent was undeniably feminine. Fishily feminine. Uriah.

In the blink of an eye, I knew I needed my wits, all of them. My foe was smarter than I, and he had Esmenet, the woman I lo—

"Come upstairs with me," would-be Uriah said through his mossy beard. "To the spelling room."

Could he make me? I didn't move a muscle. And why under all the stars was Obadiah here?

"Don't resist, Mr. Feldspar." He waved a titanium wand in front of my face, the sleeve of his cloak flapping gently. "Can you see what level I am?"

Ignoring his feminine scent, I studied the aura around him for a moment. "Gold." He and Esmenet were equally matched. If he captured her, what hope did I have?

"Good. You've certainly progressed in your abilities. Now please, lead the way."

I did.

Horror. That's what I found in Esmenet's spelling room.

Her beautiful heart etchings on the floor—the ones she used to direct her spells—had been erased. Not a trace of the shining gold remained. In their place pentagrams had been burned, black and jagged into the silky ebony planks. The five-sided stars, overlapping and intersecting at strange junctions, were all hard angles and cold lines where once graceful curves had lain.

Evil pervaded them.

The walls, once a pale lilac, had been doused in black; buckets of the dark paint had been tossed at the panels. Patches of the purple showed through, and puddles of inky pitch pooled on the floor.

Six growlers of Brown Worm sat near the eastern wall, their glass jugs shaped like a woman's silhouette. Seductive and tempting. They glittered in the candlelight like a knife blade.

Wickedness hung in the air. A terrible purpose lurked here, and I had yet to discover what it was.

But it wasn't until Uriah shoved Obadiah into the room that I spied the true horror.

Esmenet. Frozen. Just like Obadiah.

"What the—"

But before I could finish the question, someone knocked on the front door. Politely. Almost quietly.

A fleeting look of surprise raced across Uriah's features. He wasn't expecting anyone then.

Maybe it was the cops! Maybe they were responding to the note I'd sent from the restaurant. Hope flared deep inside me. I couldn't remember ever wanting a cop more badly than I did now. Even Detective Habit with her flinty eyes would be an improvement over Uriah's madness.

"Damn," Uriah muttered, his amber eyes glittering. "You know who it is?"

I shrugged again as the knocking persisted, louder this time.

"Liar," he said, scanning my face. "You think it's help."

I cursed my stupid face. I needed the impassivity of Detective Habit.

"No matter," he said. "No matter at all." As Uriah shut me inside the spelling room, I saw his features meld into Esmenet's.

I wanted to kill him.

The doorknob disappeared the moment the door closed—a new feature of the room, I was sure. I kicked viciously at the panel, throwing all my strength into it and shouting. But somehow I knew such efforts would be futile. The cops wouldn't be able to hear my bellows from this eerie place.

Desperately I approached Esmenet. Her face was frozen in a grimace of frustration. I tried to erase the furrows across her forehead, but my fingertips met a surface as hard as granite. Instead I placed a warm kiss against her icy lips.

How could I undo the work of a Gold? An evil Gold, at that.

But I had to try.

Like throwing a net randomly into a lake for fish, I threw my senses over her, Sensing what I could in her tissues and organs and cells. I wanted to snatch any little clue. Time breathed down my back.

But the spell baffled me. Initially I thought Uriah had slowed her metabolism to a standstill, but that's not what I found. Or, that wasn't all I found.

The spell had slowed the heartbeat, true, so I tried to reverse it. I shuffled things around, Grabbing and Pushing carefully until her heartbeat quickened. But that didn't change her breathing. So I quickened her breathing. But then her brainwaves didn't follow suit, and messing with brainwaves seemed dangerous.

I was perplexed and now scared for what I was doing to her. If I put her metabolic functions at different rates, that couldn't be good for her physiology. For instance, would cell division follow brain or heart cues? I Pushed everything back to where I'd found it, not wanting to experiment on my belov—

Obadiah! I could experiment on that sewer rat. If I fixed everything I could think of, bringing him back to consciousness, what would I care if I ended up giving him cancer because of telomere issues during mitosis? He'd deserve it.

Then Lyric's face flashed through my mind, glowing as she had when I'd seen her—Stars, was it this morning? She loved him. I couldn't cause her any more pain. Not even to save Esmenet.

Still, I scanned him, Sensing his metabolic functions. His functions were similar to Esmenet's—heart, lungs, brain all slowed to a standstill. Even his cells weren't dividing. Obadiah was a big frozen lump of tissue.

Not much different than usual, I thought uncharitably.

Glad for what I'd learned while working with Esmenet, I Grabbed an enzyme, anthranilate synthetase, to kickstart the creation of tryptophan. I Pushed it, ready to return it in a heartbeat if it behaved like Esmenet's. But I discovered something else instead.

The complexity of the spell was related to the magic potential of the victim. Waking Obadiah would be easy; walking Esmenet would be difficult. Obadiah was Tan, far below me now. Esmenet's Gold was beyond my reach.

Pushing one molecule in Obadiah caused a cascade of additional changes. A good cascade. Obadiah's metabolism began to speed up uniformly throughout his body. I quickened his heartbeat, and his breathing increased. Brain activity followed.

Like the bastard had a heart or brain.

Obadiah's eyelids fluttered open, and he fell into a heap in my arms. I shoved him away, resisting the urge to knee him in the groin—accidentally on purpose.

"Lyric—" he said.

Stars, the bastard loved her.

"Where is she?" I asked.

"She's gone to her mother's. The babe's due any day now, and she wanted her mother's help."

Confusion. "You mean she's—" Lyric hadn't looked pregnant, had she? Then I thought about that glow, that telltale glow. "What babe?" I asked.

Obadiah eyed me warily. "Hers," he said. "And mine."

I did a quick mental calculation and said, "You two sure didn't waste any time."

"She—" he started. "It's just that we—" Then he looked around him. "Where am I? Why're you here? Why're you doing this to me?"

"I didn't do this to you, you stupid cock—" I stopped myself. We didn't have time to fight. Although I could Sense Uriah standing on the step talking to someone in the cool night air, I knew he'd be back any minute. "How do you know Guild Chair Uriah?" I asked.

"I *don't* know him. He helped me with that pig of yours—"

"Obadiah's pig," I corrected, appreciating the name of the story for the first time. At least it wasn't "Gage's Pig."

"Whatever. But I never really talked to the man until today."

"What do you mean?"

"Dear Goddess," the beady-eyed man said. "I found a horrible potion, the one making Cantabile feel so wretched."

Confusion. "Cantabile?"

"Lyric's cousin."

Oh yeah—the cousin married to the old guy and overwhelmed by the blues. This was relevant because? "What are you talking about, man?" I seethed. "Spit it out!"

"Her supposed beloved husband, Doctor Sforzando, was giving her a potion that squashed her libido. Apparently he didn't want her putting horns on him, so he—"

"Stars!" The bonehead found a link to the rapist! "What'd you do with the potion?"

"Well, I couldn't do anything, not without making Doctor Sforzando suspicious. But right after I found it, I ran to the local guild chair and told him."

Uriah again. He was going to kill us all.

"You tell the cops?" I asked, even as I gave my intuition a free rein, morphing my features.

"No! I didn't think the Guild would want word of this getting out. You think I should have—Hey! What do you think you're doing?"

"Do I have the nose right?" I asked.

"Right here," he said, touching a small bump on his bridge. "You're missing this. But what're you doing?"

"Shh! You have to trust me. How about the eyes?"

"They look good. Hair looks good." Obadiah scratched his own head. "How'd you learn to do that?"

"Be quiet. Uriah's going to be back any second. Give me your mind," I commanded, taking his hand in mine.

Obadiah jerked his hand away. "You're a damned drunk! Why should I help—"

"Uriah's going to kill us. He's a she and she's the ringleader in these rapes. She's using the hormones to make chastity-belt potions. One of us needs to escape—she'll go after Lyric next, if she hasn't already, and Uriah's a Gold. Even together we can't overpower her. We have to trick her."

With his mouth hanging stupidly open, Obadiah slowly gave me his hand. I could Sense Uriah. He was coming up the stairs, slowly but inexorably.

With a speed I thought impossible, I showed Obadiah how to make his features resemble mine. His nose became more aquiline, his cheekbones higher and flatter, his skin smoother and more golden in color. That disgusting mole on his cheek evaporated.

The disguises weren't perfect. Micro angles on his face and mine weren't quite right, but I was counting on two things. First, Uriah didn't know either of us very well.

Second, people—even Golds—generally see what they expect to see. I knew he *could* see through my disguise—he'd proven that in the pit; but I didn't think he *would*. Would he ever suspect me of saving Obadiah after I'd attacked the wife thief in the foyer?

"Pretend to be me," I commanded. "Escape when you get the chance. Make sure Lyric's safe, then send the cops."

Just as the door swung open, I slowed my metabolism to a near standstill. Risking discovery of my deception, I kept enough brain activity to understand what was going on.

"Here's what's going to happen, and it's going to happen quickly," Uriah said to Obadiah, assuming he was me. "Your dear friend Obadiah is going to fuck your precious Wizard silly. You're going to be drunk and walk in, catching them in the act. It'll be too much for you, especially given your inebriated state. You'll kill him. You'll kill her. You'll kill yourself."

"But—but why?" poor Obadiah asked in my voice.

"It wraps everything up in a neat bow. I'd've liked to've framed you as the rapist, and maybe I still will, but this way, everyone who knows about my potions will be dead. Gone."

"But why'd you ever make those horrible potions? All those girls . . . You shattered their lives. And for what? To shatter more girls' lives."

"Shut up, you drunken weasel. When little rich wives can't keep their hairy cunts in their skirts, drastic measures are needed."

"But it goes against all of the Guild rules, raping all those girls," he said, "It goes against all Guild morals."

I had to hand it to Obadiah, he was trying really hard to understand Uriah's malicious mind.

"And it's against all the codes," he doggedly continued, "to give potions to anyone against their knowledge or will. I haven't even been to the academy, and I know that. How do you get to be Gold and still be so evil?"

"It's because the Guild allows wretched upstarts like yourself to obtain membership that it's in such trouble. They let in drunks and whores and addicts and gamblers. If I had my way, the Guild would be the bastion of wealth and good breeding that it was in the days of Alfred III."

"Alfred the Awful, you mean. The king burned Wizards at the stake if they weren't of high enough birth, or if they stayed home with their family."

"For a mongrel like you, this would be a tragedy, I agree. But I come from a long line of distinguished Wizards. My family served kings throughout time."

"Your Love Wizard comes from no noble family," Obadiah argued. He must have been guessing.

"You don't know what you're talking about, fool. Her mother was the highest-ranking Wizard in all of Lezmiri." Uriah shook his head in disgust. "And you're missing the point altogether, plowboy. Ask yourself this: when was the last time a Platinum Wizard walked this land? You seem to know your history well enough. When was it?"

Obadiah certainly did know his history, far better than I. I waited, unmoving, for his answer to come from the lips that looked like mine.

"Three thousand years ago?"

"That's right, drunken weasel, during the reign of Alfred the Awful. Wizards had freedom then."

"Highborn Wizards had freedom—freedom to torture and trick."

Uriah waved his hand and shrugged. "But free of morals and rules they achieved amazing power. They would've appreciated my chastity potions. I actually adapted it from one of their ancient texts."

"You'd do away with all of our safeguards?" Obadiah asked.

"Yes. I've done away with them for myself, and I'll be the first Platinum Wizard in three thousand years." Uriah's eyes glowed maniacally as he continued. "But enough talking, drunk. The quicker we get rid of you, the purer our gene pool will be." With his titanium wand, Uriah waved a glyph I didn't recognize, and my doppelganger's body froze. His head didn't, though. He could see, and he could talk.

"What—"

"Shut up, drunk. Shut up and watch. We'll get that ale in you soon enough. All those hormones you'll produce while watching your good friend fuck your Wizard will just bolster the case against you."

Then Uriah turned to me. My blood would've run cold, if it could have. He traced a glyph, a bastardization of the *Nauru* glyph I saw now, and my physiology returned to normal.

Once freed, only supreme self control kept me from lunging at him. I might have surprised him then, but I needed a better chance at setting Obadiah free. The last thing I wanted was to flounder around this room with an insane Gold, wasting the one small advantage we had over him. Her. It.

Uriah shoved me into the deviant pentagrams, waving another glyph, the *Chamorros* glyph but upside down. Unnatural pheromones assaulted my senses, latching onto my dopamine receptors and telling my body that the most beautiful woman alive was right in front of me, wet and willing.

Lyric. Her hair, in all its glorious shades of blond, cascaded over her shoulder. Honeys. Almonds. Silvery whites. Her pink lips were as plump and tempting as berries. Impending motherhood swelled her belly and breasts, and her fertility just made her that much more delectable. Her eyes sparkled. Her skin shone.

The spell taunted me, teased every receptor on every spell. It made me believe that this woman embodied my every physiological and emotional need.

Then I realized I didn't need the spell, not at all. Every natural chemical exuded from the woman in the spell fit perfectly into my cell receptors. I was bathing in the pheromones of my most perfect mate.

Esmenet.

How long had I been in love with her? Since I first felt her strength? Since her patience and distance let me rediscover myself? In the back of my mind, I must've known I wouldn't go back to Lyric; we'd damaged each other too brutally. But that lie—the lie that I wanted my wife back—gave me the ability to live in Esmenet's house and bed and heal.

But I was in Uriah's spell. I had an audience.

Uriah must have made Esmenet look like Lyric to tempt Obadiah, but she wasn't tempting me. She couldn't. After all these months of striving to perfect myself, making myself loveable for Lyric, I could see now that I'd been wrong. Not wrong for improving myself. But I'd set my eye on the wrong goal.

Esmenet.

No doubt, she looked just like herself to those outside the spell. And to sustain the charade that I was Obadiah, I needed to make love to this woman like I loved her with my whole heart.

I couldn't wait. My love was no charade.

"Lyric," I said for the sake of the simulation. I hoped it pissed Obadiah off.

Puzzlement crossed her expression but only for a moment. Recognition flickered quickly across her face, to be immediately replaced by a bland glaze in her eyes.

She understood the farce immediately. She amazed me.

My fingers itched to caress her ass. My arms longed to pull her tightly against me. Finally, her chest was flush to mine, her heart pounding against mine. I pressed my lips against her ear. She smelled like heaven, like spring rain and moonflowers.

In a barely whispered voice, I said, "He wants Gage to watch Obadiah make passionate love to you. Then Gage'll get drunk, rape you in a rage, and kill us all."

Esmenet slid her fingertips from my knee, up my thigh, and across my hip, sending shivers of delight. "I need to think," she breathed in my ear.

I kissed her delicate collarbone, savoring the silkiness of her ebony skin. I caressed a breast with one hand, feeling its weight like I might never feel it again. I loved her so much my heart actually ached. Oxytocin exploded through my brain, binding to opiate receptors I'd never dreamed of even a few days ago.

"That's not helping," she said, arching so my mouth could explore her neck, that tender spot behind her ear.

"We need to save him, Esmenet. Lyric's bearing their child."

"Shh," she murmured, running her fingers through my hair.

"Obadiah and Uriah are watching us."

"Shh," she said. "I don't care. Make love to me."

23

And he did.

In Gage's arms, I became living passion. The honesty of his kisses, the way he poured his heart into each velvet touch shook me to the core, told me I was loved.

"Tell me you want me," Gage said loudly, not caring that Uriah could hear. Or maybe especially loud, so that Uriah could hear.

"I want you," I said. "Surely you can Sense that," I murmured for his ears only.

"Tell me you need me." His fingers caressed my abdomen, almost as if he were memorizing each curve.

"I do. I need you. I crave you."

"And I love you, Esmenet Sokaris, with my every cell and enzyme and molecule." Emotion filled his husky whisper as he pulled me so tightly against him that I could hardly breath.

"Gage, I—"

"I know about your cursed Guild," he rasped. "But do you love me?"

I could feel my oxytocin receptors filling, and I was helpless to stop them. I didn't want to stop them. His words were binding me to him more strongly than any spell.

"I do," I said, knowing my future was forever changed. "May the Star Goddess help me, I love you."

"Then kiss me," Gage said. "And never stop." He bestowed me his lips and tongue, pervading my senses until all I could see was him, all I could feel and taste and hear was him.

As Gage nuzzled my neck and nipped it, too, I dipped my hand over his ridged stomach. When I palmed his thick shaft, it throbbed, and he hissed in a breath. I stroked him up once, then down. Up, I tormented him. And down.

His fingers tangled through my braids, clumsy with desire—adorable for his clumsiness. But the sight of his strong, bronzed hands on my black breasts took my breath away. The feeling of belonging to someone, of making love without the veil of a spell standing between us left me weak with joy.

I arched my back, pushing my breast toward his mouth. In my hand, his cock throbbed more intensely, grew hot. He captured my nipple between his teeth, and my ability to torment him ceased. I was clay in his hands, his to mold as he saw fit.

Gage lay me back in a thick pile of animal skins. I didn't know whose magic had put them there, and I didn't care. "I love you," he said again, oblivious to our watchers. "I can drink your beauty," he said. "I can get drunk on it, and your power and your strength."

I stretched beneath his gaze, giving him as much to appreciate as I could. Gage ran his palm over my shoulders and neck, my waist and stomach. He caressed my calves and thighs, and there he lingered, stroking, massaging.

Shamelessly, I opened my thighs for him, wanting his touch. Wanting him.

And he surpassed my every expectation. Gage looked at me as he stroked, his eyes burning with intensity. They were filled with desire and love. "By the Goddess," he said, "I do so love you."

I came in a heartbeat, an orgasm tearing through me like wildfire. His words, his adoration undid me. But Gage gave me no rest. Nudging my thighs apart farther, he went down, and I gasped as he sucked my clit. He sucked hard.

Under his tongue I trembled, feeling the pressure of another imminent orgasm, but he pulled back. He licked me, and his tongue felt like liquid silk.

My awareness of Uriah and Obadiah melted away into nonexistence.

"I want you," I said. "Inside me. Now."

His eyes locked on mine, Gage Feldspar slid inside me. The final piece fell into place. Every cell in my being finally felt like it had all it needed. I was bound to him, and there was no going back.

He filled me, perfectly.

He slid in deeper, and I thrust to him. He was mine. Then the dance began in earnest, making us selfish beasts taking what we wanted from each other. I rolled him beneath me and rode him, hitting the head of his cock against that magic spot deep inside me.

His mouth smothered mine, and his hand grabbed my ass. It wasn't enough. I wanted every part of me to be penetrated by him, to be touched and impaled by him. Taking his hand in mine I slid his fingers along my crevasse, and then I slid him into that tighter hole. His cock pulsed deep within me, and he groaned.

I saw stars then, and nothing existed in the entire universe but Gage and those stars. Brilliant points of light exploded behind my eyes, and I shouted his name—his real name. "Gage! I love you, Gage."

"Esmenet."

With our cry, the world shifted.

And shattered.

For a brief second, his face flashed before me, only it wasn't his—it was Obadiah's. And I caught a weird glimpse of my belly, round with child and white as snow. Lyric.

Uriah's dark magic.

The Guild Chair had discovered our charade, and he'd just figured out that he'd been duped.

24

With four Wizards fumbling maniacally without a plan, I should have been more careful. I should have tried to escape, or allied my magic with Esmenet's.

But one thought burned through my mind—lacking her wand and her spelling hearts, Esmenet would be weakened. I needed to protect her.

In kicked the experience I'd gained from all those drunken brawls with half-orcs and ogres twice my size in dark alleys and barrooms. With a clarity usually obscured by alcohol, I raced toward my opponent, plowing into Uriah with all my weight.

Uriah stayed on her feet, likely with the use of magic. I outweighed the disguised creature, so I knew I outweighed her in reality. She should've crumbled under my assault.

But I didn't stop to inquire why she didn't. Instead, I punched the side of her head, using all my weight. The bare knuckles of my left fist smashed into her skull, bone crunching bone. Then, lightning fast, the bare knuckles of my right fist rammed her, and then my left crashed into her skull again.

I've knocked out half-orcs with my combination punch,

even drunk. I'm fast and strong. And I captained our boxing team all through school. The fact that this Gold still stood was a testament to her magical strength.

I took a step back, balancing to optimize my weight. Figuring the horrible Wizard was watching my fists, I kicked out with my foot, quick as a striking snake, and landed the perfect kick on the bridge of her nose.

Not a boxing move, but then if I'd always followed the rules, the half-orcs I'd fought in the alleys would've killed me.

The creature should have been crumbling to the ground, but no. As easily as capturing a newborn puppy, Uriah caught my ankle. And she jerked it up, pulling my feet out from under me as casually as wiping her nose.

I hadn't been watching anything but the Uriah creature. Not even from the corner of my eye had I seen Esmenet or Obadiah. But when the monster snagged my ankle in its fist, I saw.

I saw the knobless door explode open, the hallway promising a freedom from this hell. I saw Obadiah flee, his feet skittering under him, almost faster than his body as he rounded the corner.

After the creature jerked up my ankle, high above my head, the inertia of my body did the rest. And I saw as I fell. Everything was upside down.

I saw Esmenet trace a glyph with her index finger as my head rushed toward the floor in syrup-slow time. And I saw the power from her fingertips crackle toward Uriah.

"Esmenet!" I shouted.

And then my world went black with a sudden *crack*.

When I came to, Uriah was pouring beer down my throat. Brown Worm.

Oh Goddess, it tasted good. Like heaven. Like spring. Like my very first orgasm.

I spit it in her face. Droplets clung to his mossy beard. Foam splattered his shirt. Uriah's eyes glittered an angry topaz, but she didn't say a word.

"Where's Esmenet?" I demanded, trying to stand.

But I was bound. With ropes and with a spell.

"You're a very clever Wizard," she said. "With some very surprising skills." She held a stein to my lips, and lifted an eyebrow. "Will you drink without a struggle, or must I force this down your throat?"

"I'll die before I drink again, you asshole." I tried to deck her. My knuckles itched for her bone. But I could move nothing but my mouth. Great. I'd have to taunt her to death.

Her wand flickered. My jaw opened, and my head tilted back. There was nothing I could do.

Bleak despair overwhelmed me. I'd quit. Quit! I had a woman I loved, and a career, too. And this fuckhead was drowning it. I wanted to kill her. I wanted to smash her into a bloody pulp, see her brains dripping off some alley wall.

I wanted to cry.

But after a few minutes, I didn't care. The entire situation struck me as hilarious. "Yer beer—beard," I howled, laughing like a hyena. "It looks like seaweed." Uriah ignored me, pouring more Brown Worm down my throat.

I guzzled it, moaning in disappointment when she emptied a growler. My drunken nose caught a scent, Uriah's scent. Only it wasn't a man's smell. With tears from my laughing rolling down my face, I said, "And I bet you have kelp dangling above your cunt, green as the ugly beard on your chin. And it adds to that oceany smell, I bet."

I howled again at my own wit.

"Something fishy about you. Fishy fishy fishy."

I was laughing so hard at my own joke I didn't see her fist fly at me. Blood trickled from my nose, over my lip, and down my chin, but no pain reached my brain. The Brown Worm was doing the thing it did best: disconnecting my body from my brain.

"Ha! Fish twat!" I chortled at her. "You even hit like a girl!"

No one ever said Brown Worm made me smart.

I saw her fist this time, knuckles inexpertly balled. But what she lacked in finesse, she made up for in rage-fueled enthusiasm. I heard the cartilage in my nose crunch to a pulp just before I lost consciousness a second time.

Still drunk I woke to a heavy sound. *Thunk. Thunk. Thunk.* It was the thud of my head bouncing across the floor while someone dragged my ankles. Uriah. She paused for a moment, poured more ale down my throat, then continued dragging me.

"Your breath smells as fishy as your twat," I said as she huffed, shoving me into the pentagrams.

"Gage," she warned, "shut your mouth."

Uriah had let her disguise melt, and now I could see her true face. She was one ugly woman. Her shaggy hair was the same color and texture as river reeds, and her teeth were shaped like whelks, cone-shaped and pointed. Just as brown and spotted, too.

"Your mother was a kelpie, wasn't she? I'm surprised they didn't kill you at birth."

"My birth," she hissed, "was far more noble than yours. But I've no time for this."

She shoved me into the pentagram, and manacled my ankles and wrists to a stake in the floor's center.

She traced an ugly glyph, a bastardized *Radula*, with her titanium wand. The terrible Gold threw all of her might into the spell, furrows of concentration lined her sandpaper skin. Even before the spell took hold of me, the power from the wand crackled and sparked.

I knew something terrible was happening to me.

"Enjoy yourself," the creature grinned, showing her whelk

teeth. The snails in her teeth-shells came out and waggled as she spoke. Or maybe it was the beer.

"I'm leaving you for a moment; I have a mouth or two to shut. Forever. But don't worry, Mister Feldspar. You'll be too busy here to miss me!"

I hoped Obadiah was smarter than he looked, that he could save Lyric and himself, too.

Tendrils within the sticky web of Uriah's perverted spell were fraying. In thrall of his awful work, all my Gold senses should have been frozen. But they returned to me, slowly and imperfectly.

What I saw was horrific.

A blurred figure writhed and jerked in the center of Uriah's terrible pentagram stars. Through the thick cotton of my distressed mind, I heard the figure slaver and scream. I Sensed . . . blood lust.

Invisible teeth from each of the Hells shredded the unfortunate, ripped him, digested him alive. Agony.

My powers and Uriah's were too evenly matched for either of us to gain the upper hand for too long. Perhaps that explained why her dreadful spell was unraveling, why I could feel.

Perhaps that could explain why I could do little more than watch the horror in her perverted pentagrams. I couldn't even cast my Senses to the center of the room.

But the figure in the center howled in mortal anguish.

Futile rage washed through my veins. My psyche had given me a chicken as a totem. But enough! I needed the strength of a panther to rip through the last shred of this spell.

As if seized by the Goddess's Hell Lover, the figure writhed on his stomach across the floor, teeth gnashing and clacking. Feet kicking. I smelled blood.

I struggled to clear my mind. Clarity shouldn't have been so difficult to achieve!

Sobbing. The figure was now sobbing.

Sweet Goddess. There was only one reason for my weakness. Only one reason. Bonding with Gage—surrendering to his love—had sapped my ability to work magic.

I'd lost my powers.

I laughed maniacally. Those wagging snails, her clammy cunt. Her clam-shaped cunt! Goddess, the room was spinning. The Uriah thing was wrong! She'd said this would be terrible, but it was hysterical!

The ghost of Esmenet's voice whispered in my mind.

It's in your brain stem, Gage. The cells there are transmuting L-tryptophan into serotonin. They're signaling you to attack, to rape, to maim.

"But you're not real!" I shouted. "You're not here!" I knew she wasn't. It was the sober part of my brain, the part that'd soaked in all she had to teach.

I was more alone than I'd ever been.

Those signals are flying across your neurotransmitters! Ignore them! Don't give in!

"Esmenet! Where are you?!"

Then I wasn't alone. The green baize walls of the Slug and Garden appeared before me. Surrounded by their comforting warmth, it felt like home. And my friends appeared, too, adding to the security.

Then the drunken rage was upon me.

Friendly faces melted away, leaving mocking men. "Stupid shit! Cocksucker!" the crowd shouted at me.

Clover, my trusted friend in the beer, shouted, "You smell like your momma's cunt, and she's been dead for six months!"

Sweet Orange flipped her blond hair over her elfish shoulder and shouted, "I slept with every man here! Every single one but you, Gage!"

Esmenet—high perfect breasts, tiny waist, full lips—jeered

at me. "You can't get it up, asshole. You worthless piece of shit, you're not even good for fucking!"

I wanted to kill her.

I lurched toward her, wanting to feel her elegant throat crunching inside my fist.

"Esmenet, you bitch."

"You smarmy day-old turd," she said. "You crow like a banty rooster, but you don't even have a rooster's balls."

I closed the distance between us, like a lion homing in on a gazelle.

"You were always shitty in bed, Gage. A bad fuck." This time the words came from Lyric's pretty pink lips.

Esmenet was gone, but the bar wasn't. Dwarves and elves and men and ogres hooted at me, cheering Lyric on. A sea of green and brown and red faces, each with angry mocking eyes. I wanted them all to shut up. I wanted to make them all shut up with my own hands.

"And I never wanted to marry you. It was my father's idea," Lyric mocked.

"Liar!" I howled.

"He wanted grandchildren with magic; he didn't know you were useless as a Wizard and as a man. He begged me to leave you years ago."

The barroom crowd waved steins in the air and gave deep-throated cheers for my ex-wife.

I wanted to kill.

"You came in two seconds, Gage." This from Robin, her chestnut hair streaming down her back. "You thought I didn't know that day by the lake, but I did. And you always came too fast."

The crowd booed me and started chanting, "Loser! Loser! Loser!" while stomping their feet on the floor and slamming their steins on the counter.

Shame and rage washed over me. "Shut up!" I bellowed. "Shut your mouth!"

"Real men don't come in ten seconds, Gage," she jeered. "You're not a real man."

I'd wipe that smile right off her face. I'd bust all of her teeth—that would wipe the smile from her mouth. Reaching for the buckle of my trousers, I said, "I'll show you a real man!"

By the Goddess, I could see!

But what I saw made me quail.

Gage was handcuffed in the center of those criminal penta-grams, writhing and screaming and frothing at the mouth.

I had to free him! I had to save him from whatever Hell Uriah had wrapped around him. So I struggled in her spell, feeling like I swam in quicksand.

But then . . .

But then I could truly Sense! I still had enough magic to Sense that Uriah was gone, that Gage was trapped in a working glyph.

I Sensed he teetered precariously on the brink of irreparable insanity.

I should've freed myself, but watching him struggle against her vile wickedness hurt my heart. I had to free him. I had no choice.

I looped my senses over him, gently, lightly.

And found his cell receptors swimming in alcohol, rage zinging from one neurotransmitter to another catalyzed by the booze.

Uriah had made him drunk! All that work Gage had put into himself to shift his membrane surfaces had been undone by her vile hand. More than half his cells were now morphed to accept alcohol molecules preferentially. I hoped Uriah rotted away in the innermost Hell.

And I couldn't save Gage! That was the most frustrating part. No Wizard in history had even been able to Grab proteins from a cell membrane. My attempts would be especially futile now, now that my love hormones were all wrecked.

I couldn't save him.

The thought tore a sob from deep inside my chest.

Then I thought of Gage—how he'd helped that dog, how he'd become invisible, how he morphed his own face. No one had ever told him that those things were too hard for his level. He just did them.

I'd have to follow his lead.

I sent my mind into Gage's body, through his skin tissue and into his blood. Into his organs. I went deeper still. I went to the cell. I went to a cell's surface. I found an alcohol molecule, just one.

I tried to Grab it. Without my wand, without my spelling hearts; with only my hamstrung skills, I tried.

But I couldn't do it.

Of course I couldn't do it. I'd bonded to him and lost my powers.

I flattened my knuckles into a professional fist, one guaranteed to knock the teeth from even a half-orc and stalked toward Robin. I coiled my arm for the perfect punch as she stood, hands on her hips, waiting. The perfect target.

But the punch fizzled.

Not my doing. I didn't hold back or stop myself. I didn't overcome biological urges and halt the spell in its tracks.

I blinked, feeling a little more sober. But I knew Uriah had poured enough Brown Worm into me to keep me drunk for hours.

The flash of sobriety lasted only a few heartbeats. Then I was again a slave to my tryptophan and serotonin, to the barroom drinkers jeering and mocking my every sexual imperfection. To the Brown Worm wiggling through me.

"You little faggot!" The barkeep taunted.

"Drunken pisser!" my friend Clover called, his forked beard expertly twined to spikes.

In the spell, rage swamped all reason. I grabbed the closest asshole—a hairy dwarf, beads of bone and a steely metal clanking in her beard—by her thick neck and squeezed. She looked at me through bloodshot eyes, a sneer on her hairy lips. I squeezed, and her eyes bulged.

I yanked my arm back to pound her, looking forward to the sound of her teeth smashing under my knuckles.

I let calm fall over me. I refused to let panic cause failure.

Alcohol is a simple thing, so easy to find in Gage's cells. It's a carbon atom with an oxygen/hydrogen pair bound to it. Everywhere I looked, alcohol stuck to a cell surface. I needed to get rid of them all.

So simple—in theory.

I tried to Grab a molecule from a cell membrane. I Grabbed. It slipped. Squinting, I Grabbed again. The damn thing slid away.

Impossible.

Gage hollered in rage and swung a fist that came up short against the handcuff. I heard blood hit the floor in fat splatters.

I needed to help him now!

A calming breath filled my lungs, permeating my blood with oxygen.

A different idea occurred to me. Maybe I was approaching this problem from the wrong direction, a too literal direction.

I'd been imagining picking up all these little bastards and putting them in tear ducts . . . but what if I just convinced them to be something else—like when I convinced breathable air to become butane in order to light a candle.

As Gage convulsed, my heart quickened. Taking a deep breath, I slowed it. Never had I needed to focus like I did now.

Concentrating on one cell, I found a bond between the oxygen and the hydrogen within the alcohol. I found a bunch of free electrons and bombarded the bond with them. Under the barrage, the hydrogen molecules released the oxygen molecules, and the alcohol was gone. Gone!

I'd done it! With one molecule, but I'd done it.

Maybe. But could I do it on a larger scale?

Gage kicked invisible foes, fury written on his face, in every muscle. Unintelligible words flew from his mouth.

I caught a thousand cells in my senses and pulled a bunch of free electrons from the surrounding substrates. They blasted the oxygen molecules free.

I took a mental step back and caught all of Gage's cells. I bombarded all the alcohol molecules with electrons . . .

And I stifled a cry of joy as they disintegrated.

Then I realized I still had my powers, at least some of them. What had my illicit love done to me?

Ignoring the booing of the barroom crowd, I squeezed the fat dwarf. I squeezed and squeezed. Oil oozed from her pores, and her gray eyes bugged. Her breath came out in ragged gasps, and the fetid stench of her panting only empowered me. As life poured out of her, heat coursed through me.

I'd never imagined such an intense pleasure from killing.

But again, my rage simply fizzled away. Through no force of my own will. I just didn't need to kill her.

Sweet Orange swaggered up to me, swishing her sun-gold hair from one shoulder to another, her perky ass highlighted by her tight green leggings. "I heard," she said in her husky voice, "that you fucked Obadiah's pig. That you love to fuck pigs."

"Pigs never complain about how fast you come," chortled Clover, his blue eyes sparkling with a malicious grin.

The half-orc barmaid started squealing like a pig, tormenting me. "You can't get it u-up," she sang. "You can't get it u-up!"

I balled my fists to pummel.

* * *

Gage Feldspar wasn't drunk. Not anymore.

But could I fix the mutations in the membrane proteins? If I couldn't, he'd be addicted, craving the alcohol, all over again. He'd be just as tortured as he was when he had arrived on my doorstep.

No Wizard in three thousand years had had the skills I needed. But I had the courage to try.

I didn't think about a mechanism. Instead, I simply imagined his cells looking and smelling the way they had this afternoon, when he'd returned home after just achieving his new Yellow status.

He'd glowed with health and vigor—a man so complete in his powers, I could easily imagine him attaining Bronze status, and Silver and Gold.

His courage and fortitude. Gage Feldspar took my breath away.

My barroom friends weren't quite right. Their words sounded fake, their smiles thick with a cruelty I'd never seen before.

I didn't believe in them.

Then I realized. The Brown Worm was gone from my blood, somehow evaporated. And without the booze, the serotonin and tryptophan were completely controllable.

I looked at the caricatures of my drinking buddies and laughed. Clover and Sweet Orange and even the ugly barkeep were my friends in a twisted way.

The creatures standing before me weren't them.

And Robin, who lurked in the back with the dart-throwing elves, loved me. When she moved away we'd both been lonely, heartbroken. We hadn't loved each other enough to marry, but our relationship had been rewarding.

I saw Lyric standing around a bunch of lady ogres. They were rubbing her belly, and it looked like they were giving her birthing advice. I loved her, and always would. But she wasn't mine anymore. I'd lost her.

And I'd grown.

Lyric had forgiven me as I'd forgiven myself. The hateful words spewed from her lips weren't real. I breathed deeply, content with myself.

I sat on a barstool and said, "Barkeep, could you bring me a lemonade, please?"

Esmenet brought it to me.

I knew that I loved her, only her. I would give my life for her.

With that thought, the Slug and Garden disappeared.

Drifting to awareness, I heard her saying my name. "Gage," she said. "Gage." Her words were soft and gentle as an early summer breeze. "Gage."

My consciousness ebbed and flowed like tiny waves on the shore, but always, her voice called me in. The moon calling the tide to shore and back to sea.

I blinked. The pub was still gone. No jeering. No beer. No brawls. But the black splatter walls of Esmenet's spelling room stared at me, reminding me that all was not well.

"Gage." Her voice was still yielding, still tender.

I sat on the cold oak floor, surrounded by the black scars of the revolting pentagrams scraped into the floor. My clothes stank of beer and sweat and vomit. And my top lip itched like mad. When I scratched it, dried blood flaked away, making me sneeze ferociously.

Gingerly touching my nose, intense eye-watering pain assaulted me. Fuck. It was broken. Again. Damn, it hurt.

Then I remembered the booze Uriah poured down my throat. I rubbed my temples, preparing for a hangover from the Hells.

And fuck, I thought, remembering all those months of conquering my cravings. I was going to have to fight that battle all over again.

Something to dread.

But I pushed the fear away, standing to my feet. Right now, my nose hurt worse than my hangover. And I didn't want the Brown Worm; I wanted Esmenet.

"Gage," she said, and never had a word, a voice, sounded as precious as hers did now.

I squinted into the darkness. Only one candle sputtered in the darkness. "Where are you?"

"Here," Esmenet called. "Can you help me?"

Stepping toward her voice, I discovered that chains still held me in the center. Uriah's spell was broken, but iron still trapped me to the floor. The black iron manacles were as ugly as the five-sided stars burned into planks. "I'm chained."

"Imagine a miniature finger pressing the release mechanism inside," she said.

I did, and it opened. Easy.

"Wow!"

"Light a candle."

I did, nearly without a thought. And caught my breath.

Esmenet lay completely supine on the floor, frozen as still as a frog in an autumn pond. I found her tattered cloak and gently wrapped it around her.

"What's wrong?" I sat next to her on the cold floor, capturing her shivering hand between my palms. "What'd that fucker do to you?" I willed my warmth into her.

"Nothing. But I'm exhausted."

"Why? What happened while I was brawling in the fake bar?"

She laughed weakly. "Is that what you were doing?" She scoffed, sounding stronger. "It looked like you'd been reincarnated as a rabid wolf."

I helped her sit, amazed my head didn't ache. "So is Uriah's body in one of these dark corners? Is that why you're so tired?"

"Not that, but . . . Are you craving a beer? Do you have a hangover?"

"Funny you should say that. My busted nose hurts worse than that hangover, and I don't want a beer. I want to get out of here, make sure Lyric—and Obadiah—are okay."

"Really? No hangover?" Esmenet stood to her feet. "You don't want even one small ale? No Badgers Best? Nothing?"

I thought for a moment and said, "My mouth tastes like blood. I wouldn't mind some water."

"I did it, Gage! I figured out how to do it!"

"A cure?" Awe. "But—I mean—I thought you said it couldn't be done."

"You inspired me."

I wanted to revel, but an icy finger of fear still clung to my mind. "We have to go," I said. "Now."

"You're right," she said, shaking her cloak out and straightening her gown. "We need to visit Mayor Astra and Chief Axiom."

I'd forgotten them. "That, too—we'll messenger them. But first we have to go to Doku Harbor."

"Doku Harbor? We don't need a ferry. What's there?"

"Lyric's mother, and hopefully everyone else." I shot a glance over my shoulder to make sure Esmenet was following me.

"Before Uriah kills them," she said.

"Uriah and her minions. She said she was going to hunt them down and kill them, just before she left."

As we raced down the hall, I asked, "Where's your wand, Esmenet?"

"In the laboratory."

I walked in quickly and snatched it. "So, what do I need to make one of my own?"

"I made you one last week," she said, unable to keep a grin off her face. "It's the moonstone one next to mine."

"This?" I asked, amazed, holding up long tapered stone.

"Yes," she said, pleased with herself. The wand reflected the candlelight with a pearly colored sheen. "Moonstone's a type of feldspar. What substance could be more fitting for you? Do you like it?"

"It's beautiful," I said, staring at it. It'd been so cold when I first picked it up, but it warmed quickly in my palm. An opalescent peach light seemed to emanate from inside of it.

"Try something," Esmenet urged me. "Cast a spell!"

I wanted to obey, but we needed to hustle out of there. I'd never forgive myself if Uriah hurt Lyric.

"Go on!"

I closed my eyes, and thought of our mission. Focusing, I pointed my new wand, perfectly balanced, first at my beloved and then at myself.

25

And we appeared at the end of my ex-mother-in-law's street, all the way across town.

"Are we in Doku Harbor?" Esmenet asked in a stunned whisper. The whites of her eyes shone as brightly as the moon in the darkness of the cool evening. "How'd you do that?"

As surprised as she was, I said, "It's one hell of a wand, I guess."

"But what molecules did you Grab?"

"I don't know. I was just thinking we really needed to hurry, that we had to get here."

"Did you—"

"What?" I asked.

"Well, I've never heard of anyone doing such a thing, but did you draw on my power somehow? I feel so weird."

"I don't know *what* I did. What do you mean, weird?"

Esmenet didn't answer for a moment. Then she shrugged her shoulders. "I don't know exactly, but we're here." I heard her braids clack as she shook her head in amazement.

"Now what do we do?" I asked. "March up and ring the bell?"

"We might try looking through the windows while invisible."

"That's a good idea, but it won't throw off the Uriah thing—she's a Gold."

"Probably. Still. You have a better idea?"

"No, not really." Focusing through my new wand, which grew warm in my hand, I found that becoming invisible was as easy as lighting a candle. The wand was great.

"Gage," Esmenet said, "I have to tell you something." I could Sense her but not see her, cloaked as she was in her invisibility spell. "Before we go any farther."

"What is it?"

"I tried to explain . . ."

"Explain what?"

"Maybe why I feel strange, why Gold Love Wizards can't fall in love. Shouldn't."

"You better explain that again, because I've fallen madly and deeply and irrevocably in love with you." In the dark, she and I both invisible, I unerringly caught her hand in mine.

"The Guild prohibits it."

"Fuck the Guild! You've seen the Chair—she's got pointy snails for teeth, and she thinks it's perfectly fine to rape young women to make potions that subjugate other young women!"

"It's more than that," Esmenet said in the frighteningly weak voice.

"Tell me!"

"When we bonded in those wretched pentagrams of hers, all of our oxytocins and serotonins redistributed themselves. We're bonded to each other. Now we have to battle all of our own hormones before we can Grab or Sense any-one else's."

"Esmenet," I said, striving for patience. "I just spelled us across the city with the wand you made for me. You just suggested I might have drawn on your power to do it."

"The redistribution won't hurt you," she said. "You don't brew love potions."

"So you're telling me you can't cast any spells?" I didn't believe her exactly, but I was afraid for her anyway.

"I'm telling you that I'm weaker, that I probably won't be able to use my spelling room." I could hear her try to get her voice under control. "I probably won't be able to make any potions."

"But that's your life," I said.

"Exactly."

I ran my invisible hand through my invisible hair. This just didn't seem fair.

Or right.

"Don't you have to wade through your own hormones when you have your menses?"

"Yes, but I can't actually work when I'm ovulating. The hormones are too funky."

"Esmenet," I said. "I just don't believe that falling in love can be so detrimental to you." I waved her invisible hand through the air in front of our faces. "Look at you!" I demanded, ignoring the irony. "You're a Gold!"

"Look at me," she repeated.

"That's what I mean. What could stand in the way of a Gold?"

"No," Esmenet said. "Look at my hand."

I looked. Her hand couldn't be seen. "What?"

"My aura."

I blinked. The blanket of light surrounding Esmenet's invisible hand had changed. Gone was the bright metallic yellow shot through with rosy hues, the quintessential Gold.

Her entire body was now bathed in a silvery white. Lightning-like streaks glittered though the aura, some electric blue, others blindingly white.

"What is it?" I asked, fear filling my veins with cold. "Did you—regress? Are you Silver?"

"Silver," Esmenet repeated numbly.

"Silver's still powerful." I swallowed, not believing that myself, not even a little bit. "And maybe the color just looks strange because we're . . ." I searched for a reason. Any reason. "Outside at night." That's it! "Maybe it's because we're standing in the moon's shadow!"

"Gage," she said, in a childlike voice.

"Here," I said, shoving her into a puddle of bright moon-light. "See? Now it's—"

I wanted to say, "Gold," but it wasn't true. Esmenet was no longer a Gold Wizard. "No," I said firmly. "Maybe it's because we're invis—"

"Gage!"

"What?"

"I'm not a Silver."

"That's exactly what I mean! You're aura looks off because—"

"Because I'm Platinum."

"But—" Shocked, words failed me. "I heard Uriah. He said he'd be the first Platinum Wizard in three thousand years. Obadiah knew it, too, and he's never wrong. That is—" Words began to fall from my mouth like water over a fall. "I mean, he's wrong about some things. Like stealing wives. You should never do that, but even that wasn't wrong. I mean I was a bad husband and now I'm not and now I have you." I took a deep breath and said, "Three thousand years!"

"Platinum," Esmenet said again, and I don't know which one of us was more moonstruck.

I wrapped my arms around her invisible self and kissed her. "Congratulations! Three thousand years!" I kissed her again, astounded that this amazing woman wanted anything to do with me.

26

Gage stepped lightly next to me, his feet making no sound on the gravel path. His invisibility spell was so thorough that he cast no shadow in the moonlight. Light poured through.

"Link your mind with mine," I whispered, "so we don't have to speak aloud."

He unerringly took my hand, and turned his mind over to me with a trust that took my breath away.

The bedchambers are on the east side of the house, his voice whispered in my head, *on the ground floor. They all have windows. Big windows.*

Great. Can we go around the back of the house?

No, there's a wall of roses. We can't get through the thorns.

Got it. We snuck around the front.

Do you Sense anyone, Platinum?

I sent my mind out while we crept around the side. Thick shrubs lined the walls, and the scent of Queen of the Night bushes tickled my nose. But nothing tickled my mind. *No. Do you?*

No, but I smell something fishy. Her cunt was fishy once her disguise was gone.

He was right. I'd smelled it, too, but playing the skeptic, I said, *The sea's not that far, Gage. We're in a harbor town. Maybe that's what you smell.*

Maybe, he said. *That's why I asked if you Sensed her.* His voice resonated in my head like a delicious secret, like something I'd always wanted and never believed could be mine. Maybe giving up my career for him wouldn't be so bad.

With the slightest pressure of his hand, Gage directed me toward a lit window—the only lit window on the side of the house. White blossoms, wide open in an invitation to nocturnal pollinators, covered the shrubs. Furry moths with huge wings hit the lambent windowpanes with small thumps.

Wait, he said before we stuck our faces to the glass.

With the link between us, I could feel him Sense the room. I felt him recognize the occupants. *Who is it?* I asked.

Lyric and her mother.

Don't tell me—Cantata.

His chuckle sent a warm tingle from my brain stem down my spine. *No, her name is Aria.*

To be cautious, I tossed my Senses out, scanning the house myself. Nothing. No sign of Obadiah, or Uriah, or anyone else besides Lyric and her mother. We crept closer to the window and looked in.

"Dear Goddess!" Gage said, aloud. After the prolonged silence, the sound waves of his voice entered the external auditory canal of my outer ear with great force and struck the eardrum madly, causing it to vibrate wildly. I put my hands to my ears to muffle the noise.

Shh! I admonished in his mind.

Why would anyone want to have a child?

Lyric was in the throes of childbirth, sweat pouring down her puffy face, pain etched in every muscle.

There was nothing pretty or dignified about the process of childbirth. Lyric's knees were spread, and she faced us, giving us a fantastic view. A horrible view.

Lyric was completely dilated, but where the babe's head should be crowning, a tiny foot hung out. Not two feet, but one. Trouble.

An older woman, presumably Aria, ineffectually twisted and pushed the little ankle. I had to stop her.

I'm going to faint, Gage said as a contraction wracked Lyric, who shouted in pain. The older woman waved her hands in helpless terror.

Where was the midwife?

"I have to go in there, Gage," I said in an actual whisper. "That lady needs help." As I raced to the front door, I said in his mind, *Stay here! In case Uriah comes back.*

He didn't answer, but from across the grass I heard him spew the contents of his stomach into the Queen of the Night bush. *I'll watch*, he said in my head. *But not through the window.*

I knocked loudly on the front door but didn't wait for Aria to answer it. I burst through the house, pausing when I found the kitchen. After I washed my hands, I hurried to the women.

"I'm the midwife," I said, coming through the door.

"Thank the Star Goddess Obadiah found you," Aria said. Relief spread across her features. "But where is he?"

"I have no idea," I said, brushing past her to the mother-to-be. Another contraction was hard upon her, and her features were so squished and flushed that I barely recognized her. Of course, I'd only seen her in a tiny hand mirror, so perhaps I shouldn't be uncharitable.

I cast my senses over the woman and immediately saw one source of difficulty. "Make her take deep, slow breaths," I said to Aria. "Take her hand and make her quit panting. The child isn't getting enough oxygen, and neither is the mother."

Then I jumped. I hadn't been consciously aware of Gage's mind link until that moment. But someone had surprised him. Something—

Lyric was hyperventilating. "No panting!" I commanded.

Brains need air. Ignoring Gage, I quickly Grabbed oxygen molecules in Lyric's blood and shunted them to the baby, whose heartbeat immediately steadied.

I sent my mind along the length of the umbilical cord. It wasn't twisted, kinked, or wrapped where it didn't belong. I shunted more oxygen into it.

We're coming into the house, Gage told me. But I ignored him. This babe could be in danger, and so could the mother.

Wishing for my lubricants, I took the infant's foot in my hand and sent my mind into the tiny creature's mind. It—no, she—was too immature to understand words and logic, so I sent her images of herself, wrapped in a tiny ball, bathing in the warm nutrients of her mother's womb. Quiet and warm and calm. I wanted her to curl back up.

I could hear our visitors enter the front door and shuffle around, not knowing their way to our room. *They knew you were here, Esmenet. They were waiting for us.*

Gently, I pushed the baby's foot back in with my fingers. With my fingertips, I nudged, convincing her that turning around would be so much more comfortable. I sent her mental pictures describing how much nicer it would be.

The girl child struggled against the muscles trapping her, but she seemed to understand what was needed. The baby shifted in happy anticipation, and the heartbeats of both mother and baby stabilized further—a definite improvement.

By the time the next contraction came, the baby's head was where it belonged, her feet tucked back in. "Push," I urged Lyric.

"As hard as you can." Amid grunting and yelling on Lyric's part, her new daughter's head and shoulders slowly emerged.

The baby looked a little blue, but not frighteningly so. I shoved more oxygen into her blood.

Seconds later, another contraction seized the new mother. "It's the last one," I said. "Then you can hold your babe—your daughter."

"Is she—" The contraction twisted her. "Ahh!"

"She's fine," I said to the alarmed Aria and to the distracted new mother. "Push!" I shouted to Lyric. "Finish this!"

I held the babe—ten fingers, ten toes, and healthy lungs—carefully in my hands. Slimy with a white, cheesy substance, she was still beautiful.

"Ahh!" Lyric shouted, "I thought you said I was through." Another contraction, but not as strong.

"Shh!" I said, wishing for towels. "It's just the afterbirth." Fingering the pulsing umbilical cord, to Aria I said, "I need a knife—a sharp one—and some towels."

She scurried away like a trained parlor maid, rather than the mistress of her own house. She came back with the cops.

"Wizard Esmenet Sokaris," said Detective Habit, "you're under arrest for instigating the rape of twenty-one women over the last twelve months and brewing immoral and illegal potions to curb the sexuality of other young woman."

These were the words I heard as I held the slimy babe, white with cheese, in my arms. Afterbirth dripped onto the floor, and I shifted my weight, giving Lyric some privacy.

"Get out," I said. "I'll join you shortly."

The babe finally began to cry, proving to everyone just how healthy her lungs were. She waved her little fists in the air and angrily squinted in the candlelight. Even covered in goo, I could see that this child would be adorable. Obadiah walked in, and his eyes softened when he saw his new daughter and Lyric.

"You are hereby stripped of your rank as Gold, and the

Guild can no longer recognize you until such time that you clear your name," said Habit. "*If* you clear your name."

"But—" Aria flapped her hands again, like a fledging bird trying to fly. "She just saved my daughter—and my grand-daughter. She hasn't— Obadiah! What have you done?"

"Towels, Mistress Aria, and a knife," I commanded.

The arresting officer and his colleagues didn't depart, but they left us in peace as we cut the umbilical cord and cleaned the babe.

After placing the swaddled newborn on Lyric's breast, the new mother made adoring cooing sounds at her new baby, whispering secret words of love and touching the child's face with her fingertips and lips.

This could have been Gage's life; he could've been the proud papa.

But he wasn't.

Uriah's here, Esmenet. His voice was husky. *And I love you.*

He was now bound by the chemistry of his blood to me.

I finally glanced up from my charges.

Obadiah and Gage were handcuffed, held by a fat cop in uniform and Detective Habit. Habit's eyes were as inscrutable as always. Chief Axiom looked at me impatiently, uncharacteristic stubble on his square jaw. Perhaps I saw a shadow of fear in his expression, but it was hard to tell in the flickering candlelight.

And Guild Chair Uriah—he wore a triumphant expression above his seaweed beard.

Wiping blood and gore from my hands with a towel, I said to Aria and Lyric, "You need to send for another midwife—"

"She's on her way," Obadiah said. The fat cop shook his cuffed hands menacingly.

"There's no need for that, Pike," said Axiom. "Just calm down."

"Great," I said, patting Lyric's arm. "The midwife can finish up the details here, but you and your new baby are safe and healthy."

"Come with me, please," said Detective Habit. I heard the horses on the street snort. "Now."

Haughtily, I walked toward the chief, who led me from the house toward the black carriage. The expression Uriah gave me as I passed her was the same one a cat would give a mouse. But exhaustion and anger kept fear from my heart.

Axiom led us to a large carriage where the hallmark black Percherons waited patiently to pull us to the station. Axiom, Habit, Uriah, and I rode in the closed coach, while Pike, the fat cop, led Obadiah and Gage to the caged area on top.

Something didn't make sense here, I thought, as we piled up the carriage steps and through the thick dark doors. Chief Axiom had behaved strangely—bursting into a room while a woman gave birth. And who ever heard of him arresting someone personally, even if that someone was me? As I slid over the seat to make room for Detective Habit, another thought occurred to me. Why would Axiom bring his entire entourage with him?

He didn't want to be alone with Uriah.

That was the only conclusion I could draw. Which meant . . . Which meant, he smelled something fishy, too: the Uriah creature.

As the coach began to rumble under us, I toyed with my feathered wand, wishing I knew the state of my powers. How had I been hampered by binding with Gage, and how much did my promotion to Platinum give me strength?

We were about to find out. I took a deep breath.

"Chief Axiom," I demanded. "What's the meaning of this?" I put far more outrage into the question than I felt.

"I think you know, Wizard," he said, in a voice as sad as his eyes. He ran his hand along his square jaw, and the action struck me as nervous. Nervous and tired. Wishing to know more, I held back. I didn't dare Sense him; it'd make me too vulnerable to the Uriah thing.

I looked out the nicked and scraped window for a minute, thinking. The harbor sparkled under the gibbous moon, its peaceful surface a sharp contradiction to my mind. The large ferry usually docked at the pier was gone, perhaps on the opposite shore. What game was Chief Axiom playing?

Uriah sat next to me, exuding evil. I thought about the women she'd caused to be raped, the women she'd subjugated. And I wanted to kill her.

But no, her death wasn't something I could seek, not and live easy in my heart. I wanted to see her imprisoned for the rest of her life. A jail could be made to hold a Gold Wizard, and I could help concoct it.

The time had come to take off the gloves.

"What's the evidence against me?" I asked. "And against Wizard Feldspar?"

"The—" Axiom started.

"That lush Feldspar constantly craves the booze," Uriah interrupted. "He rapes those girls in fits of—"

I didn't reply. I simply held up my hand, forcing her to see my new aura. It worked.

"Platinum!" roared the Uriah thing. "That's not possible! I'm to be the next Platinum, the first in three millennia!" From her belt she jerked her wand, titanium glinting dangerously inside the carriage. Moonlight filtered through the scarred glass of the window, glittered off the wand. The Uriah thing poured a resonating power into her titanium wand, and the carriage vibrated.

But the power was random and rough. She hadn't directed it toward a purpose. She hadn't organized it.

The wand—a Gold's wand—was loaded with pure fury, volatile and treacherous.

Sensing an imminent explosion, I yanked the carriage door open. Damp salty air hit my face. "Jump!" I shouted to Axiom.

The stately trot of the Percherons' massive hooves was slow enough under most circumstances, but now the ground rushed past the open door frighteningly fast. Over my shoulder I saw unharnessed energy crackling from Uriah's wand. Electric blue and hoary white sizzled over her silver-gray titanium.

I leapt.

My shoulder hit the sandy side of the road painfully, and I rolled down the embankment, clutching my own feathery wand. In my peripheral vision I saw other bodies launch themselves from the carriage, some from the top and others from the inside. Disorientation prevented me from identifying particular people.

Just up the beach, close to the ferry, localized chain lightning flashed in metallic greens and ozone blues, breaking up into a dotted line of silver as it ended. A quick glance to the sky told me there was nothing natural about this phenomenon. Uriah's wand had harmlessly discharged its power, but Goddess, the creature was powerful.

A hundred paces in front of me, a thick figure ran, its silhouette clear beneath the nearly full moon. Shadows from a copse of cattails cast eerie spikes across the sand. Then the figure ducked behind a dune near the water.

Uriah.

"Sokaris," Axiom said into my ear. I nearly jumped from my skin. The chief had snuck up behind me. "I'm sorry to spring this on you, the fake arrest and all. We couldn't contain him by ourselves. Can you capture him?"

"Sokaris!" the Uriah thing shouted across the beach in a preternaturally loud voice before I could answer. Magic enhanced her volume. "Sokaris!"

"He's a she," I answered Chief Axiom. "And it seems I'll

have the opportunity to try. Would you please see that Feldspar is uncuffed and briefed? Let him know the arrest's fake."

"He's already been freed, as has Obadiah. And Gage figured the game out himself. He's watching from behind that shack. 'Following your lead,' he said. Habit's backing him up. She's tough as hooves."

"Thanks."

"Wizard," Axiom said.

"What?"

"Good luck."

I quickly threw my Senses over the beach. Gage was closer to the Uriah thing than I was, and he was right on the shore. Relieved, I found that only we, the folk from the carriage, lurked on the beach. No other villagers or fisherman still lingered. No lovers making out in the dunes.

Focusing all of my powers into my wand, I realized my feathers felt strange, not fluffy and feathery. Glancing down, I saw a transformation underway. Long, graceful contour feathers and short downy ones were melting, morphing. Feathers from the spotted barred rock, the red and blue jungle fowl, the black ancona—all were congealing.

Under my fingertips fur erupted, stiff, oily guard hair covering thick soft underfur. In the shadows of the moon, I saw large spots emerge in the pelt, dark circles with lighter centers.

My totem was changing; my heart was no longer that of a chicken. My totem was now something with fur and spots—a tiger, I hoped.

What? I heard Gage's beloved voice in my mind. *Not a hyena? Not a giraffe?*

I grinned but didn't answer. Confidently, I strode out toward the Uriah creature's dune. "Uriah," I called, using the same magic she had to increase my volume. "According to the chief of police, Chief Axiom, you're under arrest."

"You're under arrest," Chief Axiom reiterated in his loudest voice. Still, his mortal voice sounded puny in comparison.

"Uriah's not my name," she called, emerging from behind her dune in the form she'd used in my home. "I'm Princess Rorqual, Daughter of Queen of the Deep, Inheritor of All the Seas." Her hair of reeds rippled in the light breeze, making her hair resemble snakes.

I told you her cunt smelled fishy, I heard Gage whisper for my mind only, but Uriah heard.

"You drunken fool!" Uriah thundered. Her yellow whelk teeth flashed in the moonlight.

"Fool, yes, but drunken no longer. See, if you use your powers for good rather than evil, then you progress from Gold to Platinum."

As Gage taunted her, I felt Rorqual discharge her power into her wand and prepare to strike. With a racing mind, I tried to ready myself. What glyph would she use? How would I counter it?

"Sokaris saved me, you stupid shit," Gage said across the sand. "She cured an impossible disease, and now she's Platinum."

I heard Rorqual gnash her teeth in rage as I prepared my wand.

"And you're still a Gold. All your evil was for naught." Gage's voice crackled with authority, making my heart pound in pride for him.

"We shall see," she said in her enhanced voice. Sharply, Rorqual traced an angular glyph into the salty air. Silvery sparks crackled off the wand's tip. The glyph, the *Kosrae*, sent an icy sliver of fear from my brain to my fingertips.

"Don't look at it," I shouted to my allies, preparing a counter spell. "Don't look!" The sparks didn't dissipate immediately as most glyphs did. This one hung in the air, beckoning all to admire its crazy lines, its absurd angles, its mesmerizing colors.

The arcane glyph hung in the damp air for all to see, to drive all mad.

Electricity sizzled through my newly morphed wand. Electrons leapt from hair to hair, dancing across my fingertips. I let all of the power pour into my *Suva* glyph, the gold glitter falling into the night.

The moist night air cooled suddenly, and water vapor began to condense into tiny water droplets around condensation nuclei. Encouraged by the electrons spinning from my wand, droplets fattened and began to pour, not over the whole beach, but over the horrible *Kosrae* glyph. The sudden change in temperature brought a fierce gust of wind that flapped my cloak frenetically. Finding the *Kosrae*, the wind grew.

Someone—Detective Habit—streaked past me, naked and shouting gibberish. She'd looked at the *Kosrae* glyph—and she'd lost her mind.

"Officer Pike," Chief Axiom shouted at the fat cop. "Catch Habit and lock her in the coach!"

"I'll try, sir," the fat man called, waddling quickly after the insane woman.

And then Rorqual started another glyph—the *Ielcun*.

Before I could respond, the wind and rain from the *Suva* washed the hanging glyph away, leaving us wet and cold, but sane.

Or so I thought, until Officer Pike danced past, swaying his fat hips suggestively, tossing invisible hair over his shoulder coquettishly. I could almost see his imaginary tutu. Axiom marched opposite him, toward the water, singing in a deep baritone an obscene ditty about sailors and whales.

Gage! I said in my head. *Are you—*

I can handle this one, said Gage in my head, obviously in possession of his wits. *Really. I can handle this spell—you get her!*

I didn't doubt it, even as I watched a fiddler crab grow obscenely as a result of Rorqual's *Ielcun* spell. Waving its huge red-tipped claw, the crab grew from the size of a rat to that of a small cat, but I didn't doubt Gage's ability to control it.

I needed to subdue this rogue Wizard. Ignoring the snapping sound of the crab's gigantic claw as it scuttled over the shore, potential spells crossed my mind quick as lightning, only to be discarded.

Meteor rain might obliterate our foe—but us, too. No good. I could disintegrate her cells, turning her into a pile of mush. Too inhumane, even for Rorqual.

A wet breeze assaulted my face, the weather still unsettled from the wind and rain I'd called to annihilate the *Kosrae*. I could use this! Taking advantage of the changeable weather, I pushed the wind out over the harbor, letting it increase in strength. I centered it carefully, with a bead set on Rorqual.

Rorqual's crab, growing crazily, was now the size of a pony, and it was still increasing. It waved its antenna as it snapped its massive red-tipped claw. From the corner of my eye, I caught a glimpse of its face—a spider's face. Disgusting and frightening. I had to ignore it, trust Gage to take care of the creature before it chased down the insane people.

The wind from my spell blew hard over the surface of the harbor, but I honed it carefully. A handful of fishing boats dotted the water, and the increasingly strong wind from my pelted wand pushed them right to shore. They'd lose their catch tonight, but they'd keep their lives.

Obadiah darted past me, running sideways, almost scuttling. Snapping his teeth and pinching his hands open and shut in a parody of the horse-sized fiddler, Obadiah had obviously been driven mad, too.

Gage and I were the only sane minds on the beach.

I could feel Gage's magic brewing, and Rorqual's, too. She wasn't content with just one horrible monster. I had no idea what focused growth hormones could do to a crustacean—the crab had grown to the size of a Percheron.

Tossing my senses over the harbor, I sharpened the wind just a bit, carrying it precisely where it needed to go. The wind pushed the harbor water exactly, and when the wind had piled up water on the shore opposite of Rorqual, I let it die. No more magic needed: nature and gravity could do the rest.

"Giving up?" Rorqual taunted in my direction. "Your magic not strong enough?" she shouted, even as the water from the harbor sucked unnaturally away from the shore.

The fiddler crab, drab in the moonlight, scuttled wildly over the beach. It clicked its pincher frantically. I feared for our mad companions.

Even through the wind I could hear the chief's rude marching song: ". . . and though he'd dug through tons of muck, when he spied her he wanted to fuck . . ." I gently convinced his mad mind that his innermost desire lay on the street and in the town, far from the water and the beach. I did the same for Habit, Pike, and Obadiah.

A burst of energy from Gage's direction told me he'd done something to the gargantuan crab. A heartbeat later it darted off harmlessly into the water, swimming away in the waves.

"Ha!" Gage laughed aloud. "I told it a big fat ass waited for it on the opposite shore. But what do you know? Rorqual's still here!"

My Senses told me that an ass wasn't what the fiddler would find: my wave was barreling toward us.

"I should have killed you outright, Feldspar, when I found you at the police station. I should have killed you then."

Just as Rorqual began her next glyph, I heard the massive wave from the seiche bearing down. It'd rolled over the enormous fiddler crab without slowing.

The enormous wave hit the shore just as I cast an energy-absorbing spell. I didn't want this thing to bounce back across the harbor to the other shore. I didn't want to destroy the ferry or houses or people on the other side.

In the light of the nearly full moon I saw her register the empty harbor. Where water should have been, wet sand lay. Fish flopped clumsily, sending slapping sounds into the summer night.

And then the towering tsunami came into view—menacing, deadly.

Rorqual calmly traced two consecutive glyphs: the *Hairu* and one I didn't recognize. Charged electrons from both glowed brightly against the night sky.

The *Hairu* summoned a dire shark.

"Gage!" I shouted aloud. "Get away from the shore!"

One of her glyphs—I didn't know which—had bastardized my seiche wave, spreading it. Its precisely honed surface was now diffused. The wave would now cover much of the beach.

The tsunami thundered across the harbor, towering toward us. It was taller than my brownstone—frightening enough in its own right—and the wave was carrying a dire shark.

I sent my Senses over the beach, desperately seeking Gage. And the shark.

But the brilliance of Rorqual's magic overwhelmed any signal from the shark or from my beloved. Even those lacking a molecule of magic potential would be able to see the electricity exploding from the creature. In a starburst of energy, Rorqual was transmuting, transforming somehow.

Becoming her truest self.

And then the tsunami hit.

Waves smashed over her, and the last vestiges of her humanity melted away. Glowing like a meteor, her reedy hair liquefied, and her skull elongated so that she had a long snout. Human skin—incandescent now—sloughed off, billowing around her wrists and ankles. Revealed, her true skin was greenish with fantastic multicolored whorls and stripes. The texture and patterns reminded me of thick jungle snakes that wrap around prey—hypnotizing.

Then the oversized wave receded, sucking her into the water in a froth of seething foam. Did I see a lustrous tentacle? In the diffused light of the moon on the churning water, I wasn't sure.

It'sss not over, Esssmenet. Humanity shall not have the lasssst word, Rorqual's true voice hissed in my mind. *Not even you and your moonsstone friend can ssstop uss.*

And she was gone.

So was Gage.

Fighting a growing panic I threw my Senses over the water again, ignoring all signals but his.

Nothing.

27

It took the Chair of All Guilds, Wizard Healy, more than two months to send me a new assistant.

As far as I was concerned, Healy could have taken a year. I didn't want a new assistant—I wanted Gage.

During that period of waiting I'd gotten into the habit of walking the beach, Sensing all of the watery life forms. The coronet fish, the striped bass, the mussels and clams, I could identify them all now.

But I never found the one I sought.

Chief Axiom, his mind restored by my wand, often walked with me, probably wanting to be with me when we discovered Gage's body. He'd told me that finding his corpse was just a matter of time. The harbor's water sucked in the dead, kept them a while, and then returned them, he said.

I knew he didn't want me to see Gage's fish-chewed face.

And the sea and her fish had kept Gage—or his body—for a long while.

But then, we hadn't found Rorqual's body either. I suspected Princess Rorqual, Daughter of Queen of the Deep, Inheritor of all the Seas, wasn't dead. How could the Queen of the Deep drown, even in a tsunami?

Those days were filled with a sorrow as scorching as the hot summer sun on the sand, a heat the slight breeze did little to alleviate. The smell of dead fish and rotting seaweed assaulted my nose, and I wore it home with me, dragging it around my empty house.

But the day my new assistant was to arrive, something strange filled the sea air. Even though late summer was upon us, my mind kept thinking of spring. Light zephyrs sucked away the fishy scents. Something tickled the back of my mind.

Axiom walked with me on the morning my new assistant was to arrive. Chief Axiom liked the iridescent yellows and oranges of the jingle shells, and he picked them up whenever he spied one in the sand. He wiped the sand off a yellow one as he said, "Detective Habit suspected Uriah all along." I'd restored the minds of Habit, Pike, and Obadiah, too. "She even guessed that Uriah was setting Gage up for the fall."

"What made her think that?" I asked, drawing no comfort from the warm sand under my feet. My own detective work hadn't progressed as far as Habit's, not in this direction.

"It seems Habit asked Uriah to scan Feldspar's mind one time, and Uriah didn't do it."

"But I thought he exonerated Gage then."

"Oh, he exonerated him just fine, but Uriah apparently never scanned him. Habit has enough magic to see when it's used and to see levels and such. She saw that Uriah lied about scanning Gage. Habit didn't know what to make of it, but she knew it wasn't right."

Watching the small gray waves lick the shore, I thought about the role the former Guild Chair had played in our lives. "Uriah told me not to fall in love with Gage. He said it'd ruin my ability to pull hormones for love potions."

"And you think he's right?"

Looking across the smooth water to the distant shore, I thought I could see something in the distance. I squinted and saw nothing. Finally I shrugged, then nodded. "Probably."

"That creature lied about a lot of things. What makes you think it's right about this?"

"My blood chemistry changed while working with Gage. When I fell in love, it changed my physiology."

"But have you tried yet to work with someone else? Do you know for sure?"

"I'll find out soon enough. The Chair of all Guilds hand-picked a new assistant for me. He may actually be at the house when we get there."

We walked in silence for a few moments. Axiom knew the depth of my grief; there was no reason to dissect it.

"So how's Lyric's little baby doing?" Axiom asked, changing the subject.

"She and Obadiah had the babe's naming ceremony last week, on the same day as their wedding."

"How efficient," Axiom said dryly, reminding me why I liked his quiet company. "And what did they name the babe?"

"Andesine." I dragged my toes in the damp sand. "After Gage."

Axiom scratched his jaw. "How do you get Andesine from Gage?"

I smiled a little bit. "Andesine's a beautiful crystal. It's a kind of feldspar granite." But it made me sad. What if this child, not even of his loins, was all that remained of Gage?

"I'm surprised the grandmother didn't insist on a musical name—Coloratura or something."

I smiled again.

"I shouldn't joke," Chief Axiom said. "My father's name was Postulate."

A laugh escaped me, the first in weeks. Maybe my chemistry

was reverting back. That thought made me want to cry. I didn't want to return to what I was.

I wanted Gage.

"My work here's finished," Chief Axiom said. "I've made you laugh, now let's go home."

My new assistant was waiting for me in the parlor, bags sitting neatly at his side. I didn't even ask his name. Sorrow made me rude, and I didn't look at his features. Curtly, I sent him to my renovated spelling room.

He wasn't Gage.

But that strange expectant feeling I'd had on the beach didn't leave me. I couldn't shake the feeling that something important was about to happen. Maybe Wizard Healy could work miracles.

And, of course, something important was about to happen. I was going to find out whether I could still Grab proteins and hormones for love potions.

Retrieving my wand from the laboratory and dusting it off, I thought I'd try the most basic aphrodisiac. Even emotionally crippled, if I had any magic ability left at all for brewing, I should be able manage the *Varanasi* glyph.

My new assistant, selected by the Chair of all Guilds himself for his magical aptitude, his looks, his suitability to my life, shed his robe without a drop of modesty and looked at me, waiting.

My pentagram hearts, all new, surrounded him. His penis stuck expectantly from a thatch of dark gold hair.

"The *Hiva Oa* groove, please," I said as I drew my glyph into the air.

This wasn't going to work. My heart wanted Gage. So did every cell in my body. Handpicked or not, my blond assistant wasn't going to work. His chest wasn't thick and brawny, his eyes weren't dark, and his nose wasn't crooked from years of barroom brawls.

The beautiful man standing before me wouldn't work at all—not without help.

I did the only thing I could. I twisted the *Varanasi* spell a bit, and his blond hair took on a chocolate sheen. Where it'd been shaggy and long, it became sleek, like mink. Now it was pulled back in a neat club. His skin darkened, and his muscles thickened.

Gage.

With tears rolling down my cheeks, I shed my robe and stepped into my spell.

And something wonderful happened.

Seeing what Esmenet had done with the man in the spell, I laughed. I'd been gone two months, and she was cloaking the poor guy to look like me.

I had the solution to her problem.

Gently, I pulled my stand-in from her spell, careful not to hurt him. I handed him his robe and pushed him toward the door. "Go wait in the parlor."

Then I stepped into her magic world.

I missed his face, the fan of lines around his eyes. The chocolate color of his irises. The curve of his lips.

Seeing them now, I choked back my tears. I wanted Gage back in my arms right now. I walked over to him and put my palm on his rugged cheek. "I miss you so."

"I'm right here, my love."

I didn't know how the strength of my Grabbing would be, but my wand was more powerful than ever. The *Varanasi* had been cast to perfection. The blond assistant from the Chair of all Guilds looked exactly like Gage.

I kissed him then, melting into him, surrendering to him. I knew that my memory enhanced the kiss, made it seem more real than it was. The yearning in my mind filled in Gage's smell, his taste, and the irrational part of my brain so happy to live in a dream world drank in every drop.

Lost in my fantasy, I wrapped my arms around him, savoring his heat and his strength. Something deep inside of me loosened.

For the first time in my life, I felt complete.

And as I went to Grab the first proteins, I knew it was real.

Somehow, Gage Feldspar was in my arms.

I kissed away the tears that fell down her cheeks, cupping the back of her head in my palm.

This woman had my heart. Without her I had no life, no self.

My fingertips, my palms drank in the silky curves of her hip and her waist. She pushed her breast into my hand, surrendering her mouth to mine.

"I'd rather have you," she breathed, "than anything else."

I inhaled her cinnamon scent, watching her nipples harden. I lightly touched one with my tongue.

"I love you, you know," I said, losing myself in her muscari-colored eyes. "With all of my heart." Her black lashes fell against her cheeks.

Her teeth flashed white in a slow smile.

I pushed her onto the pillowy mattress of her bed that'd just appeared behind us.

She flopped back toward the headboard, cherry with ancient runes carved into it.

Our gazes locked; I caught her thighs in my hands and spread her. Burying my face in her musk, she was wet and hot. I ran my tongue over her clit, groaning with pleasure as it throbbed beneath me.

"By the Stars, Gage," she said, arching toward me. "I love the way you do that."

"This?" I asked with a wicked lick.

"Mmmm."

I took that as a yes. "And this?" I buried one finger in her amazing heat.

An unintelligible sound came from her. My tongue took turns with my thumb caressing her nub.

"Like this then?" Two fingers. A thumb light as a feather over her clit. My tongue.

Another unintelligible sound fell from her lips, this one longer than the last. She quivered under me.

Esmenet pulled away from me and tried to climb on top of me. "Did you Grab what you need?" I asked.

"I've got you, don't I?"

Esmenet buried my cock deep inside. We came together.

I looked at her from across her spelling room. She was more beautiful than I remembered. The texture of her skin, the planes of her cheeks—I couldn't look away from her.

"What took you so long to come home?" she asked. And I realized: I was home.

"Esmenet," I said, "come here." She crossed the new floor. The floor had been redone with applewood rather than ebony. The planks were bright and cheerful against the purple walls.

I wrapped my arms around her, tightly. I crushed her to me, willing the sadness to evaporate. "I came as soon as I could."

"But where were you?"

"I was a . . . guest of Princess Rorqual and her people, including her minions who raped all those young girls."

"A guest?"

"I couldn't leave."

Esmenet shifted against me, like she was trying to crawl into my skin with me. "You smell so good. What did Rorqual want with you?"

"She wanted to teach me about her people. She tried to convince me that reestablishing the relationship between her people and ours would be good for all of us."

"Her people?"

"The Eurquale. Until the reign of Alfred III ended, they ruled by our side, counseling kinds."

"An evil race, then, if they counseled Alfred III."

"Evil and knowledge hungry. They'll sacrifice anything for knowledge. They want to know how you became a Platinum, and they're willing to do anything to figure it out."

"But there's no formula for advancing," Esmenet said. "They must know that."

"They think there is, and they want to rule on land again. They'll do whatever they can toward that end." I pushed her away so she could see I was serious. "They'd kidnap you if they thought they could get away with it."

"I'm too strong. Who could kidnap a Platinum?"

The question seemed rhetorical, so I didn't answer it. In the silence Esmenet traced her fingertips over my chest sending zings of excitement right to my cock. Again.

"So it was Rorqual who put those growlers in your room."

"Yes." I wrapped one of Esmenet's braids around my finger, admiring the shiny blackness of it. "Rorqual hated me, still hates me."

"But why?"

I laughed. "That damned pig made a fool of her. She'll never forgive me, as long as people are telling that story."

"I heard a kid jumping rope to that story the other day."

"Exactly. So when she needed to pin the rapes on someone, she picked me. She thought it would teach me a lesson."

Esmenet laughed. "Did you learn it?"

"I learned something," I said suggestively, cupping her breast.

She pushed my hand away. "Let's go to the lab and see how we did with those hormones."

"If you can't brew potions anymore, then you can get a position in the Guild. There's a vacancy, Chair Sokaris."

"You're very funny."

"No, what's funny are those scaredy cats above your doors. I liked those chickens. I glared at those new guys on the way in, and they mewled in fright. The chickens, they stood up for themselves."

"They're not scaredy cats; they're housecats. And they'll get braver with time. Even those brave chickens you're so fond of started off as tiny fluff balls."

"And what's with the street names? Manx Lane? Really. Siamese Street? You don't live on Bantam anymore. No, now it's Kitty Court."

Esmenet laughed, a rich deep sound as beautiful as her smile. "It's Calico Court, and you know it. They'll change to Tigers and Panthers and Lynx before too long."

"Must be challenging for mail delivery."

She just rolled her eyes at me. Her magic was strong enough to change the architecture of the entire city, and she knew I knew it.

28

I put a stopper in the final vial, and when Gage walked into the lab, I was still shaking my head.

"What is it?"

"Look." I laid out a small blue bottle. "One." Then another blue bottle. "Two." I pushed another toward him. "Three."

He smiled at me but obviously didn't get it. He needed more lab time. "What?"

"I made three vials from our spell. I usually make one."

"Wow!" Then he grinned wickedly. "I guess you're about to retire then." He held his hand to his brow and said in a falsetto, "Oh, I'll never brew another love potion!"

I threw an old rag at him. "Don't be an ass."

"I don't want to teach," he continued, bending backward in a parody of drama. "I want to brew! I live to brew!"

"I've never done it, but I'm pretty sure I could turn you into a toad."

"Oh, yeah? How are you going to fuck a toad? Could a toad do this to you?" Gage kissed me, hard and demanding.

"I'll let you stay human in the night, I guess."

"Three potions from one trip to the spelling room. You'll blow the world away, Sokaris. At this rate, we'll be able to give everyone in town a potion. What a happy place the world will be."

I wrapped my arms around him, savoring his strength. "I have a hypothesis," I said.

"Another one? Didn't the last one get you sneezing under my door?"

I nipped him, then said, "I think the hormones are so plentiful because we're bonded together. If I tried to pull hormones or proteins from anybody else, it wouldn't work."

Gage grinned at me. "That doesn't sound so bad."

"Selfish."

"Like you're not." His fingertips were dancing over my nipple, which was now rock hard.

"Did you come down here to distract me?"

"Yes." That rakish grin. Then, "No. Somebody's upstairs."

I stepped back, looking at him quizzically. "Somebody?"

"Chair of All Guilds, Wizard Healy."

"Stars, Gage! We're down here making out while the Chair of All Guilds is waiting in the parlor?"

"I made him a nice drink: mint lemonade. And I gave him some little sandwiches with those cucumbers I found in the market yesterday. And that goat cheese. He's quite happy."

I rolled my eyes and headed upstairs, wishing I had time to screw Gage's brains out.

The Chair of All Guilds, Wizard Healy, sat in my austere black-lacquered chair looking like he belonged there, his long legs folded neatly at the knees, his feet flat on the floor. He wore expensive shoes, the trim of which complemented his pale gold aura.

"Wizard Sokaris," he said, "I want to thank you, and you,

too, Wizard Feldspar. Without your efforts, that vile creature would still be hurting women."

Since our bonding, I was tuned to Gage. I'd never imagined such magic; our mind link seemed to be permanent. A surge of happiness and pride coursed through him, making me proud for him. He deserved his moment in the sun. Praise from the Chair of All Guilds was worth basking in, even for me.

"I'm here for two reasons," Wizard Healy said in his melodic voice. "First, I want you to take the ancient tomes we found in Rorqual's office, the ones from three thousand years ago. We have no idea where Guild Chair Uriah—" Healy held up his spidery hand, correcting himself. "No, Rorqual found them, but the information should be digested by someone powerful and undeniably good. You and Wizard Feldspar have proven yourselves to be such people."

Surrounded by my platinum aura, I shouldn't have felt so stunned, but I was. Knowledge from antiquity . . . it took my breath away. Had they known then how to cure addictions, how to manipulate cell surfaces? One could find what kills the cells or—

"I see I've left you speechless," Wizard Healy interrupted with a chuckle.

"She's imagining a cure for every disease under the sun," said Gage.

"Which is why I'm trusting these books to you. I'm also entrusting you with Rorqual's diaries and spell book." Healy placed his hands carefully on his lap. "Learn what you can about her motives."

"Yes, sir."

"Wizard Feldspar, thank you for the delicious repast, and now, if you'll excuse me, I'd like to speak to Wizard Sokaris about a . . . personal matter."

"As you wish, sir," Gage replied, taking his leave.

The old coot wants a love spell. Gage chuckled in my mind after the door closed behind him.

Shut up! I said to Gage.

"Don't worry, Wizard Sokaris," Healy said, apparently aware of our link. "I don't mind if he overhears us. I can easily pretend that he can't."

Gage remained silent, for which I was thankful. "How can I help you, sir?"

"It's of a . . . delicate nature."

"As a Love Wizard, things of delicate natures are my specialty."

"It's my wife."

"Yes, sir?" I waited.

"We're enjoying a . . . second spring, so to speak."

"Increased sex drive?"

"Ahhh, yes. That's correct."

"And you wish . . . ?" I prompted.

"It's just that she—well, this is awkward. We've always enjoyed our bed sport, but there's a certain . . . act that we've wished to try, but she's lacked the . . . courage."

"Anal sex."

A faint blush crept to his pale cheeks. "Ah, yes."

"She's willing, but nervous, and you'd like a potion to help."

Wizard Healy drew a deep breath. "Yes."

I'll get the spelling room ready. We'll use the S&M setting and—

"I'm sure we can help you, sir." The throbbing between my thighs left my knees weak.

"Thank you, Wizard Sokaris. I have the greatest confidence in you—on all fronts." A double entendre? From this elegant man?

"Thank you, sir. I'll send a messenger over tomorrow with the elixir." Would Gage choose the jasmine oil, or the pomegranate?

"Very well." And he disappeared, thank the Stars. I had a leather outfit that would be perfect, and how did Gage feel about leg spreaders?

I'm waiting for you, Gage whispered in my mind. *Your hearts are waiting.*

"I'm coming," I said, my voice thick with anticipation. The handcuffs . . . The paddle . . . I flew up the stairs.

Like it hot? Don't miss Evangeline Anderson's
PLEASURE PALACE,
coming soon from Aphrodisia . . .

"*Ty*, please . . . I need you." Her slender form moved beneath him, all cream and gold in the soft light. She looked so beautiful, like a creature made of moonlight. Her high, generous breasts were tipped with pale pink nipples and the soft mound of reddish curls between her slightly parted legs glimmered faintly like spun rubies.

"What do you need, sweetheart?" he whispered gently, running one hand down her smooth, creamy flank, loving the way she shivered and arched like a cat under his touch.

"Need you inside me, filling me up." She parted her thighs wider and he could see the pouting pink lips of her tender pussy spread wide for him, inviting him in. She was so wet for him, needed him so much. His cock was a throbbing bar of iron, urging him to do what she asked. Urging him to fill her completely and fuck her thoroughly. To Bond with her and make her his forever.

"Fuck me, Ty," she begged, writhing beneath him wantonly. He found that he was closer now, the head of his cock rubbing along that sweet, slippery flesh. She was hot inside, burning with *need for him. "Fuck me," she begged him again. "Fuck me and fill me up. Make me yours . . . always and only yours." With a groan he felt himself giving in, pressing the head of his cock into her slick entrance, feeling her warm wetness envelope him completely as he buried himself to the hilt in her sweet, tight cunt . . .*

One dream merged into another. Hypersleep seemed to last forever.

Tyson opened his eyes at last in time to see the beveled front of his sleep tube sliding open. The robe he wore was slightly damp with perspiration. Hypersleep raised your body temperature a few degrees and it felt a little like having a fever when you first woke up, he remembered. With a shrug of his broad shoulders, he peeled it off.

He tried to piece the rapidly deteriorating dream together . . . something about a gerbil and his Aunt Pinky? But he had never had a gerbil or an aunt named Pinky. And he had certainly never owned or worn a pale green striped skirt . . .

"I know you didn't . . . I did. Loved that skirt . . . gerbil chewed a hole in it and I caught blue holy hell from my mom." It took Ty a minute to realize the voice was coming from *inside* his head. He turned to see the sleep tube next to him slide open and watched as Shaina slowly opened her still-dreamy ocean-green eyes.

"Did you just talk inside my head?" he asked carefully, feeling distinctly strange about asking such a question. It seemed like something you would ask someone in a dream. He looked closely at Shaina. Was he still dreaming?

"I don't know, did I?" Her face was still relaxed from the utter oblivion of hypersleep.

"I think you did," Ty told her, beginning to feel a bit more awake himself. Her creamy skin was flushed, he noticed, and wisps of her fiery red hair had begun to curl into tiny love tendrils around her pointed, kittenish face. The white synthi-cotton robe she wore was damp and nearly transparent. He could clearly see the full curves of her breasts outlined in the emerald green of her bra. Her nipples were erect and pressing tantalizingly against the synthi-cotton fabric. Suddenly, his cock felt like a bar of lead inside his briefs. *Take it easy. Just the aftereffects of hypersleep,* he thought, and this time he was reasonably sure the voice in his head was just his own internal monologue.

"What aftereffects?" Shaina looked at him and Tyson shook his head mutely. Had she caught his thought? "I had the strangest dream," she whispered, still seemingly half to herself. "I was back in second school and there was this girl in my class, Treena Tist, that I really liked. Only everybody called her . . ."

"Treena Tits, because she had the biggest . . . wait a minute. That's my memory, not yours." Tyson felt fully awake now and more than a little disturbed. What was going on?

"Ah, I see the symbiotes are becoming active. You have been sharing dreams." The Glameron's soft voice broke into Tyson's agitated thoughts.

"Hey, when we agreed to be injected with these things, nobody said anything about sharing dreams," Ty pointed out.

I can see why you like Treena, she was really pretty.

"Could you please stop that for a minute?" he snapped irritably, looking at Shaina. Her eyes were still half-lidded and he guessed that she was having a difficult time shaking off the hypersleep. To make matters worse, he was still fiercely aroused and seeing Shaina leaning against the side of her sleep tube with that dreamy expression on her face, like a woman who'd just woken up after a night of hard loving, didn't help any. God, he just wanted to kiss her, just once. He wanted to taste those soft, pink lips . . .

Why don't you? she whispered in his mind. She thought she was still dreaming, Ty realized, but he couldn't help himself. Just one kiss . . . He stepped forward and pulled her unresisting body into his arms. She was soft and warm and smelled of that feminine musk that drove him crazy with need. He lowered his head and took her mouth the way he'd wanted to from the first time he saw her, burying his large hands in her glorious tumble of flame-colored hair and tilting her face up so that he could explore her lips thoroughly, claim her completely.

Mmmm. Ty heard her purr through the symbi-link. She wanted this as much as he did, he suddenly understood. She felt the same fire, the same need whenever they touched. He crushed her against him . . . she felt so fragile and soft in his arms. He wanted to own her—to possess her completely. Wanted to Bond with her. He knew it was the dominant D'Lonian in him coming out but he couldn't help it. Inside his head, he could hear Shaina hoping that this dream would never end.

It's no dream, Shaina. It's real. I want you. I've always wanted you. I've always known you should belong to me. His cock throbbed demandingly and he suddenly wanted to rip open her robe, peel down that flimsy little bra, and suck her ripe pink nipples until she screamed. Wanted to take her here and now, to spread her legs, mount her, fill her, fuck her until she moaned and begged for more—until she belonged to him completely and forever.

Wait a minute . . . not a dream? Shaina suddenly stiffened in his arms and Ty felt a current of fear like a jolt of electricity through their link. Her eyes widened as she came fully awake. She slid out of his arms, although he didn't want to let her go, and backed carefully away from him, her frightened green eyes never leaving his face. Tyson realized with an inward wince that she must have heard his last thought.

Oh my Goddess . . . can't believe . . . Shaina's thoughts were nearly inarticulate and the air in the small sleep chamber was suddenly charged with nervous tension.

"I, uh, didn't mean that the way it sounded." He approached

her carefully as she continued to back away. "Look, McCullough, I'm sorry."

She shook her head mutely. She was thinking that he looked like some kind of a wild animal with his hair sticking up all over the place and his eyes like molten gold in his dark face. His teeth were so white and sharp. She had heard rumors about D'Lonian men and she wondered if they were true.

What rumors? That we bite our women's heads off during mating? Ty thought at her, fiercely sarcastic. He had never pegged Shaina as being a racist.

"I'm *not* racist . . ." *Just scared* . . . she finished to herself, but Ty heard it. Of course he did; he heard everything, and so did Shaina.

"You," he roared, turning to the Glameron who was standing quietly by and watching them as though he was viewing a particularly engrossing vid. "A little help here, damn it!"

"Certainly." Faron stepped forward calmly and turned first to Shaina. "Mistress McCullough, Master Tyson is enamored of you and has been from the first moment he met you. His caring and deep concern for your safety are what cause him to treat you in a less than civil manner sometimes."

"Master Tyson"—he turned back to Ty—"Mistress McCullough both desires and fears you. Her fear stems from both inexperience and the somewhat exaggerated rumors she has heard about the extreme sexual appetites of D'Lonians, which I understand makes up a large part of your heritage. Were she not a virgin—"

"That's not exactly what I meant," Tyson growled, cutting off the Glameron's calm speech. "What I meant was how do we turn it off?" Across the room, Shaina was rapidly reciting prime numbers inside her head to keep from thinking any embarrassing thoughts he might overhear, but her face was red with mortification at Faron's blunt revelations. Ty wondered if she really was a virgin.

"Yes, I bloody well am. Does that make you feel happy? Or is it more smugly superior? Just one more thing that you're good at that I'm *not*," Shaina yelled at him, her face crumpling into tears of embarrassment. Damn it all to hell, now he had made her cry when hurting her was the last thing Ty ever wanted to do . . .

"How do we turn it *off*?" he demanded, feeling ready to strangle somebody, preferably Minister Waynos, who had talked them into this in the first place. But the fat little bastard was light years away at this point. Through the symbi-link he could hear Shaina thinking much the same thing. *Well, great minds think alike,* he thought, *although they don't usually have to hear each other do it.*